DADDY'S HOME
Pamela Bauer

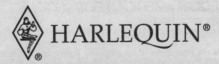

TORONTO • NEW YORK • LONDON
AMSTERDAM • PARIS • SYDNEY • HAMBURG
STOCKHOLM • ATHENS • TOKYO • MILAN • MADRID
PRAGUE • WARSAW • BUDAPEST • AUCKLAND

ISBN 0-373-70863-7

DADDY'S HOME

Copyright © 1999 by Pamela Muelhbauer.

This edition published by arrangement with Harlequin Books S.A.

Visit us at www.romance.net

Printed in U.S.A.

"You're a hero, Daddy."

Brittany held out a newspaper clipping. "This is what I brought for Show and Tell."

Tyler frowned. In his daughter's hands was a story of the airplane crash. The headline read: Local Man Is Hero.

"My teacher says you were very brave—the way you saved that lady." The child gazed up at him.

He shifted uneasily on the sofa. "I'm not a hero, and the newspapers shouldn't have said I was."

Brittany's face fell. "But my teacher said—"

"And your teacher's right," Tyler's mother interjected. "You father's just being modest. He most certainly is a hero. Anybody who saves another person's life is a hero."

Brittany moved over to stand in front of Tyler. "Are you mad at me for bringing the newspaper to school?"

He gave her a squeeze. "No, sweetheart, I'm not mad. It was very nice of you to bring me for Show and Tell." He gave her an extra hug. "I love you, Brittany."

"I love you too, Daddy. And you are too a hero."

ABOUT THE AUTHOR

You need two things if you're going to survive winter in the Midwest—warm clothes and a sense of humor. Pamela Bauer possesses both. That's why she often uses Minnesota as the setting for her romance novels. She believes there's something special about this land of 10,000 lakes that makes it the perfect setting for stories about love and family. It also happens to be the place where she fell in love with her own real-life hero, her husband, Gerr.

Daddy's Home is this award-winning author's twenty-first romance for Harlequin. Not surprisingly, it too is set in Minnesota, and has a hero who knows how to warm a woman's heart. It's a story full of Midwestern charm, which will leave you feeling good about love, about life and about family.

Books by Pamela Bauer

HARLEQUIN SUPERROMANCE
605—I DO, I DO
670—MERRY'S CHRISTMAS
792—BABE IN THE WOODS

HARLEQUIN AMERICAN ROMANCE
668—THE PICK-UP MAN
718—MAIL ORDER COWBOY

This book is dedicated to my father, the most honest man I know.

Thanks, Dad, for showing me what a hero can be.

CHAPTER ONE

"DADDY'S HOME!"

Tyler Brant barely had the door open when his six-year-old daughter flung herself at him. If there was one thing he would never grow tired of, it was the feel of her small, warm body clinging to his.

"I've missed you," he said, lifting her so that he could twirl her around in a circle. He gave her a hug before setting her down.

"I missed you, too, Daddy."

"Why are you dressed like a squash, sweetheart?" Tyler asked, smiling at the face painted the same orange as the costume she wore. Covering her legs were bright green tights that matched the stemlike satin cap hiding her blond curls.

"I'm not a squash. I'm a pumpkin!" she said, shoving her hands onto a waist that was stuffed with padding.

"And a very pretty pumpkin at that. Did Gram make that for you?"

"Uh-huh. She sewed it on the sewing machine and sprinkled all the sparkly things on," Brittany answered, wiggling in delight. "I get to be in the parade."

"And what parade is that?"

It was Tyler's mother who answered. "It's the Anoka Pumpkin Festival on Saturday. They've invited Brittany's class to ride on one of the floats," Millie Brant explained, walking toward Tyler with a tape measure draped around her neck. She greeted him with her usual kiss on the cheek. "Welcome home."

"Isn't it a little chilly for a parade this time of year?" Automatically, his brow creased as he shrugged out of his topcoat.

"She'll be dressed in warm clothes," his mother replied.

"We get to throw candy to the little kids watching the parade," Brittany added.

Tyler hid his smile.

"Are you going to come and see me, Daddy?" She looked at Tyler with big, round blue eyes so like the ones her mother used to flash at him. He saw Susan every time she batted those innocent eyes at him, and a pain caught somewhere between his heart and throat.

"I'd like to, but I'm afraid I have to work," he answered.

The little face fell. "You always have to work."

Guilt settled in Tyler's stomach like a big old rock. It was true he put in long hours—longer than the average father, but he had responsibilities. Something a six-year-old didn't understand. He looked to his mother for support.

She didn't give it. Instead, she gave him a familiar look of reprobation. "You've just spent four days working away from home. Surely you can take a Saturday off.''

''Not this Saturday,'' he responded soberly.

''But, Daddy, don't you want to see me be in the parade?'' Brittany asked.

''Of course I do. Let's sit down. I brought you something.'' He grabbed her by the hand, reached for his overnight bag and moved into the living room. He pulled his daughter down beside him on the leather sofa. She watched with wide eyes as he unzipped his suitcase and pulled out a small pink bunny.

''A Beanie Baby!'' Brittany cried out in delight, taking the soft stuffed animal into her hands. ''Thank you, Daddy.'' She wrapped her arms around his neck and gave him a kiss.

''The tag says her name is Hoppity and that she likes to play hopscotch,'' Tyler pointed out.

''She's a girl! Oh, good. I have to show Walter.'' She scrambled to her feet and hurried out of the room.

''You're not always going to be able to buy her off with a stuffed animal, you know,'' Millie said.

''I'd love to go to the parade, but it's just not possible,'' he stated, working hard to keep the irritation from his voice.

He could see his mother was not about to back down. ''What's so important on Saturday that you're willing to miss seeing your daughter in a parade?''

''What's important is getting two hundred people back to work. That fire in Hibbing destroyed a brand-new factory that would have provided income for a couple of hundred families. I have no choice but to meet with the contractors and go over the blueprints. The longer it takes to get the place rebuilt, the longer those people are out of work.''

''Let someone else look at the plans.''

''It's not that easy. I'm the president of the company. With that title comes certain responsibilities,'' he tried to explain, but his mother only shook her head.

''We've had this conversation before, Tyler. There's no point going over it again. It won't accomplish anything.''

''Mom, you know I spend every free minute I have with her. What more can I do?''

''Spend more free minutes with her,'' she answered. ''She's growing up and you're missing the important milestones in her life. I understood your need to bury yourself in your work after Susan died, but I thought that after the plane crash you'd come to your senses and realize how precious life is. I was wrong. Nothing's changed. Work is still the number-one priority in your life.''

At the mention of his late wife's name, Tyler's insides twisted into a knot. He had thought time would ease the pain of losing her, yet nearly five years had passed and each time he heard her name, he relived the fiery automobile accident that had taken her life.

''All right, Mom. You've made your point,'' he said with more anger than he intended. Seeing the hurt look on her face, he immediately apologized. ''I'm sorry. I didn't mean to snap at you.''

"What's wrong, Tyler? You've been so edgy these past few weeks."

"Nothing's wrong," he lied. "I'm fine. I've had a lot on my mind lately."

"You look tired. You should have taken some time off after the crash," she said in a motherly tone. "Instead of rushing back to work, you should have been home resting. Everyone needs time to recover from trauma."

"Not me. I needed to work," Tyler corrected her, trying not to think about the experience. Two weeks ago he'd been in a small commuter plane on his way to assess the damage the fire had done to his electronics plant when the pilot had tried unsuccessfully to make an emergency landing.

In one horrifying instant, the plane crashed into the bank of the river. Bodies were flung into the icy waters. Eight of the ten people aboard drowned. By some strange quirk of fate, Tyler and one other passenger survived. Just as had happened the day of the car accident, Tyler had been allowed to walk away.

A shudder unsettled every nerve in his body. He had to force the image from his mind. The last five years had taught him that if he wanted to be of any use to his daughter, he needed to keep the past in the past. Reliving events wouldn't change a thing.

Just then, Brittany rushed into the room waving a red folder. "I got something for you, Daddy," she announced. "It's my work from school."

"Then you better show it to me now." Tyler smiled as the little girl climbed onto his lap. With his arms wrapped around her, he watched as she opened the folder. First she pulled out a black cat made from construction paper, then a page with several words printed a couple of dozen times. Finally came a drawing done in crayon—three stick people and a rectangular house.

"This is Gram, that's me and that's you. See? I colored you a beard 'cause it was before you had your cushun." She glanced at Tyler's now-whiskerless face.

"It's concussion, Brittany," her grandmother automatically corrected her.

"Con-cush-un," she repeated. She placed her hand on Tyler's jaw. "I like you without your beard. It's smooth."

She tipped her head to stare at his only visible injury—an inch-long scar on the underside of his jaw. A piece of metal had sliced open his skin and come dangerously close to severing an artery in his neck.

"Does it hurt?" she asked.

"Not anymore," he answered honestly.

"Are you going to grow another beard?"

Before he could answer, his mother said, "I hope not. You're such a handsome man, Tyler. It's a shame to hide your good looks behind all that hair."

Tyler ignored her comment. He knew that his keeping a full beard had always been a source of irritation for his mother. During his years in college, he had been both long-haired and bearded—about as scruffy as he could be.

Then he met Susan and everything changed. She not only cut his hair for him, but she shaved his face.

She insisted that if he was going to fit into the establishment, he needed to look the part. And in those days, he would have done anything for Susan.

"Look at this, Daddy." Brittany stuck a red-and-pink finger painting close to his face.

"Very nice. I like the bright colors."

"Do you know what it is?"

"Why don't you tell me?"

"It's a cherry pie."

"Ah. That's why you used so much red."

"Red's my favorite color." She shoved the painting back into the folder, then pulled out some newspaper clippings encased in plastic. "This is what I brought for show-and-tell."

Tyler frowned. In his daughter's hands was an article about the airplane crash. The headline read Local Man Is Hero.

Brittany held it in her outstretched hands, waiting for him to take it. He didn't want to look at it. He turned to his mother. "You let her take this to school?"

"She saw your picture in the paper and wanted to bring it for show-and-tell," Millie said with an apologetic lift of her eyebrows.

Brittany smiled proudly. "My teacher said that you're a hero, Daddy. She said you were very brave."

He shifted uneasily on the sofa. "I'm not a hero and the newspapers shouldn't have said I was."

Brittany's face fell. "But my teacher said—"

"And your teacher is right," Millie interjected. "Your father's just being modest. He most certainly is a hero. Now why don't you go change out of that costume. Gram still has to iron on the pumpkin's face.''

''All right, Gram.'' Brittany shoved the newspaper article back into the folder and looked at Tyler. ''Are you mad at me for bringing the newspaper to school?''

He gave her a squeeze. ''No, I'm not mad. It was very nice of you to want to bring me for show-and-tell.'' He gave her an extra hug. ''I love you, Brittany.''

''I love you, too, Daddy,'' she responded, but the words were subdued.

As soon as she was gone, his mother said, ''Every little girl wants her father to be a hero.''

Tyler rubbed the tight muscles in his neck. ''Fine. I can be her hero while we're here in this house, but she doesn't need to know everything that happened in Hibbing, and I would appreciate it if you wouldn't encourage her to talk about it.''

''She's a child. She has questions.''

He frowned. ''Why did you give her the newspaper?''

''I didn't *give* it to her. Tyler, your picture was on the front page. She saw it when we were in the grocery store. It's rather difficult to pretend you weren't in that crash when it's been in the papers and on television.''

''I don't know why the media have to hound me. I'm sick and tired of them intruding in my life,'' he said, loosening his tie. He walked over to the sideboard and poured himself a Scotch on the rocks.

"There's nothing wrong with being a hero, Tyler," she said gently.

"Mom, please, not you, too." He took a swallow of the fiery liquid.

"You saved Kristen Kellar's life. At least that's what she says."

He grimaced. "Of course she would sensationalize everything. She's one of the media. A reporter. And you and I both know they feel that title gives them the right to invade everyone else's privacy. Have you forgotten what happened after Susan died?" He made a sound of disgust. "They were at the cemetery with their cameras."

"That was awful," she agreed solemnly, "but Kristen Kellar isn't a reporter. She's a news anchor," his mother added. "And a darn good one. She reports the news accurately and with sensitivity."

Again he made a sound, this time of disbelief.

"Well, she's told the world that without you she wouldn't be alive. I guess that makes you a hero."

"I think the eight people who died on that flight would disagree."

"You can't possibly think you're responsible for their deaths?" She looked at him with a look of horror. "Tyler, the plane split in two. There was no way you could've saved their lives."

He took another swig of the Scotch. "Since you weren't there, I don't think you know what I could or couldn't have done."

He set his glass down with a bit more force than necessary. Again, he knew he'd been sharper with her than he'd meant to be. What was wrong with him anyway? Lately, he seemed to fly off the handle at the slightest provocation.

"I'm sorry, Mom. Maybe we ought to change the subject. There's no point in arguing over something that's in the past. I've been living out of a suitcase for the past four days and I need a shower."

"And you're tired, aren't you?" His mother became all maternal once again, fussing over him as though he were a child instead of a thirty-five-year-old businessman. "There's plenty of time for you to rest before dinner, if you like. I'm going upstairs to finish Brittany's costume and leave you to unwind on your own." She gave his arm a gentle touch, then headed for the stairway. She stopped in midstride. "Oh, by the way, your mail is on the console in the hallway, and I left your phone messages on your desk."

Tyler nodded and watched his mother climb the steps to the second story. Then he walked over to the console where several days of mail had accumulated. He flipped through the pile until he came to a pale pink envelope. His name and address were handwritten and there was no return address.

He opened the envelope and found a single sheet of pale pink stationery. At the top printed in gray ink was the name Kristen Kellar, her address and phone number.

Dear Mr. Brant,

Please forgive me for taking so long to contact you, but as you are probably aware, I've been in the hospital until very recently. I wanted to speak to you before I was moved from the Hibbing hospital, but unfortunately that wasn't possible. Since I was told that you suffered only minor injuries and that you were discharged after a few days, I assume that you are in good health and have returned to work.

The purpose of this letter is to express my gratitude, although the words "Thank you" seem inadequate for expressing what's in my heart. I don't want to think about what the outcome might have been if you hadn't been on that flight. The value of your strength and determination cannot be measured. Please know that I will always remember the help you gave me.

Sincerely,
Kristen Kellar

Tyler stared at the feminine handwriting until he no longer saw words, but images. An engine on fire. Panic among the passengers. A plane torn in two. His heart began to race, his palms to sweat. He remembered the look on Kristen's face as she had frantically struggled to free herself from the twisted wreckage of the plane.

With a grimace, he crumpled her letter in his fist. He turned his attention to the other mail, determined to forget the crash.

He would forget. He had taught himself a long time ago to block out those images that had the power to play games with his emotions. And the memory of that plane crash was one of those images.

He was a survivor. Always had been, always would be.

So for the rest of the evening, Tyler didn't once think about Kristen Kellar or the crash. He played a board game with Brittany, sat with her while she watched *The Little Mermaid* video for the umpteenth time and then, despite his mother's warning, let her eat a giant chocolate bar while he read her a bedtime story.

After she'd fallen asleep, he went into his office and worked until midnight. When he finally crawled between the covers, he was weary, but it was a welcome weariness. He'd have no trouble falling asleep tonight.

And he didn't. Only it wasn't a peaceful sleep. No matter how exhausted he was, he couldn't prevent the dream.

He was in the broken half of the plane.

"I can't get free," a woman cried out to him, blood streaming down her face. "The seat belt is stuck."

Tyler hurried to her side only to discover the seat belt wasn't preventing her escape. Her right leg was trapped. With a strength he didn't know he possessed, he managed to bend the metal bar pinning her leg.

"We have to get out of here," she urged. "Look." Her eyes widened as she stared at the open end of the plane. The aircraft was slipping into the water.

"It's all right. We'll be okay," he assured her as water seeped into his shoes.

They were jostled as the plane sank lower. "I can't swim!" she cried as water rose around them.

Tyler reached for her. "Just hang on to my back," he instructed.

He felt two arms around his neck, but they soon lost their hold. He tried to reach her hands, but she was swept away by the strong current.

"Help me! Please, help me!"

He swam after her, but every time he thought he'd reached her, she slipped from his grasp. Over and over he tried to grab her hand until she was finally sucked under.

Gasping for breath, Tyler awoke with a start to find Brittany at his bedside.

"Daddy?"

He gulped in deep breaths, trying to calm his unsteady limbs as he swung his legs over the side.

"Daddy, will you help me find Tudie?"

For a moment, he was too shaken to speak. Finally, he asked, "Is he lost?" relieved that the cries for help were over a teddy bear and not a human being.

"I had him when I went to bed, but he's not there now," Brittany said in a tiny voice. "And I get scared when Tudie isn't sleeping with me."

"There's no need to be scared," Tyler said reassuringly, pulling her into his arms. "Daddy will help you find him, then I'll tuck you both in real tight so he doesn't get lost again, okay?"

Tyler thought how ironic it was that he was telling her not to be scared when he was the one who was trembling. He carried Brittany back to her room, turned on the light and set her down beside the bed.

"Sweetheart, it's no wonder Tudie disappeared. There's no room for him here," he told her as he pushed aside a collection of stuffed animals and dolls.

A quick look behind the bed proved his suspicions were correct. Tudie lay suspended between the mattress and the wall. Tyler fished him up over the brass headboard to the delight of his daughter.

"Thank you, Daddy." She welcomed the bear with open arms, kissed her father on the cheek and climbed back up onto the bed.

Tyler tucked her in, kissed her forehead, then turned out the light. As he crawled back into his own bed, he smiled to himself as he thought about his daughter and her beloved bear.

However, it wasn't Brittany occupying his thoughts as he fell back to sleep. It was the beautiful but bleeding face of the news anchor. Dark lashes framed frightened blue eyes, the once flawless skin now badly lacerated. He had tried to stop the bleeding, but pieces of glass and metal were embedded in her skin. He still shuddered when he thought about it.

He had done his best to forget that face. Done his best to put the plane crash behind him. He *had* put it behind him. It was others who wouldn't let him forget. His mother. Kristen Kellar. If she hadn't sent him the letter, he wouldn't have had her image haunting him tonight.

Well, he would tuck the memories away in a remote corner of his mind again. The crash was in the past. He had survived. She had survived. End of story.

He was not a hero. Not even close to being one.

THE DOORBELL RANG and for one brief moment Kristen Kellar wished she had the time to wash her hair, change out of her sweats and apply some makeup before answering it. Then the moment passed.

She had spent too much of her life fussing about her appearance. In the past three weeks, she'd discovered that it was hard to worry about her outward appearance when she felt so awful.

She struggled to her feet, reaching for the crutches propped against the sofa, and hobbled over to the intercom to hear her fiancé's voice say, "It's me."

Good grief! What was Keith doing at her apartment in the middle of the day? She should have washed her hair. Or at least changed her clothes. Keith always looked as if he'd stepped off the pages of *GQ*.

"Kristen, are you there?"

"Yes." She buzzed the lobby door open, then smoothed her hand down the front of her gray sweatshirt. When she heard a knock at the door, she checked through the peephole before releasing the dead bolt.

Standing on the other side with not a hair out of place, looking every bit as polished as he did on television each night, was the man voted the Twin Cities' number-one news anchor, Keith Jaxson. In his arms were flowers, lots of flowers.

Ever since the crash, he'd seemed distant and a bit impatient with what he considered her slow recovery. She knew he'd been disappointed by her request for a leave of absence from work. But now here he was bearing flowers, and she pushed such thoughts aside.

Her smile faded, however, the moment he spoke. The flowers weren't from him.

"Mailman." He grinned as if he'd said something witty. "Bob was going to have a messenger bring these over, but I said I was coming to see you and I might as well take them. I thought that the gifts and flowers would have stopped after a couple of weeks, but they just keep coming."

He didn't drop a kiss on her mouth as he stepped into the apartment but simply marched past her and headed for the dining-room table. Actually, he hadn't kissed her since before the crash...unless one counted the light brushing of his lips across her forehead he had given her in the hospital.

"Bob says he's never seen anyone get so many get-well wishes. You are one popular lady." He set the flowers and a large shopping bag filled with cards and packages on the table. "It's a good thing my ego's healthy, isn't it?"

"Isn't it, though," she murmured, wondering how she had never noticed just how self-centered he was. As he passed the mirror in the dining room, he smoothed his perfect hair.

"There are two more bags in my car. I can get them now or when I leave. Which do you prefer?" He didn't look at her, but rather past her, as if there were a roomful of people behind her.

"It doesn't matter," she answered as she hobbled toward the sofa.

"Then I'll get them later."

"Fine." She eased herself down onto the sofa.

Instead of coming to sit beside her, he stood at the edge of the glass-topped table, his hands in his pockets. "So how are you feeling?"

"Okay."

"Good." There was an awkward silence, then he tugged on his ear, saying, "I suppose the leg's starting to itch under that cast."

She ignored his comment. "Aren't you going to sit down?"

He shifted from foot to foot before finally settling on the chair across from her. He unzipped his black suede jacket but didn't take it off.

"I'm supposed to say hi from everyone at the station and tell you they miss you," he said with the same smile he used during his newscasts. The one that made women's hearts skip a beat. Kristen knew how easily that smile came to his lips and didn't return it.

"I'm sure Janey doesn't miss me. She's been wanting more air time." It was no secret around the station that Janey Samuels's goal was to be one of the evening anchors, and Kristen knew Janey would make the most of every minute of her absence.

"The less time she's in your chair, the less chance viewers will have to grow fond of her," Keith continued.

"And what's that supposed to mean?"

"You said the doctor's given you a clean bill of

health. Maybe you should think about coming back to work.''

"My leg's in a cast! What do you suggest I do? Sit sideways on the set and stick it out behind the desk?''

''You wouldn't have to do the entire thirty minutes on the set. You could sit in the newsroom and have the camera shoot a head shot. No one needs to see your cast.''

"And what about this?'' She pulled her hair away from her face and turned her head so that her puffy, discolored cheek was in full view.

He didn't try to hide his discomfort. ''Makeup will take care of that,'' he said weakly.

Her laugh was without humor. "I doubt it.''

"How do you know if you won't try? Bob told me he sent a makeup artist to the hospital and you refused to talk to her.''

''What's the point? I told you I'm not ready to go back to work. That's why I asked for a leave of absence.''

"Eventually, you'll be going back. Wouldn't it make sense to have a professional come here and show you how to apply the makeup? That way, you can practice so by the time you're ready to return, you'll feel comfortable.''

From the way he was staring at her, Kristin couldn't help but wonder if the practicing-at-home part wasn't for his benefit. Did he want her to wear the makeup so he wouldn't have to look at her scars? Not for the first time she had the feeling that he was repulsed by her swollen and bruised face.

She let the hair fall back across her cheek and angled her head to hide the scars. "Why are you pressuring me about this?"

"I'm not pressuring you," he denied. "It's just that I miss you at work, and in the hospital you told me you wanted to get back to the newsroom as soon as possible."

That was before the bandages had been removed from her face and she had seen the damage.

"I've changed my mind. I need more time to get my strength back."

"You told me a few minutes ago that you were feeling fine."

"I am. I'm just not ready to return to work."

"Your viewers will be disappointed." Then he gave her his heart-stopping grin and said, "I'll be disappointed."

It didn't stop Kristen's heart for even a moment.

"Have you read KC's column lately? Even she misses you," he added.

KC was a gossip reporter who had followed their romance with a fervent passion, never missing an opportunity to mock the two of them in her biweekly newspaper column under a special subheading— "Amorous Anchors."

"What she's really missing are the opportunities to make fun of us," Kristen said cynically.

"It's true we've been a target of her offbeat humor, but we should feel flattered," he said in a patronizing tone. "She says she gets a ton of calls from irate readers whenever she prints something unfavorable about us. I think that's why she does it. She loves to be controversial.''

''You mean she loves to dig into people's private lives,'' Kristen pointed out.

''It's all done in good humor.''

''You didn't say that when she reported that you needed to get rid of some of your big hair.''

He automatically smoothed a hand over the side of his head. ''She was right. I did have big hair when I arrived in Minneapolis. But the point is this. If KC misses the amorous anchors, the viewers do, too. They've come to expect that it'll be the two of us doing the news. We're the team they want to see. Just ask Bob.''

Kristen knew that Bob Yates as the news director had only one concern and that was ratings. If he thought another anchor could sustain those ratings, he wouldn't care if Kristen ever returned from medical leave. The fact that Keith was over here encouraging her meant that so far Janey hadn't done the job. That gave Kristen little comfort. Because if they were losing viewers, it meant another station was gaining them.

''You and I are like friends to many of those people who tune into Channel 12 each evening,'' Keith continued. ''They're concerned about you just the way they'd be concerned for a friend who was injured. Just look at the stacks of mail over there.'' He nodded toward the dining room.

Kristen knew what he said was true. In the five years she'd been at the station, she'd met many of the people who comprised their target audience. They were warm, friendly, caring members of a community she had grown to love.

"I'd like to say I could return next week, but..." She didn't finish, knowing perfectly well that it would be a mistake to go back to work in her present condition. "I really don't think I'm up to it."

"You could always ease back into it. Actually, I've come up with a way for you to do just that."

Suspicion began to creep into Kristen's mind when she saw Keith's eyes sparkling as if he had a great secret. "And what's that?"

"I've talked Bob into giving me the okay to go ahead with a *Profile in Courage.*"

These profiles were special features the Channel 12 news team produced to highlight community members who had performed acts of extreme bravery. "So how do I fit in?"

"I want you to work with me." He leaned forward, his face full of enthusiasm. "Guess who we're going to profile."

She gave him a blank look.

"Who is one of the most heroic men in the Twin Cities?"

Great. Now he was making it a guessing game. "I don't know," she said impatiently.

"It's someone who's important to both of us."

Kristen couldn't think of a single name.

"Tyler Brant," he finally revealed.

"Tyler Brant?" she repeated, her heart skipping a beat. "Has he agreed to the interview?"

"Not yet, but I don't foresee any problems in that area. Why would there be? We're not doing an investigative report. We're paying tribute to him. The viewers will love it!''

But would Tyler Brant? Kristen wondered. "He didn't strike me as the kind who would want the attention.''

"Are you kidding? Every guy likes to be called a hero.''

"Maybe,'' she said thoughtfully. She didn't tell him that she had tried several times to contact Tyler only to be told he was unavailable. Even after she'd left her name and phone number, he hadn't returned her calls.

"Not only is the man a hero,'' Keith continued, "but he's a well-respected member of the community. And there's an added benefit. If we do a profile of the two of you, we'll allow the viewers to see what you've been through the past couple of weeks and let them know that you're on the road to recovery.''

"Wait a minute. You said this was about Tyler Brant. Why would you profile me?'' she asked, uneasiness churning her stomach.

"Because he saved your life.'' He looked at her as if he were telling her the sky was blue.

"I don't want to be the subject of any show,'' she stated firmly.

"Why not? You said you were upset with the inaccuracy of many of the reports on the plane crash. This would be a way to set the record straight.'' He gestured toward the piles of mail in her dining room. "Just look at all those cards and letters. The viewers are worried about you. If we did a segment where we covered the crash, your hospitalization, your re-cuperation—''

''Stop right there,'' she interrupted him, holding up both hands in protest. ''You're not thinking about bringing a crew here?''

''All we'd need are a couple of shots of you at home. We have plenty of video from the crash site. If we interviewed a few doctors and nurses at the hospital, then close with you in the newsroom, stay-ing abreast of what's going on, we can show the public that you're still very much a part of the news team.''

Kristen could hardly believe what she was hearing. ''You're joking, right?''

''No. Why would I joke about your work?''

She stared at him in disbelief. ''Keith, you can't honestly think I'd want to be the subject of such a program?''

''Why not?''

''Because I don't want my personal life broadcast to the world, that's why,'' she protested. ''And I can't believe you could be so insensitive as to even suggest such a thing.''

He looked like a little boy who had been told he couldn't play baseball until after his homework was done. ''It's a news story, not an exposé,'' he re-minded her.

''It's an invasion of my privacy. Do you know how many times I've had reporters banging on my door since it happened?''

''Because your story is news. You were heroically rescued from a plane crash that killed eight other people. You survived, Kristen. You've worked in this business long enough to know that your situation is exactly what interests the public.''

She knew what he said was true. And at one time she would have understood exactly why he was suggesting she be the subject of the in-depth segment. As a journalist, she was familiar with the attitude members of her profession had about the stories they were covering. After all, she herself had often stuck a microphone into the faces of grieving relatives, crime victims—people who wanted to be left alone. Now she was on the other side herself. And she didn't like it.

''I'm not allowing anyone to come here and film my private life,'' she said firmly.

''All right. You don't need to have the camera crew come here. We'll skip the personal angle and shoot it from a career perspective.''

''You won't shoot it at all,'' she assured him. ''I mean it. I will not be the subject of any features— for you or anyone else.''

''You could have complete control over the content. Heck, you could even do the final edit,'' he proposed reluctantly.

''No.''

''Will you at least think about it?''

''No.''

If there was one thing Keith was used to getting it was his own way. When he stiffened his shoulders and tightened his mouth, it was obvious that he wasn't pleased with her refusal. Kristen discovered his handsome features weren't so handsome when he pouted. Actually, he looked quite ugly. Funny how she'd never noticed it before.

"Obviously, this crash has affected you emotionally. Why don't I give you time to think about it and call you later?" he suggested, rising to his feet, his hands automatically smoothing the wrinkles in his creased pants.

Kristen realized that his bringing the flowers and mail had simply been an excuse for him to come over and talk business. He hadn't come out of concern for her but because he wanted to do the feature segment and he needed her cooperation. Not only was she disappointed in him but in the Channel 12 news team, too. They didn't want her; they wanted her story. It was a sobering thought.

"I'm not going to change my mind, Keith," she told him.

His expression hardened. "Now what kind of attitude is that?"

She took a deep breath in an attempt to control the emotions swirling inside her, but it didn't help. "It's the attitude I have, and if you weren't so worried about how my absence is affecting your ratings you could take a moment to support me rather than try to put me through more stress." He looked startled by her outburst.

"Maybe you should mention these emotional periods you're having to your doctor. He could probably recommend some medication—"

"I don't need any more medication," she snapped. "What I need is a fiancé who understands what I've been through."

"I'm trying to understand, but you won't leave this apartment." He sighed. "Look, would you at least think about allowing the makeup artist to come for a visit? I'm emceeing the celebrity auction for the Children's Hospital next Saturday and I want you to be with me."

But only if you can cover your scars. He hadn't said the words aloud, but she knew what he was thinking. "I can't go."

"You won't even consider it?"

"I don't have the energy."

"You might feel differently by Saturday."

Kristen knew she wouldn't. Come Saturday, her cheek would still be swollen and bruised. The doctor had said four to six weeks. It had only been three. But she knew that—even if her face had been fine— she wasn't ready to face the outside world.

"Don't count on that happening," she said firmly.

He shook his head. "If you come with me to the door, I'll get those other two bags of mail for you."

She stared at him in disbelief. Did he honestly think it was easy for her to hobble around after him? If she used her crutches at all, it would be to beat him over the head, not to walk to the door so that he could hand her a couple bags of mail.

"Forget the damn mail," she barked at him.

He didn't say another word but quietly left. Without even kissing her forehead.

Strangely, Kristen was not disappointed.

CHAPTER TWO

"I DON'T THINK this is a good idea."

"Just do it. Please." Kristen sat in her usual position on the sofa with her leg propped up on the ottoman. Her best friend, Gayle Shaefer, knelt in front of the VCR, a couple of videocassettes beside her.

Before she inserted one, she asked Kristen, "Are you sure it wouldn't be better to see someone who's experienced in dealing with this kind of thing?"

"You think I need therapy?"

"I think talking to someone who understands what happens to a person who's been in a plane crash is probably a better way to get on with your life rather than looking at a bunch of taped footage," Gayle said candidly.

Kristen shook her head. "I'm not going to see any more doctors—and that includes psychiatrists, psychologists or whatever. I don't want to talk about the crash, Gayle." She ran her fingers through her hair. "I've done enough of that with my mother. It's all she ever wants to talk about when she calls."

"She's probably trying to sort through her own feelings. After all, she nearly lost her daughter."

Kristen knew Gayle was right. The problem was,

while talking about it may have been therapy for her mother, Kristen didn't need any reminders of how close she had come to losing her life in the plane crash.

"I didn't die. I have a broken leg and—" she gestured to her left cheek "—and a face that's messed up."

"And both will heal," Gayle reassured her in the voice Kristen had come to rely on over the years. "You'll go back to work and your life will be normal again."

"Yes, well, if I'm ever getting back to work, I need to look at those tapes. So let's see what you've got."

Gayle looked as if she wanted to protest, but didn't. "Okay, if you're sure you're ready for this."

Kristen wasn't sure. All she knew was that she needed to do something to try to make her life normal again. Ever since the accident, she'd been mired in a quagmire of emotions that were unfamiliar to her. Guilt. Self-pity. Uncertainty.

None of them made any sense. She was alive. She'd survived an ordeal in which others had died. Yes, her face had required plastic surgery, but it would heal. She should've been grateful and happy. Yet she wasn't. She was this pathetic bundle of nerves.

"Let's do it," she told Gayle, clenching her hands in her lap.

Gayle pushed the play button. Within seconds, Kristen was shivering as images she remembered all too vividly appeared before her eyes. Gayle didn't move but stayed in front of the VCR, ready to stop the tape should the experience become too much for her friend.

As the images continued, Kristen wondered whether she should have listened to Gayle. She watched as the camera scanned the crash site, capturing all that could be seen of the broken plane left projecting out of the water.

Kristen lost control when she saw a man's hat floating on the water. "Oh my G—" Her hand flew to her mouth as she choked back a lump of emotion in her throat. "No wonder everyone said it was a miracle we made it out." Then she started to weep.

Gayle popped the tape out of the VCR. "That's enough." She went over to the sofa and put her hand on Kristen's shoulder. "I'm sorry. I know this is hard for you."

"I'm o-okay," she choked out on a sob. "R-really. Show me the other one," she said, sniffling as she reached for a tissue.

"I will not!"

Kristen blew her nose. "Gayle, please. I'm okay."

"No, you're not."

"I am and I have to see it. I won't break down again. I promise. It was just the shock of seeing the plane."

Gayle didn't look convinced, but she finally slid the next cassette into the VCR. "Here's the tape that came from our Hibbing affiliate."

For Kristen, seeing the crash reported in a matter-of-fact tone by another reporter did not have the same emotional impact as the unedited footage. Although she shuddered once more at the scenes of the shattered airplane, she was able to separate her emotions from the images on the television so that she was no longer reliving the crash. Until her picture appeared on the screen.

It was one of the publicity photos the station used regularly. Next to it was a picture of Tyler Brant—the man who had saved her life. He wore a business suit and tie, his dark hair neatly trimmed, his eyes showing no emotion whatsoever. It was a typical business photo that could have been in the pages of any corporate report. There was no smile on his face.

Kristen watched the entire report, then rewound the tape with the remote until she came to the shot of Tyler Brant. She listened again as the reporter explained that Tyler had been on his way to Hibbing to check out the damage a fire had done to his electronics plant. She freeze-framed the tape.

"There he is. My hero." She stared at him thoughtfully, trying to connect the austere-looking man in the photograph with the one who had carried her for miles in the cold, refusing to let her perish in the wilderness.

If she were to close her eyes, she thought she might be able to feel his warm breath on her cheek, hear his voice commanding her, "Stay with me, Kristen. Don't you dare go to sleep. Do you hear me?"

His arms had had a strength that she'd needed, and even if she hadn't just seen his picture on the screen, she still could've recalled every detail of his face.

It was not as photogenic a face as her fiancé's. It

had no dimples, no flirtatious sparkle in the eyes, no dazzling smile that would cause a woman's heart to miss a beat. His thick, dark beard had been matted with blood, she recalled, his dark eyes compassionate, despite the pain he must have felt.

"I think he looks like a mountain man in a business suit," Gayle commented. "What's he like as a person?"

If anyone else had asked that question, Kristen would have said she hadn't had time to get to know Tyler Brant. However, Gayle had always been the one person she could talk to without guarding her words.

She shrugged. "He didn't say much. I did most of the talking. He wanted me to because he was worried I'd fall asleep, which is not a good thing to do when you're suffering from hypothermia. You probably know as much about him as I do just from watching the news."

"Does he have a sense of humor?"

Kristen shot her a look of exasperation. "How would I know? We were fighting for our lives. Although," she added thoughtfully, "he did laugh when I told him I couldn't leave the plane without finding my gold cross—you know, the one my grandmother gave me."

"Let me get this straight. The plane was sinking, and you were worried about your necklace?"

"It was special to me...and people aren't always rational in times of distress," she said in her own defense.

"Since you're not wearing it, I assume you never found it," Gayle remarked.

She shook her head. "He did look for it, though."

"He must be strong, considering how far he carried you."

"Mmm-hmm. And it was so cold. Our clothes were wet, which made me even heavier, yet he never complained."

"He risked his life to save you."

She nodded. "That's why I feel this...this debt. Like I need to do something for him. Does that make sense?"

"Of course it does. Have you spoken to him since the crash?" Gayle asked.

She shook her head. "He's never returned my phone calls."

"Maybe that's why you're having trouble putting all this behind you. Maybe you need to see this guy so you can move on with your life."

Gayle's suggestion wasn't new to Kristen. She'd had the same thought herself. Ever since the crash, Tyler Brant had been in her thoughts a lot. She longed to know how he was coping. Whether the crash had changed his life. Did he question why he was chosen to survive while the others had died? Did he ever think about that day? Did he ever think about her?

That last question was the one that nagged her the most. Did he feel a sense of responsibility for saving her life? While she was in the hospital, she'd expected him to visit or at least call.

He hadn't.

On several occasions, she'd tried to reach him at his office only to be told he was unavailable. Then she'd been bold enough to call his home only to have some woman tell her he was out of town on business. Finally, she had put her thoughts in a letter and mailed it to him.

Still, she'd heard nothing from him. Obviously, he didn't want to see her again. And yet he'd been so kind that day of the crash. He'd seemed so interested in her, asking about her family and giving her the impression that because they had survived a tragedy together, they would always share a special bond of friendship. Then he had left the Hibbing hospital without so much as a goodbye.

"I'm not going to force him to talk to me. If he doesn't think we have anything to say to one another, I'm not going to push the issue," she told Gayle.

"But it's not over for you, is it?"

"Not yet," she answered quietly. "But it will be when I'm not cooped up in this apartment. This cast on my leg is making me feel claustrophobic."

"Maybe we can drive around in the car and listen to the police scanner," Gayle suggested.

Kristen gave her a weak smile.

"We could take in a movie."

"And drag this monstrosity of a cast down those narrow theater aisles? No thanks."

"Then I'll go get us a couple of videos."

"You should go home. You have a daughter who needs you."

"It's Tom's turn to take her to her swimming lesson. He can easily get her ready for bed."

"He's been doing that far too often because you've been over here fussing over me. Go home and be with your family. Please."

Gayle glanced at her watch. "It is getting late. Are you sure you're going to be all right?"

Kristen nodded. "Positive. I have everything I need. A good book, the remote control and a bottle of diet soda. What more could I want?" she quipped.

She didn't fool her best friend. "There's a light at the end of the tunnel. You just have to be patient."

Kristen nodded. "I know."

Gayle ejected the rewound tape and slipped it back into its case. "You know any time you want to get back into the swing of things you can always tag along with me. You don't have to go back to the news desk."

"Thanks for the offer, but I'm not ready to go back yet," she said a bit more defensively than she intended.

Gayle placed an understanding hand on her arm. "Then don't. Take whatever time you need to feel like your old self again."

Long after Gayle had gone, Kristen thought about those words. Would she ever feel like her old self again? How could she when she was having difficulty remembering who that person was?

It was true that she'd been through the kind of thing that caused people to reassess their priorities in life. To stop and smell the roses, so to speak. But it was more than that. It was…

It was what? she wondered. Why did she feel so restless? Why did she have periods of weakness even

though the doctor had said there was nothing wrong
with her physically? Why did she want to cry for no
apparent reason? And why could she not stop thinking about Tyler Brant?

TYLER DID NOT HAVE a good day. It shouldn't have
surprised him. He'd had a restless night. When he
hadn't been tossing and turning, he'd slept fitfully,
and most of his dreams—none of them pleasant—
had involved Brittany.

In each of them, she was out of reach. At the top
of an escalator, astride a painted horse on a revolving
carousel, in a car speeding away from his home. She
would call out to him for help, yet although he could
see her, he couldn't reach her.

They were the nightmares that had haunted him
often during the past five years. He didn't need a
therapist to interpret their meaning. He had a fear of
losing his daughter. What father didn't?

That's why he hadn't been pleased when his
mother had announced that Brittany was going on a
field trip with her class. To the Science Museum, of
all places. How was one teacher with the help of
three parents going to keep track of twenty-two first-
graders in a place that big?

He'd been tempted to keep Brittany home from
school that morning. The last thing he needed was to
spend his day worrying about her getting snatched
by some pervert wandering the halls of the Science
Museum. He knew his fear was irrational, yet he
couldn't stop himself from imagining all sorts of awful things that could happen to his daughter. It was

only when his mother said that she would go along on the trip that he had signed his consent.

Then he'd had a flat tire on the way to work. Not only had he missed his meeting with the director of marketing, he'd had his lunch appointment canceled at the last minute. To top it off, the entire afternoon had been spent with engineers trying to figure out a solution to a mechanical problem that kept automatically shutting down one of the assembly lines.

By the time he arrived home that evening, he was tired and irritable. He wasn't the only one. Brittany whined her way through dinner, which only confirmed one thing. The trip to the museum had been too much for her. As much as he wanted to tell his mother this, he wisely held his tongue and patiently put up with Brittany's whining.

When the phone rang shortly after dinner, it was his mother who answered it. "It's Keith Jaxson from the Channel 12 news!" Excitement danced in her eyes. "He wants to speak to you."

Tyler groaned. Had he known the media were still pursuing that story, he would have let the answering machine take the call. He'd managed to avoid all reporters up to now.

"Yes, this is Tyler Brant," he said into the receiver.

"Mr. Brant, Keith Jaxson with Channel 12 news. How are you this evening?"

"I've been better, Mr. Jaxson." Tyler could see no reason for social niceties.

"I'm sorry to hear that. I won't take up much of your time. The reason I'm calling has to do with

Kristen Kellar.'' He paused as if waiting for Tyler to ask what about her, but he didn't. There was only dead air, which Keith quickly filled. "Here at Channel 12 news, we all miss her terribly and we're doing everything we can to help her get back to work as quickly as possible."

"I don't understand what that has to do with me, Mr. Jaxson," Tyler said.

"I'm sure you're aware that Kristen has a huge audience here in the Twin Cities—an audience that's very concerned about how she's doing. Because they're so interested, we'd like to do a special report to show just how hard Kristen's working to recover from the plane crash. What she's been through is remarkable and the public ought to see just what a strong, determined lady she is."

"That's all fine, but I still don't see what it has to do with me."

"Why, you're the reason she's here to tell her story. It wouldn't be complete if we didn't include an interview with the man who saved her life."

"I'm afraid that's not possible," Tyler stated in no uncertain terms.

"It wouldn't have to be a long interview, just a brief visit to either your home or office—"

"No." Tyler cut him off before he could finish.

"You're a hero, Mr. Brant," Jaxson reminded him.

"No, I'm a man who works long hours so I can come home to some peace and quiet and not have to worry about the media invading my privacy."

That silenced Jaxson momentarily. "I apologize

for disturbing you. I had hoped that you would want to say a few words about the remarkable courage Kristen has shown, but I see that I was wrong.''

''Yes, you were, Mr. Jaxson. And I would appreciate not being contacted again by your station. I have nothing to say on the subject of the plane crash,'' he said with a note of finality that nobody could mistake.

As soon as he'd hung up, Tyler could see that his mother was upset. However, she didn't say anything to him but went about the business of clearing away the dinner dishes, her mouth tightly set in a grim expression of disapproval. She disappeared into the kitchen only to return a few minutes later. She reached into the pocket of her apron and pulled out a fistful of papers.

''What's this?'' he asked as she dumped the pile in front of him.

''The messages that were on the answering machine when I got home today. Someone from Channel 12 was trying to get ahold of you. I didn't realize it was Keith Jaxson.''

Tyler didn't say anything but glanced through the crumpled papers. They were all from Channel 12. Most from a producer named LeeAnn. All said to please call regarding Kristen Kellar.

''They just won't leave me alone,'' he complained, shaking his head in disgust. ''When are they going to get it through their thick skulls that I want nothing to do with them?''

Irritation simmered inside him. Maybe if he hadn't had such a rotten day, he might've simply ignored the messages and gone to bed. But he *had* had a bad day. And he was furious that there were people out there determined to invade what little privacy he had. So he planted a kiss on Brittany's cheek, reached for his coat and went out to his car. It was time he put an end to this once and for all.

He was no hero.

KRISTEN WATCHED JANEY and Keith on the six o'clock news. Saw the two of them bantering the way she and Keith had bantered in what seemed like an eternity ago. It had been only four weeks, but it was the longest four weeks of Kristen's life. Janey was a natural. She had the look, and as Kristen was painfully aware, looks were everything in television.

Janey acted as if the anchor desk were hers. So confident, so at ease. With Kristen's job. With Kristen's fiancé. Kristen knew she should be worried. She wasn't.

She told herself that if Janey could maintain the ratings while she was on leave, that was all that really mattered. She didn't want her job back. At least not yet. So why did she feel like she was on the outside looking in?

Maybe Keith was right. Maybe she had had too much time to think. Maybe the only way to get back on the inside was to go back to work.

Maybe not. She tossed a pillow at the television, frustrated with her indecision. She wasn't happy staying at home recuperating, yet she really didn't want to return to the newsroom.

When the intercom buzzed from the lobby, she

was tempted to ignore the sound. It couldn't be Keith since he was at the station, and Gayle had a class on Wednesdays. When the buzzing persisted, she hobbled over to the intercom.

"Who is it?" she asked, her voice laced with an impatience she didn't try to hide.

"Tyler Brant."

Kristen gulped. *Tyler Brant.* The man of her dreams. The man she'd been trying to reach for weeks. The man she needed to thank.

"Come on up. I'm number 211." She pressed the button to open the lobby door.

As she waited for him to arrive, anxiety sent a rush of adrenaline through her body. Why was he here? Did he want to talk about the crash and the impact it had had on his life? Maybe when he read her letter, he had sensed her need to thank him in person for saving her life. Could it be that he needed to talk to her as much as she needed to talk to him?

When he knocked on her door, her mouth went dry. For weeks, she had rehearsed what she would say to him. Now her mind was a blank. Maybe "thank you" was all that was really necessary.

She peered through the peephole and got a shock. The person standing outside her door looked nothing like the man who had rescued her from the icy waters of the river. Gone was the thick, dark beard that had covered his jaw. There was nothing, not even a mustache, to darken the lower portion of his face.

She unlocked the dead bolt and opened the door. Her eyes met his, and she felt an instant connection. They may have spent only a few hours together, but it seemed like so much longer. She'd been right to believe that for the rest of her life she would feel linked to this man in some intangible way.

Instead of saying, "Hello, how are you?" she blurted out, "You're okay," as a way of greeting him, then felt ridiculous. Of course he was okay. He was better than okay. He was healthy, virile and looking strong. She needed to explain her inane remark. "In the hospital they told me you had come through everything with only a few minor injuries, but I never got to see you, so I guess I never really believed you were all right."

He only said, "May I come in?"

His voice was stiff and formal, not at all like the way he'd talked to her after the crash. His eyes were cold and distant.

"Please." She motioned for him to step inside. "Would you like me to take your jacket?" she asked, leaning on one of the crutches for support.

"No, I'll keep it, thank you. I won't be staying long."

She shivered, wondering what had happened to the man who had talked so tenderly to her after the crash. She hobbled over to the living room. He followed.

"Have a seat," she said, noticing how disorderly her apartment looked with the pillow and blanket on the sofa, books and magazines scattered across the coffee table, the end tables littered with glasses and empty plates. She started to fold the blanket, then realized there was no point in trying to straighten up the place now. "Can I get you something to drink?"

she asked as he took a seat on one of the moss-green wing chairs.

"No, thank you."

He looked around the apartment, his expression revealing nothing of what he was thinking. Kristen was grateful. She didn't want to see disapproval in his eyes.

Instead of sitting on the sofa across from him, she took the chair next to his. It put him to her right, which meant she could keep her scarred cheek away from his view. As long as she didn't look him straight in the eye, he wouldn't notice it. Since leaving the hospital, she had become adept at looking at people from an angle.

And the angle from which she viewed Tyler Brant told her his face was very different from the one she had etched in her memory. She found it fascinating that facial hair could change a man's image so drastically. Without the beard, he looked much younger. He was also extremely good-looking, something she hadn't really appreciated before. For four weeks she had thought of him as someone who'd rescued her, not as a man she might be physically attracted to.

"You're probably wondering why I'm here," he began.

"I assume it's because of my letter," she said almost shyly. Now that she was in the same room with him, she suddenly felt like a character from one of those old adventure movies. And she was afraid that that was exactly how she would sound if she tried to thank him for saving her life. Like some helpless, simpering female gushing over a big, strong, macho man.

She needn't have worried. He was no superhero, she quickly discovered.

"I wish you hadn't sent me that letter," he said, still no emotion in his voice.

To her dismay, she blushed. "I simply wanted to thank you, Mr. Brant," She shifted uncomfortably on the chair.

"It wasn't necessary. I did what anyone would have done in my position."

There was no hint of friendliness in his tone. No softening of the lines on his face, no understanding in those dark eyes. Nothing about him resembled the man who had worked frantically to free her from the plane and carry her to safety. The man sitting next to her could have been a complete stranger instead of the man who had tenderly administered first aid to her wounds.

"I don't believe that's true," she told him.

"You're entitled to believe what you want, Ms. Kellar."

Kristen felt as if he had dealt her a blow. Why was he behaving this way? She had thought that when she saw him again it would be a warm, friendly meeting with hugs and smiles. Instead, she was sitting next to him feeling awkward and wishing that he'd leave.

"If you didn't appreciate my letter, why are you here?" she asked, seeing no point in wasting any more time.

"I think we need to get something straight."

Kristen's heart pounded in her throat. "And that is?"

"I'm not going to do any interview regarding the plane crash—not for you and certainly not for your boyfriend. I don't want him calling my house bothering my family and I won't tolerate being stalked just so the two of you can improve your ratings." The words were spoken so quietly Kristen might have thought he wasn't overly upset. But one look in his eyes told her he was extremely upset.

She swallowed with difficulty, then said, "First of all, I didn't arrange for anyone to call your house. In case you haven't noticed, I'm not working at Channel 12 at the moment and I have no intention of being a part of any story that has to do with the crash." She leaned closer to the lamp that separated them. Then she turned her head and pulled the hair away from her cheek. "Do you honestly think I want the world to see this?"

Unlike Keith, Tyler Brant didn't flinch at the sight of her scarred face. Nor did he look uncomfortable. For the first time since he'd entered her apartment, she saw something other than coldness in his eyes. For several moments, they simply stared at each other without speaking, as if they were once more two people struggling to survive. Kristen was the first to look away.

He was the first to speak. "I'm sorry," he apologized, his voice sounding more like the one she remembered. At first she thought the apology was meant for her scarred face. But then he added, "I thought you were involved in the TV report. Your name did come up several times,''

"It shouldn't have," she said quietly, pulling the hair back down across her cheek. She moved away from the lamp, sitting back in her chair. "Believe me, Mr. Brant, you don't have to worry about my wanting to do a follow-up story on the plane crash. I have no desire to relive that awful day."

"I'm glad to hear that. Can I count on you to use your influence with management to stop any plans to the contrary?"

She chuckled sarcastically. "I'm only an anchor-woman."

"I've seen the ratings. You're very popular in the Twin Cities."

"That was before this happened." She was unable to keep the bitterness from her voice and immediately regretted letting him see her self-pity. She reached for her crutches and rose to her feet. "Look, I don't know if it'll help, but I'll talk to my boss at the station. Now if you don't mind, I'm rather tired. I haven't recovered my full strength since the crash." She didn't look at him but at her crutches as she maneuvered through the maze of furniture in the living room.

"You don't need to see me to the door," he told her. "I can find my way out."

"All right." She watched him walk away, unable to help noticing his broad shoulders. No wonder she had found such comfort in his arms. Tyler Brant was not a weak man, either mentally or physically.

They didn't exchange another word. It wasn't until

after Kristen heard the door shut that she sank onto the sofa, laid her head on the pillow and pulled the blanket over her shoulders. Any hope she had been harboring that he felt a connection to her was gone. He was just a guy who had done what he had to do in an emergency situation. Now he wanted to forget it—and her. That much had been evident tonight.

"Some hero," she muttered to herself, then swallowed back a tear that threatened but never did fall.

CHAPTER THREE

TYLER CHASTISED HIMSELF all the way home from Kristen's. He shouldn't have gone to see her. He could've telephoned and accomplished the same results. It would've been the wiser thing to do because he wouldn't now be haunted by the look on her face when she'd shown him her swollen, bruised cheek.

He could still see that angry, defensive stare she'd given him as she thrust her face under the light. She'd thought he'd be shocked into some kind of negative reaction. What she hadn't realized was that—compared with the way her cheek had looked when he'd last seen her—her face looked remarkably good.

She must have had the top reconstructive surgeon in the country. It only made sense. She made her living based on her looks. Maybe he should have said something positive about her face.

But he suspected that no matter what he might've said, she would've interpreted it as pity. And it was obvious she was already immersed in enough of that herself. Besides, he doubted that she would've believed him if he'd told her it didn't look as bad as she thought it did.

There probably wasn't a thing he could've said

that would've eased her pain. Not even the truth, which was that he was surprised at what the plastic surgeon had accomplished

Even if some scarring remained, her beauty would still be intact. Until today, he had attributed part of her attractiveness to the skill of makeup artists. But tonight there had been no makeup, no fake eyelashes, no designer wardrobe, no hairstyle created by an expensive salon. Tonight he had seen the woman, not the TV news anchor.

Gone was the self-confident, smiling face that still appeared in ads for the Channel 12 news. In its place was a hauntingly sad face that tugged on his emotions. He wished that his anger with Keith Jaxson hadn't kept him from acting like a decent human being. It wouldn't have cost him anything to show her some compassion.

The problem was, would compassion be all that he needed to give her? The minute she'd opened the door to him, he'd felt as if he were opening a can of worms better left undisturbed. Every instinct inside him warned him that as much as he wanted to help Kristen Kellar, he couldn't allow himself to be drawn into her life.

After what happened when Susan died, he knew better than to let his heart dictate any course of action. Tough was what he needed to be. Emotionally and mentally. It was the only way he would survive. And he had to survive. For his daughter's sake.

Kristen Kellar would just have to find her way out of the darkness without his help.

IN THE DAYS THAT FOLLOWED, Kristen saw little of Keith. He told her his involvement with a celebrity basketball game was taking all his free time, but she suspected that he simply didn't want to be around her. As Gayle often said, it was a good thing Keith hadn't become a doctor. He was seriously lacking when it came to bedside manners.

So she was surprised when he offered to take her to the doctor on the day her cast was to be removed. Knowing how much he disliked being around hospitals, she saw it as a sign that he was making an effort to fix whatever was wrong between them.

Although it was a cold, gray November day, Kristen felt as though the sun were shining when she walked out of the hospital minus the cast. On the way home, Keith invited her to lunch at the Chinese Lantern. When she suggested they get takeout, he agreed and told her he wanted to have some time alone with her.

As they sat across from each other at her kitchen table, it felt almost like old times. She could feel the tension seeping out of her body as they talked.

"It's a good thing it's almost winter," she commented as they ate Szechuan chicken with their chopsticks. "My leg's looking pretty puny."

Keith smiled his perfect smile and said, "The good news is that you're no longer confined to this apartment. It's time you get out and do things. Have some fun."

"You're right," she agreed, although the very thought sent a ripple of fear through her. She pushed aside her half-eaten meal and concentrated on her tea. "I'll have to get back into things slowly." She emphasized the word "slowly."

He reached across the table and squeezed her hand. "I'm glad to hear you say that because we need to make plans."

"Plans?"

"Mmm-hmm," he said, turning his attention back to his food, which he ate with enthusiasm. "You know, for our trip?"

Anxiety crept through her nerves. "Trip?"

"To the Bahamas. For Thanksgiving." He gave her a broad grin. "You haven't forgotten about it, have you?"

She hadn't forgotten. She knew they were supposed to meet his family for the holiday, but she'd assumed that because of what had happened those plans would be postponed. She opened a packet of artificial sweetener and added it to her tea. "You still want to go?"

"Of course. It'll be good for us. We'll get away from the cold. Spend some time with my family."

She took a sip of tea, then looked at him over the cup. "Maybe we should stay here. I know how to roast a turkey. We could have a quiet dinner for two at either your place or mine."

"On Thanksgiving?" He shot her a look of disbelief. "It's a day to be with friends and family. My mom says there'll be twelve of the Jaxsons there. And Bob's already arranged the schedules so we can both be gone at the same time. Can't you just see it? Four days and nights on the white sand beaches, lying in the sun, drinking piña coladas. It'll be great

for you. We'll tan up that puny white leg of yours."
He looked at her with excitement beaming all over
his face.

Kristen was not excited. The four days and nights
on the beach sounded wonderful, but there was one
huge problem Keith didn't know about.

There was no way she was ready to get back on
an airplane. Not yet.

"You're not saying anything." Some of the excitement faded from his face.

"It sounds lovely...."

"But?"

She wet her lips before she tried to explain. "It's
not that I don't want to go. I do. But the last time I
was on a plane, it crashed." She had to clutch her
hands in her lap to keep them from trembling at the
memory.

"I know it was a traumatic experience for you, but
you have to remember that plane crashes are rare.
Especially among the big airlines. I think your
chances of ever being involved in one are something
like one in 250,000."

"Well, I lost to the odds, didn't I?" she said
grimly.

He groaned and threw down his napkin in frustration. "It's not going to happen again, and you can't
even think there's a possibility it might."

"That's easy for you to say."

"Yes, it is, because I understand the laws of prob-
ability. It's far more dangerous to drive your Audi to
work each day than it is to get on a plane." When
she didn't say anything, he tried another tack.

"Come on, honey. You're not going to let fear keep you from doing something you want to do, are you? Do you really plan to let fear run your life?"

"You can put away your amateur psychology. It's not going to work." She started clearing the dishes.

"Are you saying you won't even think about it?"

"I can't think about it. It's too soon." She scraped the remains of her lunch into the garbage disposal and turned it on, not wanting to look at her fiancé. Because she knew there wouldn't be understanding in his eyes—only impatience.

Actually, he was angry. "This isn't like you, Kristen."

"What isn't like me?"

"The way you've been behaving. Ever since you've come home from the hospital, you've been moody and indifferent. You haven't been interested in anything I have to say. You haven't cared whether we even spend any time together."

"Don't try to make me the villain in all this, Keith. In all the time I've been cooped up here in my apartment, I can count on one hand the number of times you've visited," she snapped, still keeping her back to him as she rinsed dishes in the sink.

"And whose fault is that?"

She turned around then and glared at him. "Well, I can tell by the tone of your voice you don't think it's yours."

"Because every time I come over, I feel like I'm on a roller coaster with your emotions. You're either angry or depressed or anxious or tired." He rose to his feet and came to stand in front of her.

"Well, excuse me," she drawled. "I was in a crash that almost killed me."

"Which is all the more reason why you should be deliriously happy. You're alive!"

Kristen stared at him in disbelief. He just didn't get it. It was because she was alive that she was having problems. She had survived; eight others hadn't. Not a day passed when she didn't question why she had been given the chance to live. It was a terrible burden to carry, one that had her questioning almost everything in her life.

Keith grasped her by the shoulders. "What I want to know is what happened to the woman I fell in love with? The one who loved being with people? The one who always had a smile and chose to look at the glass as being half-full instead of half-empty?"

"I guess you'll have to accept that she's changed," she said soberly.

"Well, it hasn't been for the better."

The look on his face sent a chill through Kristen. She didn't want to cry, but she couldn't keep the tears from misting in her eyes. "I'm trying to get my life back together, but I feel as if my whole world has been turned upside down. Last month there wasn't a cloud on my horizon. Now…" Her words trailed off on a sob.

The sight of her tears made him pull her into his arms and hug her. "I know it's been tough, but you have to get on with your life. You can't wallow in self-pity."

She pushed him away, swallowing back the tears. "Self-pity? Is that what you think this is?"

He groaned again. "I don't know what it is. All I know is that you have to make some effort to move forward. I can't take much more of this."

"Is that some kind of ultimatum? Either I get happy or else?"

He left her question unanswered, only saying, "You're tired. You'd better get some rest." He started for the door, grabbing his jacket on the way. "I've got to go or I'll be late for work."

And Kristen added one more to the total number of days that had passed without his kissing her.

TYLER DIDN'T EXPECT that he'd ever see Kristen Kellar again. But it bothered him that he'd been so abrupt with her. He'd blamed her for something she hadn't done, and the more he thought about it, the more he realized that he owed her an apology. When his mother showed him KC's column one morning, he called Kristen to tell her he was coming over to see her.

According to the gossip columnist, there were problems in paradise. The engagement was all but a thing of the past and her job at the television station was looking pretty uncertain, as well. Rumor was that her injuries from the plane crash were more serious than the station had reported earlier.

None of these things should have been any concern of Tyler's. Whatever happened to Kristen Kellar was none of his business. Or at least he didn't want it to be. But he couldn't forget the way she looked when he'd been at her apartment. So alone. So lost. So vulnerable.

She looked as if she needed someone to take care of her. He raked a hand through his hair as he drove. He had made a habit of staying away from women who were emotionally needy. Yet here he was driving over to check on one he hardly knew and bringing her flowers.

As he parked his car, he made a promise to himself. "You are going to go in there, see that she's all right, apologize and leave. That's it."

All it took was one look at her and Tyler knew he couldn't keep any such promise. When she opened the door, he saw that the cast was gone from her leg. Instead of wearing sweatpants cut off at the knee, she had on a pair of dark leggings and a long, baggy white sweater that hid her slender curves. Even without the cast, she looked more fragile than the last time.

She didn't smile when she saw him. He wasn't surprised. He'd given her no reason to do anything but scowl at him.

"Mr. Brant," she said, standing with her hip propped against the door, her body language telling him he was not welcome.

"Tyler," he corrected her. "These are for you." He handed her the bouquet of flowers. "I should've sent them to the hospital."

"It wasn't necessary, but thank you." She took the flowers from him.

"Can I come in?"

She looked as if she wanted to say no but finally stepped aside. Her hair was shiny and it bounced as she walked. She still combed it so that it fell over her left cheek. He could tell she'd been expecting him by the order in the apartment. Unlike the last time he'd visited, there were no dirty dishes in the living room.

"You're probably wondering why I'm here," he said as once more he took one of the chairs in the living room.

"When you called, you said you wanted to apologize." This time, she chose to sit across from him on the sofa. "And as I told you on the phone, it's not necessary. I know you were upset about the way the media have been prying into your life."

"That doesn't justify the way I behaved, but I want you to know I..." He hesitated as the truth hit him like a ton of bricks.

He was here not simply to apologize but because of the way she had looked at him. As if he could give her something no one else could give her. He'd responded to her in a purely masculine way.

"I want to set the record straight," he finally concluded.

"Well, you can consider it straightened," she said with an indifference he found annoying.

At that point in the conversation, he should have excused himself and headed for the door. The air had been cleared. There was no reason for him not to walk out of her life and not look back.

But something kept him sitting in that chair. Maybe it was the haunted look in her eyes. Or maybe it was because he could smell the faint aroma of her perfume. Or maybe it was because he simply liked looking at her. Whatever the reason, instead of getting up to leave, he said, "I see the cast is gone."

"Gone, but not forgotten," she remarked dryly.

"I broke my arm as a kid and I still remember what it was like. Heavy. Itchy." He shook his head wistfully. "Your leg's going to be okay, isn't it?"

She nodded. "The doctor said it healed remarkably well."

She looked everywhere but at him when she talked. Tyler wondered what was going through her mind and finally asked, "And what about the rest of you? Has that healed remarkably well, too?"

Her head jerked up. "It's been a slow process, but I'm getting there."

"I'm glad to hear that." The silence that followed quickly became awkward. Tyler ended it by saying, "I should probably go."

Just as he was about to get up, she said, "Do you ever wonder why we were chosen?"

"Chosen for what?"

"To survive."

The question caught him off guard. "I don't think we were *chosen* exactly. It just happened that way."

She looked at him then, her eyes filled with uncertainty. "None of the others had a chance to escape," she said quietly. "Why us?"

Tyler knew exactly what she was saying. He would have been lying if he'd told her he didn't ever question the reason for their survival. But it was a subject he kept tucked away in the back of his mind in a file he didn't want to access. That's why he breathed a sigh of relief when his pager beeped.

"Is there a phone I could use?" he asked.

She pointed to the one on the end table, then stood. "I'll be in the kitchen."

Tyler waited until she was gone, then phoned the number showing on his pager. It was the security guard at the plant wanting to let him know that a missing set of keys had been found. Nothing that needed his immediate attention.

Kristen didn't know that. He could easily have said he was needed at the plant and left. He didn't. He wandered into the kitchen where he found her filling a kettle at the sink.

"I thought I'd have a cup of tea. Would you like one?" she asked over her shoulder.

He glanced at the counter and saw a can of clam chowder for one. He had a pretty good idea that it was going to be her dinner as soon as he was gone.

"You like seafood?" he asked her.

"Yes, why?"

"I know a great place where they make good clam chowder." He saw her glance at the can of soup. "Want to come with me?" The words were out before he could question their wisdom.

"Now?"

"You haven't eaten, have you?"

"No, but—"

"So let me buy you a bowl of real soup."

"That's not necessary," she said, blushing.

"You don't need to eat?" he asked, trying for a lighter tone.

It didn't work. "You don't have to buy me dinner." She set the kettle on the stove.

"I'd like to."

"It's a nice gesture, but..." She paused as if considering whether or not she should tell him the reason for the "but." Finally, she said, "I find it's better if I don't go out in public"

"Better how?"

She looked a bit uneasy as she said, "Being on television makes me the object of attention. I prefer to stay home rather than have people staring at me."

"Did you feel this way before the crash, too?"

"Not really. With a job like mine, I expect to be recognized, but what I don't want is pity." She hugged herself as if suddenly cold.

"Then you'll like this place with the great clam chowder. It's small, and all the people who go there only want a quiet dinner."

She raised an eyebrow. "Really."

"Really," he repeated. "So will you come?"

From the way she hesitated, he thought she was about to turn down his offer. Then to his surprise, she said, "I'll get my coat."

KRISTEN DIDN'T UNDERSTAND why Tyler had asked her to dinner. Even worse, she didn't understand why she'd accepted. She didn't want to go out in public, yet here she was in his car on the way to a restaurant where people would stare at her.

Even though the swelling had gone down and the bruising had disappeared, the surgery had left subtle differences in her face that seemed more noticeable to her than to others—at least that's what Gayle told her. And although she could hide most of the scarring with makeup so the rest of the world didn't see, she knew what lay beneath the creams and powders.

As they pulled into the parking lot across from an old warehouse in downtown Minneapolis, Kristen felt her muscles tense. Neon signs identified several bars and restaurants in the building. Tyler led her through a door with an overhead sign flashing Eddie's in red lights with an arrow pointing up.

They climbed two flights of stairs before he pushed open a door that led into the restaurant. The atmosphere was casual, the lighting dim. Piano music drifted across the room, muting the sound of clinking silverware. They checked their coats at the small counter inside the door, then waited to be seated.

Judging by the maître d's enthusiastic greeting, Tyler was a regular guest. Their host led them to a table for two in a corner of the room, smiling knowingly as he held Kristen's chair for her.

Before she could sit, however, Tyler said softly, "Why don't you take this one. That way you can see the piano player."

Kristen knew a better view wasn't the real motive for his suggestion. In his chair, her left side would be hidden from the other guests.

"Thank you," she said, changing places with him. Suddenly self-conscious, she fumbled with her napkin, adjusted the silverware and took a drink of water. Then she glanced across the room to where a woman sat at a piano playing a medley of pop tunes. "This is an interesting place."

"I like it because you can hear yourself talk and

because Eddie makes the best clam chowder in town."

"Then you come here often?"

"Not anymore. At one time, Brant Electronics used to be just around the corner, so we spent a lot of time here."

They hadn't been sitting there long when a couple walked by. Kristen reached for her purse on the floor.

When she straightened and looked at Tyler, he asked, "What bothers you more? That they'll recognize you as the Channel 12 anchor or that they'll see your scars?"

She looked into his eyes expecting to see pity, but there was none. There was merely an interest she found comforting.

"Both," she answered honestly. "Before the accident I knew people often thought I looked different from the way I looked on television, but maybe now they're wondering if that difference isn't because of the accident. Everyone knows I've had plastic surgery."

"That sounds like a normal concern someone in your situation would have."

"I haven't been out in public much since the crash." She toyed with her silverware again and finally said, "Look. Maybe this wasn't such a great idea."

"Wait. Give me a couple of minutes," he said, getting up from the table. He was only gone maybe two or three minutes before he returned with the maître d'. He bent and whispered in her ear, "We're moving."

They followed the host to a door marked Private. It was a banquet room with several long tables. Tyler pulled out a chair for her at the end of one of them, as the maître d' left only to return moments later with a tablecloth, silverware, wineglasses and a bottle of sparkling wine. When he finished setting the end of their table, he poured them each a glass and said, "I'll send someone in to take your order."

As soon as he was gone, Tyler asked, "Is this better?"

She nodded. "Thank you."

"You're welcome."

Another silence stretched between them and again Kristen had to wonder why he'd brought her to dinner. Not once on the way over in the car had he mentioned the crash, and from the sober expression on his face, she wondered if he wasn't regretting his invitation.

Finally, she said, "I'm sorry."

"For what?"

"For your having to sit in here. You can't hear the music."

He shrugged. "I didn't come for the music."

"Why did you come?" she couldn't resist asking. "Or maybe I should ask why did you bring me?"

His eyes met hers. They looked uncertain, something she was convinced was a rarity. Tyler Brant appeared to be a man who knew what he wanted. "Maybe I just don't like to think of anyone eating soup for one."

She lowered her eyes. He felt sorry for her. That was the last thing she wanted to hear. "I'm usually not alone. You forget I have a fiancé.'' She waved her diamond solitaire in front of him.

''Then the crash hasn't delayed your wedding plans?''

''No. Why should it?''

''KC's column in the paper said—''

''Do you always believe what you read in a gossip column?''

''I usually don't read the gossip column.''

''Good, because it's very often just based on hearsay.''

''Then you haven't put your personal plans on hold?''

''No, nothing's changed,'' she answered, knowing perfectly well that her answer wasn't the truth. However, her relationship with Keith wasn't something she wanted to discuss with Tyler Brant. She lowered her eyes, worried that what she was thinking might be reflected in her eyes.

''That's good,'' he answered.

''Yes, it is,'' she agreed with a false confidence. ''What about you? I know that you were on your way to Hibbing to survey the damage from a fire to one of your plants that day. Is your life back to normal again, too?''

''Yes. Busy as usual. Never enough hours in a day, it seems.''

''You have a daughter, right?''

''Yes. Brittany. She's six.''

''What's she like?''

He smiled affectionately. ''Precocious. Knows far too much for a six-year-old.''

"Does she know about the plane crash?"

He nodded grimly. "She saw my picture on the front page of the newspaper when she was at the grocery store with my mother."

"Did it have any lasting effect on her?"

"No, she's fine," he answered.

"What about you?"

"I'm fine, too."

Kristen felt a wave of disappointment. She'd been hoping he'd give her some hint that he, too, hadn't completely recovered from the emotional trauma of the crash.

"You're lucky," she told him.

Any warmth that might have been in his face disappeared. He looked her straight in the eye and said, "No. I wouldn't exactly call myself lucky."

She wanted to ask him what he meant, but the appearance of the waiter preempted any further conversation. At Tyler's suggestion, Kristen chose the evening special along with a cup of clam chowder.

When the waiter left, Tyler asked, "Do you know when you'll return to work?"

"Is that your way of asking me if what KC said about my losing my job is also true?"

He gave her an apologetic smile. "Is it? Is there a chance you might lose your spot on the news?"

She shrugged. "I shouldn't, but working in television is not like going to work in an office."

"Are you saying they can replace you because you've had to take some time off to recover from the accident?"

"No. But as I said before, I don't know how viewers will react to the way I look now. And in TV that's what counts. The viewing audience can be fickle. And no station manager likes to see the ratings drop."

Again, she wasn't being quite truthful. But she was reluctant to admit that the issue wasn't simply one of whether or not the station would replace her, but rather one of her own loss of confidence in her ability to be successful in the anchor spot.

"However, my boss assures me I have a job whenever I want to return."

"I'm glad to hear that. You're good at what you do."

His compliment gave her a warm, tingly feeling. "So you've seen me on the air?"

He smiled then—a wonderful smile that turned the tingle into a shiver of pleasure. "I doubt there's anyone in this area who hasn't. You look like you were born to sit in that chair."

"I guess it's really a dream come true. As a child, I always wanted to work in television. I just never thought it would happen."

"Why is that?"

"Well, for one thing, I was very shy."

"Now that I find hard to believe."

"It's true," she assured him. "My mother had to drag me by the hand to school. That's when she decided to have me enter child beauty pageants. She figured that competing in the pageants would give me self-confidence, make me more outgoing."

"And did it?"

She shrugged. "It did help me get used to being in front of an audience and I did learn how to be comfortable in an interview, but I never really enjoyed the competitions the way some of the girls did. I would gladly have traded the crown, sash and trophy for a chance to be a regular kid. One who went in-line skating in the street and played softball in the park."

"You didn't get to do those things?"

She shook her head. "Mom was always worrying that I'd skin a knee or bruise a shin. Besides, there wasn't much time for play. There were dance lessons, piano lessons, voice lessons, sessions with a personal trainer, costume fittings..." She sighed wistfully at the memories. "I guess it probably wasn't any tougher than what athletes go through when they train for competition."

"You don't strike me as the competitive type," he observed.

"I'm not," she told him, pleased by his comment.

"But Mom was?" he prodded gently.

She nodded, then felt embarrassed. "That's not to say she was some kind of crazed stage mother. It wasn't like that. She was always so proud of me, even when I didn't win."

"I find it hard to believe you could ever lose a beauty contest."

She wasn't sure what was making her flush—the wine or his compliments.

"When you can't remember the words to the song

you're singing and you fall on the runway, you don't take first place," she told him with a grin.

Noticing her glass was nearly empty, he refilled it for her. "How old were you when you won your last pageant?"

"Fifteen. I finally convinced my mom that if I didn't have self-confidence by then, I'd never get it." She shook her head as she remembered the day she and her mother had argued over her decision.

"Did it cause friction between you and your mother?"

"Friction is an understatement. I think Mom really enjoyed the pageant life. It was her opportunity to meet with other mothers, to watch me do my song-and-dance routines and get recognized for it. When I stopped, some of her social life stopped, too."

"Do I detect a hint of regret in your voice?"

"No," she said quickly. "But I know Mom really believed pageants were good for me. And they were also an opportunity to get scholarships for college. All during high school she reminded me of that."

"The 'don't do it for me, do it for college angle,'" he said in understanding. "I heard the same argument when I told my dad I was quitting football."

"And we both went to college without pageants or sports," she mused.

He shook his head in agreement. "Their hearts were in the right place."

She sighed. "I believe my mother's was. But I also know she never gave up hope that I'd go back to the pageants. I think her dream was that I'd be Miss America.''

''I think my dad thought I'd quarterback a Super Bowl game.'' he said with a chuckle.

Just then, the waiter arrived with their meal. Kristen was grateful for the interruption. She hadn't intended to talk about her childhood, and now that she had she felt self-conscious.

During dinner they made small talk, asking and answering questions the way strangers do when they first meet. Yet to Kristen, Tyler wasn't a stranger. She felt a connection to this man. In fact, she was surprised at how easy it was to be in his company. Unlike Keith, he didn't appear to be uncomfortable in her presence. Not once did she sense that he was avoiding looking at the scars on her face.

Eddie's may have been a quiet, secluded spot, but the nightclub downstairs was very popular with local celebrities. Security guards lined the hallway as Kristen and Tyler tried to leave the building.

Just as Tyler was about to usher her out the exit, the door to the nightclub opened and out stepped a couple of faces Kristen recognized. One belonged to a reporter; the other a photographer. The reporter took one look at Kristen and headed straight for her.

''Kristen Kellar, what brings you to Minneapolis's hottest nightspot?'' He thrust a microphone under her chin as the photographer zoomed in on her.

She automatically tried to shield her face from the camera. ''Please turn that off,'' she begged, stepping backward in search of an escape route.

Tyler stepped in between Kristen and the reporter, his arm snaking out to wrap itself around her. "The lady's not giving any interviews," he said gruffly.

"You're Tyler Brant...the local hero," the man began, but Tyler quickly cut him off.

"Back off. I said the lady doesn't want to speak to you."

"Can you tell us...?" the reporter persisted, but Kristen didn't hear the rest of his question because Tyler had swept her out the exit and into the parking lot.

As he rushed her to his car, he muttered, "Don't those people ever give up?"

"I'm sorry. I should have handled it better," she apologized.

Most of the ride back to her apartment was accomplished in silence. Although Tyler assured her he had already dismissed the unfortunate incident, she knew that the evening had ended on a rather sour note. And she wasn't sure if the change in his mood was because of the encounter with the reporter or because he'd been reminded that she was a part of the media he detested.

As he parked in front of her building, a plane flew overhead. Instinctively, Kristen shuddered, startled by the sudden noise. As she unfastened her seat belt, she realized her hands were trembling.

Tyler noticed.

"I guess it's kind of like being shell-shocked," he commented as his eyes met hers.

"It doesn't bother you?" she asked, surprised by how calm he appeared to be.

"No." He reached across to undo her seat belt for her.

As he did, she said, "You never answered my question earlier this evening. Don't you wonder why we survived and the others didn't?"

When he didn't respond immediately, Kristen thought he wasn't going to answer at all, but he eventually said, "If you try to make sense out of what happened that day, you're going to drive yourself crazy."

"Are you saying the reason my legs suddenly become weak and I start to tremble is because I'm trying to understand what happened to me?"

His gloved hands had tightened into fists and he stiffened. "Trauma affects everyone differently."

"I just wish I could sleep at night."

He looked at her then. "You have nightmares about the crash?"

"Don't you?"

"No." The answer came so quickly and abruptly she wondered if it might be a lie.

"I often dream that I'm in a cemetery looking for someone, but I can't figure out who it is I'm looking for."

Again he was silent for a moment. Then he said tersely, "I've learned the best way to deal with trauma is to put it behind you. Far behind you."

"And do you have a method for doing that? A method that works?"

"It's something only you can figure out."

"In other words, I suffer alone."

He leaned closer to her. "You're not alone, Kristen. You have a fiancé, friends...your family."

Who don't understand, she wanted to cry out. But it was obvious from his attitude that he didn't want to analyze any feelings about the crash. He had managed to put the past behind him. He expected her to do the same.

"So life goes on," she said with a hint of sarcasm.

"Yes, it does."

Kristen didn't try to pursue the subject. "I'd better go inside," she said, opening her door. "Thank you for dinner. I had a nice time."

He went around the car to help her with the door, but she was already out and had closed it by the time he got there.

"Would you like to come in for coffee?" It was an automatic, polite gesture on her part. She knew he'd decline.

She shouldn't have been disappointed, but she was. It was only after he left that she admitted to herself the reason why. It wasn't because she wanted to discuss how he really felt about the crash. It was because she liked being with him. Tyler Brant made her feel good.

She looked down at her ring and a wave of guilt washed over her. For the first time since the crash, she had enjoyed the company of a man. She had felt like a woman. A whole woman.

Later as she lay in bed unable to fall asleep, she

realized that guilt was once again keeping her awake. This time, it wasn't the guilt of having survived a tragedy. It was the guilt of being engaged to one man and wanting another.

CHAPTER FOUR

THE FOLLOWING AFTERNOON, Gayle stopped by on her lunch hour to bring Kristen a French Silk pie.

"I thought your endorphins could use a rush," she said as she swept past her to the kitchen. "I know mine can." She set the pie down on the counter and pulled a knife from the drawer.

"I haven't had lunch yet," Kristen protested as her friend began slicing.

"Silly woman. This *is* lunch," Gayle said with a grin. "But if you insist, I brought salad, too." She whipped out a plastic bag from her oversize purse. "You have any dressing that isn't fat free?"

Kristen could only smile and shake her head. "If you keep bringing me lunch, there isn't a chance I'm going to be called skinny when I go back to work."

"That's my goal," Gayle boasted. She ran a critical eye over her friend. "I'd say a diet rich in chocolate will help."

"Coffee or tea?" Kristen asked.

"Tea. But you sit. I'll get it."

"At least let me set the table," Kristen pleaded.

"All right, but I'm in charge of lunch." Suddenly, Gayle noticed the flowers on the table. "Oh, my. Those are gorgeous!"

"Yes, aren't they? If you need a tomato, I have some in the refrigerator," Kristen said, not wanting to answer questions about the flowers.

The diversion worked. Gayle scrounged around in the refrigerator for some vegetables. When she surfaced, she said, "I tried calling you last night, but there was no answer."

"I went out for dinner," Kristen said, pulling silverware from the drawer.

"Well, good. I'm glad you're finally getting out again. So where did you and Keith go?"

"A place called Eddie's, only I didn't go with Keith. I went with Tyler Brant."

That stopped Gayle in her tracks. "I thought you said the last time he visited he made it perfectly clear what he thought of you and the station."

"That's why he came over last night. He wanted to apologize." Kristen reached for two ceramic mugs from the cupboard.

Gayle's eyes moved to the flowers. "Are those from him?"

"Mmm-hmm."

"And he took you to dinner?"

"Yes."

"Must have been some apology."

Kristen nodded. "He's a gentleman."

"That's not what you were saying after the last time he visited. You told me he was downright nasty about Keith's wanting to interview him."

"Not exactly nasty. 'Upset' would be a better word."

Gayle shot her a curious look as they sat down across from each other at the table.

"I can't say I blame him," Kristen continued. "Until you've been on the other side of the camera, you don't realize how intrusive it can be." Seeing her friend bristling, she added, "I don't mean that as a criticism. It's just that being a victim changes a person's perspective."

"You're a journalist," Gayle reminded her.

"Yes, and I believe the public has a right to know the facts of a story. But take last night for instance. We were coming out of the restaurant, minding our own business, when some young, hotshot reporter spots us and shoves a microphone in my face."

"Who was it?"

"That new guy over at Channel 7."

"Not Burns?"

Kristen nodded soberly. "It was awful. You know what I've been going through since the crash, and then to have this…this…kid asking all sorts of personal questions and the camera getting it all…" She shivered at the memory.

"Kristen, you're in the business. You know the guy was only doing his job."

"No, he was being totally insensitive. He had no regard for my feelings. All he cared about was getting a story," she said with a grimace.

"The line between the public's right to know and a celebrity's right to privacy is a fine one," Gayle pointed out.

"That may be true, but until I became the headline

story, I never realized how horrible it was to have a camera aimed at your face.'' She shivered again.

"Not all of us are insensitive when it comes to filming," Gayle said, clearly taking offense at the unintended criticism.

"You're the best photographer I know, which is why so many reporters want you assigned to their stories," Kristen said reassuringly.

"You're not saying anything I haven't said myself," Gayle told her. "I've worked with people who will do or ask anything to get a story...including your fiancé."

Kristen sighed and set down her fork. "I know. He just doesn't get it. He's the one who's behind this whole *Profile in Courage* segment. I've told him I don't want anything to do with the darn thing, but he doesn't listen. He just keeps hammering away at how good it would be for us."

"Good for *him* maybe. You have to remember something. He's working with a handicap—his ego." Kristen shot her friend a warning look, and Gayle held up both hands palms out and said, "Sorry. I won't say any more."

It was no secret that Gayle and Keith didn't get along. Ever since they'd worked together at the same cable station early in their careers, there had been friction between the two of them.

"So tell me what this Tyler is like," Gayle said, changing the subject.

"I don't know much about him. I think he's the kind of man who purposely keeps people at a distance. It would probably be easy to stereotype him as cold and uncaring, but there's more to him.''

''You mean beneath the stone there beats a warm heart?''

''Exactly. You should hear the way he talks about his daughter. She's the light of his life.''

''And his wife?''

Kristen shrugged. ''He didn't mention her except to say she died in a car accident when Brittany was a baby.''

''So he's eligible.''

''I don't know that. For all I know he could have a significant other at home, although I rather doubt it. His mother lives with him and helps care for Brittany.''

''I'm surprised you went out at all,'' Gayle remarked.

''There's no reason for me not to, now that my cast is off.''

''That's what I've been trying to tell you.'' She used her fork for emphasis.

''Well, you were right. I enjoyed myself.''

''As in a woman enjoying a man's company?''

''I told you. He knows how to treat a woman.'' She knew there was no point in denying that she'd enjoyed being with Tyler. Gayle had the power to see right through her lies.

''Very interesting,'' she drawled with a twinkle in her eye.

''Nothing happened,'' Kristen insisted, again feeling guilty about Keith. ''It was all very proper.'' She took a sip of tea.

"Well, that's good, because you do have a fiancé who might not appreciate a man's bringing you flowers, taking you out to dinner and making your heart thump."

Kristen set her mug down with a thud. "Who says my heart thumped?"

"Didn't it?"

To her annoyance, Kristen blushed.

"I knew it did. I could tell by the tone of your voice. Are you going to tell Keith you went out with this guy last night?"

"If he asks. I mean, I won't lie to him, but last night was not what you seem to think it was. I'm engaged. I wouldn't do anything to harm that."

"Your loyalty has always earned my admiration, but I'm wondering if Keith appreciates it," she said in a skeptical tone.

She shrugged. "Even if he doesn't, it's important to me."

This time, Gayle was the one who sighed. "You know, if you don't want to answer this next question, you don't have to. But I have to ask anyway. Are you sure everything's okay between you and Keith?"

Again, Kristen knew there was no point in lying. "No." She tossed her napkin aside and pushed her plate away. "I feel as if we're only going through the motions. We're engaged to be married, yet I feel as if we've become strangers ever since the plane crash."

"You don't fall out of love with someone because you've been in an accident," Gayle pointed out.

"I didn't say I'd fallen out of love with him."

"You just said you've become strangers. What's wrong?"

Kristen wished she had the answer, but she didn't. "He says I've changed. Or rather, the crash changed me."

"As if 'change' is a dirty word, right?"

She nodded. "Change can also be frightening, especially when it makes you feel as if you don't know who you are anymore."

"Is that how you feel?" Gayle asked gently.

It was difficult for Kristen to put into words exactly what she was feeling, but she knew that if anybody would understand, it would be Gayle. Seeing the compassion in her eyes gave her the courage to say, "I know I'm not the same person I was before I boarded that flight. It's like one minute I was a promising young news anchor engaged to the guy I thought was the man of my dreams, and then I take a plane ride and...poof." She snapped her fingers. "I wake up a different person."

"It's only natural that you're feeling a bit uncertain about things," Gayle tried to reassure her. "You've been through a trauma. And it doesn't help that you had to have plastic surgery on top of everything."

"It's not my face. I mean, it is and it isn't." She searched for the words to try to make her friend understand. "When I look at Keith, I see someone whose primary concern is his appearance, and I think maybe that's how I used to be."

Gayle held up both hands. "Now wait a minute. It's one thing to be concerned, another thing to be obsessed. You were never obsessed with your looks.''

"No, but I placed way too much importance on my physical appearance.''

"It's the nature of the business,'' Gayle reminded her. "Looks are important in our industry. It's unfortunate, but true.''

"Yes, and now you know why I'm uncomfortable.''

"You haven't changed physically, Kristen. When you return to that anchor desk, everyone will see the same face they're used to seeing in that chair.''

"I'm not so sure,'' Kristen admitted warily. "I don't just have scars on my face, Gayle. Those can be covered with makeup. But what about the emotional scars inside me? Will I be able to hide those?''

"Those will fade in time, just like the ones on your face.''

Kristen wanted to believe she was right, but she couldn't help feeling afraid. And the fear was in not knowing what the future would bring.

She reached across the table to give Gayle's hand a squeeze. "Thanks for letting me talk about this.''

"You should be talking about this with Keith,'' her friend said bluntly.

"He doesn't want to hear it.'' Kristen couldn't keep the sadness from her voice. "I don't know what's going to happen to us, but I know something is wrong when a man I hardly know can make me feel more like a woman than my own fiancé.''

"So Tyler Brant did make an impression on you, didn't he? Did he make a pass at you?''

Kristen laughed. "No, so you can take that hopeful look off your face."

"So this attraction is one-sided?" she said with a contemplative gaze.

"I wouldn't exactly say I'm attracted to him. I mean he's not good-looking in the same sense that Keith is, but he's got something."

"He's sexy." Gayle didn't beat around the bush but came right out and said what Kristen had been thinking. "Keith is Ivy League good-old-boy handsome. From the pictures I've seen of him, Tyler Brant looks more like he's fought his way to the top taking a few knocks along the way."

"I think you're right. He started his own company when he was only twenty-three."

"Aha. A self-made man. Must go after what he wants. Do you think you'll see him again?"

"There's no reason to."

"You mean besides the fact you're attracted to him?"

"Gayle, the guy saved my life. It's no wonder I feel something toward him. You would, too, if you were in my shoes."

"Yeah, gratitude." She wagged her finger at Kristen. "Just admit it. You find this guy sexy."

"And what if I do? I'm engaged to Keith. And as you said, love doesn't just stop."

"Who are you trying to convince? Me or you?" She pushed away from the table and got to her feet. "Time for chocolate. When logic fails, I say go to something you know will never let you down."

"Better make mine small," Kristen warned.

Gayle simply harrumphed.

TYLER'S SOCIAL LIFE consisted mainly of professional obligations and time with his daughter. Most Saturday nights he spent with Brittany. He looked forward to their evenings together, but it did mean that his free time was limited. That, however, didn't prevent a couple of his well-meaning friends from trying to arrange dates for him.

What they didn't realize was that Tyler wasn't interested in long-term relationships. Actually, he hadn't really been interested in dating at all. Until he met Kristen Kellar.

Now he found himself wondering what it would be like to spend more time with her. She had been on his mind a lot since their dinner on Tuesday. So it came as no surprise when at a wedding on Saturday—his thoughts drifted to her.

Weddings were never easy when you were single, Tyler realized as he sat at a table with several employees who had come to celebrate the marriage of the director of sales at Brant Electronics. There were three married couples at Tyler's table. He was there with his six-year-old daughter.

As much as Tyler loved Brittany, he couldn't help imagining what it would be like to have Kristen sitting beside him instead. She was elegant, graceful, beautiful. And she could probably dance without stepping on his feet. And she wouldn't tug on his coat sleeve and say, "Daddy, I have to go to the bathroom."

Which is exactly what Brittany did halfway

through the reception. Tyler led her out of the hotel ballroom and to the bank of elevators in the lobby. Because the wedding reception included a dance that would go late into the night, Tyler had taken a room at the hotel. This way, when Brittany became tired, he could put her to bed. She loved the idea of sleeping overnight at the hotel.

Rather than use the rest rooms outside the ballroom, Tyler decided to take his daughter back upstairs where he wouldn't have to worry about her going into the rest room alone. While he waited for the elevator, he noticed television anchor, Keith Jaxson, approaching.

At first, Tyler thought Jaxson might recognize him, but then he remembered that all the videos from the crash would have shown Tyler sporting a beard. It was obvious as the anchor approached that he didn't know who Tyler was. They were simply two people waiting for the same elevator.

To Tyler's surprise, when Keith Jaxson stepped through the open doors, he pressed the button with the number five on it. He wanted the same floor as Tyler and Brittany.

Brittany chatted all the way up while Keith Jaxson remained facing the front, his eyes on the row of numbers flashing over the door. When the elevator stopped at the fifth floor and the doors slid open, he stepped out ahead of Tyler and Brittany.

"This way," Tyler urged his daughter, aware that they were following Keith Jaxson.

"Can we stay until the dancing starts, Daddy? I know how to do the chicken dance and the macarena.

Remember last time we went to a wedding with Gram and I got to dance, too?''

"Sure, Brittany. We'll stay for the dancing," he answered, wondering where Jaxson was headed.

He soon found out. Jaxson stopped only a few doors away from Tyler's room.

Tyler was grateful that his daughter took small steps for it meant they were far enough behind that the anchor would be able to get inside before they passed. Only Jaxson didn't have a room key. He knocked on the door and waited while Brittany and Tyler drew closer.

Tyler heard a woman's voice say, "It's about time. I thought maybe you had changed your mind."

"Not a chance."

From the tone of their voices, it didn't take a genius to figure out that the couple was having a romantic liaison. But why would Keith Jaxson and Kristen rent a hotel room for a romantic tryst? He saw Jaxson go inside and heard the door slam shut. But just as he and Brittany passed, the door opened again. A pale, thin arm snaked around the door and hung the Do Not Disturb sign on the knob.

Then, for just a brief moment, Tyler caught sight of the head that went with the arm. It had brown hair, not blond. Kristen wasn't the woman in the room.

"Daddy, hurry. I have to go bad." Tyler didn't realize that he wasn't moving until Brittany tugged on his hand.

"All right, I'm hurrying," he told her, slipping the small card through the lock on the door.

While Brittany used the bathroom, Tyler stared out the window. Kristen had been so insistent when she told him her wedding plans hadn't changed.

An unfamiliar anger heated Tyler's veins. What kind of man was this Keith Jaxson? And how could Kristen pretend that everything was okay in their relationship…unless she didn't know the guy was cheating on her.

That made his protective instincts surge. The question was, what should he do? Tell her? He'd look like a first-class heel. Yet he couldn't bear to think of her marrying a guy who couldn't even be faithful before the wedding.

He needed to put it out of his mind. It was none of his business what either of them did. They were a couple of narcissistic celebrities who probably deserved each other.

Only he wasn't sure that Kristen was self-centered. At first he had thought vanity had been the reason behind her self-consciousness, but after having dinner with her, he'd changed his mind. It was obvious that the emotional trauma she'd suffered went much deeper than the scars on her cheek.

He wondered if Jaxson wasn't the one having a problem with the slight imperfection on her face. Again, anger rumbled inside him at the thought of Kristen being hurt by a man who couldn't accept her as she was.

He wished he had never gone to see her. Now he was in the awful position of caring what happened to her. And as much as he hated to admit it, he did care. All he had to figure out was how to change that.

Because Kristen Kellar was engaged to another man. And because Tyler Brant had come to a decision five years ago. When it came to women, there was only room for one in his life.

His six-year-old daughter, Brittany.

"I'M READY TO GO BACK to work."

As soon as Kristen said the words to her boss, doubts began to creep into her mind. After so many weeks, she finally felt the need to be doing something. She just wasn't sure that she was ready to be in front of a camera. On the other hand, maybe Keith was right. Maybe work was the tonic she needed.

"That's great, Kristen," Bob Yates said with a grin. "We've missed you around here. When do you want to come back? Probably not until after Thanksgiving, I imagine, since you and Keith are planning to get away for a few days, aren't you?"

That question made her more than a little uneasy. Either Keith hadn't told their boss she wasn't going on the trip or her fiancé still harbored hopes that he could convince her to change her mind.

"Actually, I thought Thanksgiving week might be a good time for me to start," she told him.

That raised an eyebrow on Bob's face. "You want to work the holiday?"

She shrugged. "I might as well. I don't have any other plans."

"I thought you and Keith were going to the Bahamas."

"I'm not going. As for Keith, I'm not sure what his plans are." Which was the truth. Ever since she'd told him she wouldn't be getting on an airplane and going anywhere, he had stopped talking about the trip. She had no delusions that he would put off his own vacation to stay home with her.

"Is there anything I should know about the two of you?" Bob asked.

"What do you mean?" she asked with a false naiveté.

She could see he was uncomfortable; he was tugging on his ear as he did whenever he had to broach an unpleasant topic. "Well, I guess you might as well know. There have been rumors floating around here..." he began to explain uncertainly.

She looked down at her diamond engagement ring. "That we might not be the Mr. and Mrs. of television news?"

"*Are* the rumors true?" When she didn't answer, he said, "I don't want to pry, Kristen, but I need to know."

"Why? Because the ratings might go down if the public finds out we're not the happy couple everyone hoped we'd be?" She didn't want to sound defensive, but she had a hunch she was about to be reprimanded for Keith's behavior.

He lifted his eyebrows. "They certainly went up when the news got out that you two were dating. You know I've never liked the idea of office romances, but I did stand behind both of you."

"Because you saw what happened to the ratings," she returned cynically.

"That's not fair. I supported you before the viewers even suspected it. I stuck my neck out for you with management, and you know it." He used his cigar as a pointer.

Kristen had to admit what he said was true. Although at first he had discouraged her from getting involved with Keith, once he'd seen there was no stopping their romance, he'd been their biggest champion.

"I know you did, Bob, and I appreciate it," she said sincerely.

"So you need to be up-front with me about this. Are you and Keith having problems?"

She could see the anxious expression on his face and decided to answer honestly. "Yes. Ever since the crash, there's been this…this…" She paused, flailing her hands helplessly. "I'm not sure how to describe it, but things are definitely not right between us."

He squeezed his eyes shut and grimaced, then quickly pinned his poker face back in place. "I was worried something like this would happen."

"I'm sorry."

He waved away her apology with a flip of his hand. "Naw, it's not your fault. I'm the one who should've known better. I should've pulled one of you off the 6:00 p.m. when it became evident that you were more than co-workers." He went silent, flopping down in his chair and puffing on his cigar with a renewed vigor.

"There have been some challenges for both of us since the crash. Every couple has to overcome obstacles in their relationship," Kristen told him, despite knowing perfectly well that there was a lot more wrong with the relationship than she wanted to admit.

"And your obstacle is…?"

What was it? She wondered that herself. The fact that she had survived a plane crash? That she needed time to recover emotionally from the disaster? That she wanted a man who loved her for what was inside her, not what was on the outside?

"We're working through some problems," she answered, trying to exude a confidence she didn't feel.

"And if the problems can't be worked through? If you break your engagement…what then?"

"It doesn't mean we can't co-anchor the 6:00 p.m. report," Kristen pointed out. "We're both professionals. We were doing the news together before we ever started dating. People aren't just tuning in because they want to see a couple of lovebirds. They like our news program."

He stroked his jaw unhappily. "I wish I could share your optimism, but the ratings speak for themselves."

"So what are you saying, Bob? That we can't be on the same set if we're not romantically linked?"

She could tell by the way his smooth dome turned a light pink that that was exactly what he was thinking. He gave her a contrite look and said, "No, of course not. I just need to figure out what this will mean for the ratings if for some reason you don't end up as Mr. and Mrs."

"We're good anchors, Bob. Both of us."

"I know that, but you know what the determining factor is in so many decisions around here," he said uneasily.

"Numbers," she said solemnly.

He rubbed a hand over his bald head. "Let's not create a problem where there may not be one. Let's talk about getting you back on the set. How are you feeling? You don't look like the leg's giving you any trouble."

"No, it's not. The doctor says it healed remarkably well. I've been given the okay to return to work."

"That'll make the viewers happy." He leaned forward in his chair, his arms on the desk. "And your cheek? It looks as if it's healed well."

"Yes, it has," she confirmed, wishing she didn't want to squirm under his scrutiny.

"Then you won't need any more surgery?"

His words put her on the defensive again and scraped at her self-confidence. "Does it look like I need more surgery?"

"No, it doesn't. I only asked because I know that reconstructive surgery often requires several procedures before the doctors are satisfied. You look like the same old Kristen to me."

She didn't believe him for a minute. She wasn't terribly disfigured, but she wasn't the same old Kristen, either. But she hadn't come to the station to discuss her appearance but rather her job. She only wished the two weren't so closely linked.

"So there's no reason for me not to return to the anchor chair at six and ten starting next Monday," she stated unequivocally.

"If you're sure you're ready?"

"I'm ready," she told him.

"Good. Then we'll see you next Monday."

ONLY ON MONDAY, Kristen didn't go back to work. After spending the weekend making preparations for her return to the station—laying out the makeup that would hide her scars, choosing a suit from her wardrobe, having her nails done—she had trouble falling asleep on Sunday night. When she finally did doze off, it was a restless slumber interrupted by nightmares. None of them made sense, yet every one of them left her feeling fearful and anxious.

It came as no surprise to her that Monday morning she awoke with a headache. As she padded into the bathroom for some tablets, she felt weak and dizzy. The thought of sitting beneath the hot studio lights was enough to cause her to break out in a sweat. A look in the mirror confirmed what she already knew. She wasn't ready to be put under the microscope in front of the public.

So she did the only thing she could do. She called Bob Yates and told him she wasn't feeling well. When he suggested that her plan to return may have been premature and that she probably needed to extend her leave of absence, she didn't argue.

Keith, however, didn't agree. When she phoned him to tell him he didn't need to stop by and pick her up on the way to the studio, she could hear the annoyance in his voice.

"What do you mean you're not going in because you're sick? Is it the flu?" he demanded to know.

"Maybe. I don't know. I just don't feel well. I guess I haven't completely recovered."

"I thought you told me the doctors had given you a clean bill of health?" he said accusingly.

"They did, but that doesn't mean I'm ready to return to work."

"Physically you are."

She resented the tone of his voice. "What's that supposed to mean?"

"Are you sure this dizziness isn't psychosomatic?"

"You think I'm imagining that I feel dizzy?"

"Not imagining, but maybe you're using your health to avoid facing things."

"No!" she vehemently denied. "I'm not trying to avoid anything!"

"Are you sure?"

"Yes, and I'd appreciate it if you didn't try to play doctor. I have a team of medical professionals who do that job."

"Kristen, the makeup covers your scars. No one will be able to tell that you've even been injured. You'll look just the way you've always looked."

No, she wouldn't, but that wasn't even the issue.

Annoyed with his assumption that she didn't want to go to work because of her scars, she snapped, "I'm not staying home because of my face. I told you. I'm not feeling well."

"When will you feel well?"

She sensed a testiness in his voice. "I don't know. Bob's extended my medical leave indefinitely."

"What?" She could hear the barely controlled anger in his voice. "But we've already run the promos for your return. The viewers are expecting you to be there tonight."

"Then you'll have to explain that I'm not going to be there," she retorted. "I need more time."

"Time for what?" he asked impatiently.

"To get my strength back," she retorted.

There was dead air for several seconds before he finally said, "I'm worried about you, Kristen. You're spending way too much time alone."

"And whose fault is that?" she asked.

"Come on, that's not fair. I've been begging you to go out with me, but you don't want to do anything but hole up in that apartment of yours. I'm getting tired of eating alone."

She felt the familiar weakness that had plagued her ever since her hospital stay. "I don't want to argue with you, Keith. This isn't a discussion we should be having on the phone."

"I agree," he said soberly. "I'll call you when I get back from the Bahamas."

"So you are going without me?" Even though it was what she'd suspected he'd do, it still hurt to know that he didn't care enough to spend the holiday with her.

"Kristen, you could come if you wanted to."

"No, I can't."

He sighed. "Not if you won't try to get on with your life instead of dwelling on the crash."

Get on with her life? He had no clue as to what she'd been going through. Did he honestly believe she could just pretend that nothing had happened?

That she hadn't survived a tragedy that had taken the lives of eight other people?

She searched for the words to explain to him how she was feeling, but none came. There was no point in trying to make him understand. He was sure he had all the answers. Kristen wasn't sure she even knew the questions.

Finally, he said, "I've got to go. Get some rest and then we'll talk some more."

And with those words, he hung up the phone. Kristen could only stare at the receiver. Who was this man who called himself her fiancé? She studied the glittering diamond solitaire on her finger. At one time, it had represented so much hope. So many plans for the future. Now it only reminded her of what had changed in her life. She took it off and tucked it away in a drawer.

CHAPTER FIVE

THANKSGIVING WAS the one holiday Millie Brant insisted the family celebrate together. That meant Tyler's brother, Marshall, and his wife, Lynn, came down from Duluth, his younger sister, Renee, flew in from California and his great-aunt Clara got a one-day pass from the nursing home to spend the day with them.

For Tyler, Thanksgiving was just another opportunity to miss Susan. Like his mother, Susan had always made a fuss over the holiday. Even before Brittany was born, she'd hang stencils in the windows, decorate the house and spend days baking and cleaning in preparation for the Thanksgiving meal. Maybe that was why the aroma of pumpkin pies baking in the oven always made Tyler more aware of the emptiness in his heart.

Tyler had known that the holiday wouldn't pass without his brother and sister asking about the plane crash. Although Marshall had driven to the hospital in Hibbing to see Tyler, Renee had only spoken to him over the phone and now needed to see for herself that her big brother was truly all right. Despite his assurances that he was perfectly fine, she couldn't resist giving him a spontaneous hug every now and then.

What Tyler lacked in enthusiasm for the holiday was offset by his mother's joy at having her three children under one roof at the same time and Brittany's youthful exuberance for the traditions of the celebration. She began Thanksgiving morning parked in front of the television, where she watched Macy's Parade march down the streets of New York.

During one of the commercial breaks, the Channel 12 news team made a plea for donations to Toys for Children, a charity drive being sponsored by the station. Tyler noted that it was Keith Jaxson and Janey Samuels, meteorologist, Tom Miner, and sportscaster, Dean Watson, who were doing the public service announcement. They were identified as the Channel 12 team. Kristen Kellar was nowhere in sight.

Tyler wondered if it had been her choice not to appear with the others or if the decision had been made by someone at the station. He'd noticed that when promotional spots for the news appeared on the screen, it was still Kristen's smiling face in the group photo. Maybe the rumors hinted at in KC's column were just that. Rumors.

Tyler didn't want to think about Kristen, to wonder how she was doing. Yet he couldn't help himself. Was she with Jaxson at this very moment? Or had she found out about his unfaithfulness and ended their relationship? Was she spending the holiday with her family? Or was she alone?

It was this last possibility that haunted him. Unable to resist the temptation to find out, he excused himself from the family room, went into his office and dialed Kristen's number. The phone rang at least half a dozen times before she finally answered.

"Hello?"

"It's Tyler Brant." She didn't say anything. "How are you?" he asked, imagining her sitting on her sofa in her apartment.

"How do you think I am?"

It wasn't said in a flippant tone, but rather in an almost woeful one. "You don't sound very good. Are you feeling all right?"

"I'm not sure I'll ever feel all right again." She sighed, then quickly added, "Forget I said that. I'm just tired. Why are you calling, Tyler?"

"I just wanted to wish you a happy Thanksgiving."

She chuckled sardonically. "Oh, that's right. We have so much to be thankful for, don't we?"

"Kristen, you are okay, aren't you?"

"Sure. I'm fine. How are you? Is your family together for the holiday?"

"Yes. What about yours?"

"Most of them are in Wisconsin. I didn't go this year."

She sounded lost and forlorn.

"Where's your fiancé?"

She didn't answer his question but said, "Look, it was sweet of you to call, but I really must go. I have something cooking on the stove."

"Kristen, you're not alone, are you?"

Again she ignored his question and just said,

"You have a nice day, Tyler. Happy Thanksgiving to you."

The click told him she had hung up. He stared at the phone for only a few seconds before taking action.

As he walked back out into the family room, he carried his jacket and his keys. "I have to run an errand. I'll be back in time for dinner," he announced to his family gathered in the room.

"An errand? It's Thanksgiving. Where on earth could you possibly need to go?" his mother wanted to know.

"I have to check up on someone who hasn't been feeling well," he answered.

"Now?"

"Yes, now." He bent to give Brittany a kiss, saying "Keep Auntie Renee company, okay?" He gave his sister a wink, waved at the others and headed for the garage.

All the way to Kristen's apartment, he wondered if he was behaving foolishly. For all he knew, she wasn't alone. After all, she hadn't said Jaxson wasn't there. Maybe she was simply in a bad mood.

So why was he heading toward her place?

Because his instincts told him she needed someone to check on her. Because he needed to be that someone. Because he knew what thoughts were going through her head, and because he understood the reason for her sadness.

And perhaps most important of all, because he wanted to see her again.

UNFORTUNATELY, SHE DIDN'T want to see him. She made that perfectly clear when he rang up from the lobby. "This isn't a good time for me," she muttered.

"Kristen, let me in. Please."

The silence that greeted his request made him wonder if she had said all she was going to say. He pressed the bell again. There was still no answer. Just when he accepted the fact that she didn't intend to let him in, he heard the buzzer indicating she had opened the door.

When he arrived at her apartment, she was waiting for him, clinging to the partially open door as if she needed it for support. She wore a sweatshirt and a pair of jeans. "Why are you here, Mr. Brant?" she asked.

"I thought we agreed it's Tyler," he said as he stepped around her into the apartment.

"All right. Why are you here, Tyler?"

He shrugged. "I just thought I'd stop by and say hello."

"I appreciate your coming by, but this really isn't a good time for me."

He could see the shadows beneath her eyes and something tugged on his heartstrings. She looked so unhappy he had to fight the urge to take her in his arms and comfort her. "Bad day?"

"Bad week," she said.

He reached around her shoulder and closed the door. "I don't smell any turkey cooking."

"I'm not having turkey," she said, her arms wrapped around her waist.

He looked around the apartment and saw that they were alone. "Where's Jaxson?"

"Out of town."

"What kind of man leaves his fiancée alone on Thanksgiving?"

"My fiancé is not your concern," she stated flatly.

"No, but you are." He glanced at her left hand and noticed the diamond solitaire was missing. "I want you to come and have dinner at my house."

"Today?"

"Yes. Turkey. Mashed potatoes. Gravy. You know, the usual Thanksgiving menu."

"I can't go to your house for dinner," she protested, wandering into the living room.

He followed her. "Why not?"

"Because...because I can't. You have a family."

"A small one."

"But they don't know me. You hardly know me." She sank onto the sofa.

He chuckled. "I wouldn't say that. You're in our living room practically every night."

"That's not me."

"Then who is it?" he asked, sitting down beside her.

She shrugged. "I'm not sure, but it's not me."

"Then why don't you come and let me get to know the real Kristen Kellar?"

She looked at him then, puzzled by his statement. "Why are you doing this? You told me you didn't want to be a hero, yet here you are, charging into my home like some knight on a white horse."

"I'm no knight," he assured her.

"Maybe not, but don't tell me you're not here on some kind of rescue mission. You think I'm sitting home all alone feeling sorry for myself."

"Are you?"

"No. Yes." She heaved a sigh. "Does it matter?"

"It matters to me," he told her.

"Why should it? You're perfectly well-adjusted. Me—my life hasn't been the same since the day of the crash. I'm tired all the time, yet I can't sleep. I can't work—" She stopped abruptly, then said, "I'm sorry. I forgot. You don't want to hear it."

He could feel her pain as if it were his own. Yet how could he help her without dredging up those very emotions he had worked so hard to keep buried? "You have to put the crash behind you, Kristen."

"Now you're starting to sound like my fiancé." And it was obvious by her tone of voice that she wasn't complimenting him.

"I'm nothing like your fiancé," Tyler stated emphatically.

She looked at him and said, "No. You're not."

"So will you come to my house for dinner?"

"I don't think so. I appreciate the invitation, but I'm really tired and I think I'd better go to bed."

Tyler was sure her fatigue was due to her depressed state. What she didn't need was to spend the day alone in her apartment. "How about if I bring you home right after dinner?"

"That's not a good idea. I've taken some medication...." Her voice trailed off.

"Then we won't give you any wine. Now, where's your coat? We need to hurry or we'll be late."

"I can't go like this!" She gestured to her sweat-shirt and jeans. "And I don't have any makeup on."

"You're a beautiful woman with or without makeup, Kristen," he said sincerely.

"But my scars—"

"Are barely noticeable," he interrupted. "I promise you nobody will make you feel uncomfortable."

"How many people will be there?"

"Counting you, eight."

"Eight!"

He could see the panic in her eyes. "It's not as bad as it sounds. All adults except for my daughter." He held out his hand to her. "Come on. Let's go get your coat."

She didn't take his hand. "Tyler, I really am too tired."

"What if I tell you I won't take no for an answer?"

From the look on her face, he could see that she was puzzled. "I don't understand why you're doing this."

"Well, you know what? I don't understand, either. But I'm here and I'm not leaving without you."

She shrugged and made a sound of frustration. "At least give me five minutes to change into something a little more appropriate for a holiday dinner."

"All right. Five minutes."

She took longer, but the time was well spent. When she emerged from her bedroom, she wore a light blue top covered with sequins and a long black skirt. With her pale blond hair draped loosely on her shoulders, she appeared almost ethereal.

"You look lovely," he told her, noting that she had applied makeup so that no traces of the scars were visible. On her lips she wore a soft shade of red that called attention to her perfectly shaped mouth and made him wonder what it would be like to kiss it.

"Thank you. I still don't think this is a good idea," she told him as she slid her arms into her full-length wool coat.

It was a sentiment she echoed several times on the way to Tyler's home. When she finally quit protesting, Tyler glanced over and saw the reason why. She'd fallen asleep. In repose she was even more beautiful than she was when she was awake, and he felt something stir inside him.

She was still asleep when they reached his home. He called her name several times. Not even the slamming of his door woke her. He opened the passenger side and nudged her shoulder. Still, she slept.

Finally, he lifted her into his arms and carried her inside. He was greeted with looks of surprise and a barrage of questions.

"What's happened?"

"Is she all right?"

"Does she need a doctor?"

"Oh my goodness! It's Kristen Kellar!"

"Who's Kristen Kellar?"

The last question was answered by his mother, who excitedly proclaimed Kristen was the Channel 12 anchorwoman. The woman Tyler had saved in the plane crash.

"She doesn't need a doctor. She needs sleep," Tyler said as he carried her through the house. "Where should I put her?" he asked his mother.

"She can sleep on my bed," Brittany offered, hurrying to keep up with her father.

"Brittany's room is probably best," his mother agreed, so Tyler carried Kristen up the stairs to the second floor. He was grateful when his daughter was the only one who followed him into the bedroom.

"How come the lady's sleeping in the middle of the day?" she asked.

"Because she's really tired and she took some medicine. Please move all those stuffed animals from your bed."

Brittany scrambled to do as she was told so that Tyler could place Kristen on the bed.

"Is she sick?"

"No, she's just tired."

"But her cheeks are red." As soon as her father had placed Kristen on the bed, the youngster reached up to touch her forehead with her small hand. "She feels hot to me, Daddy."

Tyler placed the back of his fingers against Kristen's forehead. It was definitely warm. Deliciously so. And soft. He wondered how other parts of her might feel, then quickly reprimanded himself. What was he thinking?

"We need to take off her coat." With Brittany's help, he carefully removed the coat.

"Are you gonna take off her clothes?" Brittany asked in a near whisper.

"I don't think that'll be necessary." Tyler placed the coat across the foot of the bed.

"They'll get all wrinkled," Brittany warned. "Gram never lets me sleep in my clothes."

"I think hers will be okay," Tyler assured her, trying to ignore an imagination that teased him with a variety of images of an unclothed Kristen.

"I can get her shoes." Brittany carefully removed the black suede heels and set them on the floor beside her bed. "She's pretty, isn't she?"

"Yes, she is," Tyler agreed.

"I like her top. It's all sparkly."

"Maybe she needs a blanket."

"She can use my red one," Brittany said, offering the afghan her grandmother had crocheted for her.

Tyler draped it across her slender form.

"Should I stay here and watch her to make sure she's all right?" Brittany asked.

"I think you should come down and have dinner first. Then, if she's still asleep by the time you're finished, you can pull guard duty, okay?"

"Okay." She placed her hand in her father's and allowed him to lead her out of the room. "Gram said she's the lady you saved from the plane crash. Is she really?"

"Yes, she is."

"Is she the newslady Gram always watches on TV?"

"Yes."

By the time they reached the dining room, Tyler felt as if they had just played twenty questions. He was in no mood for a second round with the rest of his family, which is what he knew would happen if he gave them a chance.

He didn't. "I would really appreciate not having to answer any questions right now," he said to the group gathered for dinner. "Let's get on with Thanksgiving." His family nodded in understanding.

As he took his place at the table, his mother asked, "Would you like us to wait a bit longer before serving?"

"No, it's all right. There's no telling how long she'll sleep."

"Very well."

Although nobody questioned him, Tyler could see the curiosity in everyone's eyes. They must be wondering what had prompted him to leave so suddenly only to return carrying a woman who was sound asleep. As much as he loved his family, he realized that—all things considered—sleeping through dinner wasn't a bad idea. What Kristen didn't need was to feel obliged to explain her situation to a group of strangers, even if they were nice strangers.

So maybe he had been wrong to insist she come back with him. Maybe he'd been selfish. In his eagerness to see her again, he hadn't considered what she needed, let alone what she wanted.

Of course, he hadn't exactly figured out what he wanted, either.

THE FIRST THING KRISTEN SAW when she opened her eyes was an array of stars. Big luminescent stars of varying sizes glowed above her.

It only took her a moment to realize she wasn't in her own bed. So where was she? As her grogginess faded, she remembered why she wasn't in her own bed. Tyler had insisted she have dinner with him. She had fallen asleep somewhere between her apartment and his house.

So she was now in the awkward position of being a guest in one of his bedrooms.

"Walter, would you please be quiet so I can read?"

In the strange, dark room, the sound of the clear, high-pitched voice was startling. Kristen sat up with a jerk but saw no one in the darkness.

A few moments later, she heard, "You're talking again, Walter. If you're not going to listen to me, I won't let you come with me and Gram when we go to the park."

As Kristen's eyes adjusted to the absence of light, she noticed a dim glow in the corner of the room. In its shadow was a small figure.

Kristen reached for the lamp on the nightstand beside the bed. As light illuminated her surroundings, she saw she was in a child's domain and the child was inside a pup tent pitched in the corner. It had to be Brittany Brant's bedroom, Kristen concluded as she eyed the child-size table and chairs, a chalkboard, miniature kitchen appliances made out of hard plastic and dolls galore.

With the light on, the stars lost their luminescence, becoming cream-colored plastic shapes. But what caught Kristen's eye was the rainbow. Bands of purple, pink, yellow and green stretched from one corner of the room, up over a ceiling painted sky blue, then down the opposite wall. Not only had she slept beneath a blanket of stars but under a rainbow, too.

"You're awake!"

At the sound of the little girl's voice, Kristen glanced toward the pup tent and saw a blond head poking through the end flap.

"Yes, I am."

"Okay. I'll be right out."

The head disappeared briefly, then the flap was pushed aside and out crawled the little girl, a book in one hand and a flashlight in the other. As she approached the bed, Kristen could see that Tyler's daughter was a beautiful child. She wore a red jumper over a white blouse, with her blond curls held away from her face by a matching red barrette. Kristen looked for some resemblance between Brittany and her father but couldn't see any.

"You must've been really tired. You slept a long time," Brittany said with concern in her young voice, setting her flashlight and book down on the nightstand.

It was then that Kristen noticed the photograph. A woman with the same blond hair as Brittany's and the same blue eyes smiled at her from the frame. Tyler's wife. Brittany's mother.

"Yes, I was tired," Kristen admitted, setting aside her curiosity about the woman in the picture. "Thank you for allowing me to use your bed."

"You're welcome. Gram said it was okay to put you in here. Uncle Marsh and Aunt Lynn have the yellow room and Auntie Renee's in the green room."

Green room, yellow room, rainbows and stars. Kristen didn't expect Tyler would have such a home.

"This is a lovely room. I especially like the rainbow."

The child grinned. "Did you see my glow-in-the-dark stars?"

Kristen nodded. "I did." She glanced toward the tent. "Who were you talking to in there?"

"Walter."

Kristen hadn't heard any other voice, and there had only been one shadow on the canvas. She suspected Walter was a figment of Brittany's imagination. "Does he want to come out, too?"

"Uh-uh. He stays in there most of the time. He's shy."

"I understand. Maybe you should leave him the flashlight," Kristen suggested.

"It's okay. He likes the dark."

Suddenly aware of just how dark it was, Kristen pulled her hand out from under the red crocheted afghan and checked her wrist. "Oh my gosh. It's after eight." She let her head fall back against the pillows.

Brittany leaned over her, pressing her right palm to Kristen's brow and her left one to her own forehead. "I think my dad's wrong."

"About what?"

"He didn't think you were sick, but you're hotter than me. Feel." She reached for Kristen's hands, lifting one to Kristen's forehead, the other to her own brow.

Actually, Kristen thought Brittany's skin was warmer than hers, but the face staring into hers was so serious she didn't have the heart to contradict its owner.

"I'll get the thermometer." Brittany tucked both of Kristen's hands back beneath the afghan as if she were a nurse and Kristen her patient.

Kristen watched her scurry out of the room to return shortly with a thermometer in her hand. She pulled it from the case, slid a protective plastic covering over the tip, then stuck it in Kristen's mouth.

"It's probably the flu," Brittany diagnosed, again acting as if she were a nurse. "We sent six kids home yesterday with temperatures." She smoothed out the wrinkles in the afghan, making sure that Kristen was neatly covered. "I hope it's not strep 'cause then you have to get a shot." She made a face as if she had sucked on a lemon. "You don't have a sore throat, do you?"

Kristen shook her head vigorously. A few moments later, the electronic gauge on the thermometer beeped and Brittany removed it from her mouth. She held it up for Kristen's inspection.

"What does it say?" she asked warily.

"Ninety-eight point six," Kristen answered. "I don't have a fever."

"That's good." She slipped the plastic covering into a wastebasket, then returned the thermometer to its case. "Would you like some water?" she asked, reaching for the glass on the nightstand.

Kristen's mouth was dry. She raised herself up on one elbow, accepted the glass and took a long drink. "Thank you."

"You're welcome. Does your tummy hurt?"

"No."

"That's really good. It's yucky when you have to throw up." She hopped up alongside Kristen and sat on the edge of the bed, one leg bent beneath her, the other dangling over the edge. "Ms. Grayson says it never fails. Right before Thanksgiving...just like that." She snapped her fingers. "The flu bug hits."

"Who's Ms. Grayson?"

"My teacher. I help her when kids get sick because I'm gonna be a nurse when I get big."

"And do you like Ms. Grayson?"

"I do, but some kids say she's mean. That's because she makes you sit inside during recess if you're naughty." Brittany continued to study Kristen's face intently, as if she was fascinated by it. "I can see why my dad likes you. You have a pretty face."

Uncomfortable under the little girl's scrutiny, Kristen pushed herself up into a sitting position so that there was some distance between them. "You know who I am?" she asked the child.

"Uh-huh. Gram told me you're the lady my dad rescued from the plane crash."

"Your Gram's right," Kristen confirmed, feeling the usual twinge of anxiety at the mention of the crash. "My name is Kristen."

"I'm Brittany." She offered her hand to Kristen in a very serious manner.

"I'm pleased to meet you, Brittany," she said, taking the little fingers in her own.

The child returned the compliment, then observed, "You look different than you do on TV."

Kristen shifted uneasily. "You mean because of my face."

"Uh-uh. Your hair's different."

Kristen smiled. "You're right. It is different. I'm letting it grow."

"So you can wear it in a pony?"

If she were honest, she would have said, "So I won't remember the old me." Instead she said, "I wanted to try something different."

Her answer satisfied Brittany, who quickly changed the subject. "Do you want to see my turtle?"

"Sure."

Brittany scrambled off the bed and over to one of the bookshelves lining the walls. She reached for a glass bowl filled with a bit of water and lots of rocks. "His name is Speed."

"Speed?" Kristen repeated.

"We bought him last summer at the pet store because he moved faster than any of the other turtles there. Isn't he cute?" She lifted him out of the terrarium and shoved him under Kristen's nose.

"Yes, he's very cute," Kristen replied, breathing a sigh of relief when Brittany put him back in the bowl. "Do you have any other pets?"

"Uh-uh. I wanted to get a dog, but I can't. Gram's got allergies."

"What about Walter?" Kristen glanced toward the pup tent.

"What about him?"

"Does he like dogs?"

"Of course. Do you have one?"

Kristen shook her head. "I'd like to but I can't have one in my apartment building."

"Did you have one when you were little?"

"No. All I had was a couple of fish."

"We've got fish. Lots of 'em. They're downstairs. Wanna see?"

"Maybe later," Kristen told her, reluctant to go downstairs and meet Tyler's family. Actually, it was something she was hoping to avoid. The thought of calling a taxi and slipping away without anyone noticing was a tempting one.

Brittany bent her head toward the little tent. "Walter's asking me something." She jumped off the bed and ran to the tent. She stuck her head inside briefly, then turned back to Kristen and said, "Walter wants me to tell you he thinks you're nice."

"That's good...isn't it?"

"Oh, yes. Walter doesn't like to be around people—except me. You want to meet him?"

"Sure."

Brittany motioned for the invisible Walter to follow her to the bed. Grabbing a handful of air, she said, "Walter, this is Kristen." In an aside to Kristen, she said, "He's kinda shy at first, but he'll talk once he gets to know you."

Kristen smiled, waved her fingers and said, "Hi, Walter." Brittany beamed.

"Walter, you better go clean up that mess you made in my office," Brittany ordered her imaginary friend.

"Your office?"

"It's not really a tent. It's my office where I work."

"Oh." Kristen remembered Tyler saying how precocious his daughter was. She could see what he meant. "What kind of work do you do?"

"Reading, mostly. I can read the fourth-grade books and I'm only in first grade," she said proudly. "And I've already read fifteen books for the readathon at school."

"That's great. I like to read, too," Kristen admitted.

"I have lots of books." Brittany pointed to the shelves. "See?"

"You sure do. Have you read all of them?" Kristen asked, eyeing the collection.

The little girl looked at Kristen as if she'd asked a ridiculous question. "Of course! They're my books. Sometimes I let my dad read them to me 'cause he likes to think I'm still a baby." She rolled her eyes in an endearing way. "I better go get my dad and tell him you're okay. He's been worried about you. That's why I stayed in here. I told him I'd watch you."

"Why, thank you, Brittany. That's very sweet of you. And I appreciate your letting me use your bed. I didn't plan to come sleep the day away."

"Are you hungry?"

"A little," Kristen admitted.

"Good. We've got lots of turkey." She took Kristen's hand.

"You know what? I can eat something when I get

home.'' Kristen swung her legs over the edge of the bed and looked around for her shoes.

"But my dad said you were going to eat with us," she protested.

"Well, I was, but as you can see, I fell asleep and missed dinner."

"You missed most everything. Auntie Clara had to go back to the home. She gets cranky when she's tired. And Uncle Marsh and Aunt Lynn had to visit her side of the family. But Auntie Renee's still here and Gram, of course."

The fact that several guests had already left eased Kristen's apprehension slightly, but she still didn't feel up to meeting strangers. It would be embarrassing enough having to face Tyler after having fallen asleep on him.

She was tempted once more to call a taxi. But one look at this sweet child's face told her she couldn't run out on her or her family. So with Brittany's help, she slipped on her shoes and washed up in a bathroom that Brittany called her own. Like the bedroom, it had a rainbow across the ceiling and plastic stars that glowed in the dark.

As Kristen stared into the mirror over the sink, she noticed that some of her makeup had rubbed off while she'd been sleeping. Faint traces of her scars could be seen.

Normally, she carried makeup in her purse, but she hadn't wanted to keep Tyler waiting. And, of course, she hadn't expected to fall asleep. She did the best she could freshening up, then opened the door to find Brittany waiting patiently outside.

"Ready?" she asked Kristen, who was sorely tempted to be honest and say no.

Instead, she nodded and accepted the little hand stretched out to her. As the girl led her through the house, she could see that Tyler's home was as elegant as it was large. A crystal chandelier lit the winding staircase taking them to the first floor while plush carpet cushioned their footsteps as they walked. It was the kind of home Kristen expected to find on the Parade of Homes tour. Exquisitely crafted, beautifully decorated and not a thing out of place.

Flames flickered in the stone fireplace as they entered the family room. At the sound of Brittany's voice, three heads turned in their direction. Kristen wanted to turn and run as fast as she could.

"Kristen's hungry, Gram," Brittany announced as she led her into the room.

She was ready to deny Brittany's declaration when her eyes met Tyler's and something happened. She found she couldn't speak. Not a word. What she saw in those eyes was reassurance, understanding, concern...and something else that made her mouth go dry.

"I told her we have lots of turkey," Brittany explained to her aunt and her grandmother.

Before anyone could respond, Tyler said, "Mother, Renee, this is Kristen Kellar. Kristen, my mother, Millie, and my sister, Renee."

Both women greeted her cheerfully, getting up to offer her their hands and friendly welcomes. Kristen could see the family resemblance in all of them, as three pairs of eyes, warm and caring, gazed at her.

"I'm sorry I missed dinner. I...I've been rather tired lately," Kristen said weakly.

But she needn't have worried that her excuse sounded lame. Renee said, "There's no need for an apology, Kristen. Tyler told us you're still recovering from the crash. And rightly so. It must have been awful!" She shivered as she added, "We're just glad you're here with us."

Kristen didn't miss the way Tyler stiffened at the mention of the crash. He quickly changed the subject saying, "She probably wants to eat, not sit around and talk."

Before she could confirm or deny his statement, Millie said, "Of course she does. Come with me, Kristen. I put some dinner aside for you. All we have to do is zap it in the microwave."

"That's really not necessary. I don't want to put you to any trouble," she told the woman who, apart from her gray hair, didn't appear old enough to be Tyler's mother. There wasn't a line on her face and her figure was as slim as her daughter's.

"Oh, it's no trouble," Millie said with a smile, hooking her arm through Kristen's. "It's a thrill for me to have you in my kitchen. I've been a fan of yours for a long time."

It was a reaction Kristen often encountered. Although she would have liked to shy away from the recognition today, she sensed a genuine concern in Tyler's mother. It was impossible not to warm to Millie Brant. So Kristen smiled graciously and accepted the overture.

"I'll help," Brittany offered, grabbing Kristen's other arm.

When Renee was about to follow them into the kitchen, Tyler said, "We don't all need to watch her eat."

"I'm sorry, Kristen. Do you mind if we join you?" Renee asked.

The warmth generated by the Tyler women had her saying, "Not at all. Please do."

Tyler shot her a questioning look, which she ignored. In the kitchen, she sat on one of the stools at the breakfast counter at Brittany's suggestion. Then the little girl began helping her grandmother by setting a place for their guest.

"Chocolate or white milk?" she asked Kristen, holding up a glass tumbler in her hand.

"Maybe she wants coffee or tea," Renee interjected.

"No, milk is fine." Kristen smiled at Brittany. "White, please."

Kristen found her self-consciousness evaporating as Tyler's family did everything they could to make her feel welcome. Tyler, she noticed, stood to the side, keeping his distance.

The Brant women set a virtual feast of leftovers before her. So much food that there was no way she could eat it all. To her relief, Renee and Millie each took a piece of pumpkin pie, while Brittany had a dish of ice cream. Tyler had nothing.

They talked about things connected to Thanksgiving. When Brittany mentioned watching the Macy's Parade on television that morning, Kristen related the story of how the annual event had been one of her first assignments as a reporter. That had Brittany's eyes widening and prompted a discussion of floats and balloons, as well as music, movie stars and cartoon characters.

When Kristen had eaten as much as she could, she gently pushed her plate aside. "That was wonderful. Thank you."

"Aren't you going to have pie?" Brittany wanted to know.

Kristen held up her hands defensively. "Oh, no. No pie for me. I really should be getting home."

That brought a moan of protest from Brittany. "Oh, don't go home already," she begged, batting her blue eyes at Kristen. "We have to play charades."

"It's a family tradition," Renee explained. "We sit in front of the fire and play charades to end our Thanksgiving celebration on a fun note."

Kristen took a peek at Tyler, who looked as if fun was the last thing on his mind.

"If it's a family tradition, I wouldn't want to intrude."

"Good heavens, you're not intruding, Kristen," Millie declared. "We'd be delighted to have you stay." Her sentiments were quickly echoed by Renee.

"You have to stay 'cause there's not enough of us," Brittany added. "Daddy won't play. He's the referee. Uncle Marsh and Aunt Lynn aren't here now, so if you go home, we can't play." Then Brittany turned to Tyler and said, "Daddy, tell her she should stay. You said she was spending Thanksgiving with us. Charades is part of Thanksgiving.''

From the look on Tyler's face, Kristen expected Tyler to support her suggestion she go home. But she was coming to realize that he seldom did what she expected.

To her surprise, he said, ''We could use another player.''

''And we can make it a short game,'' Renee said temptingly.

Logic told her one thing. Her emotions told her another. She followed her emotions. ''All right. I'll stay. For one game.''

She only wished the whoop of delight had come from Tyler, not Brittany.

CHAPTER SIX

KRISTEN COULD HARDLY believe that it was nearly midnight by the time she left the Brant home. One quick game had turned into several long ones, with more laughter than Kristen had heard in a very long time. Even Tyler couldn't help grinning as they mimed and giggled their way through the charades.

When Tyler carried an exhausted Brittany to bed, Millie and Renee persuaded Kristen to share a cup of tea with them. It was an offer she was happy to accept. The two women made her feel at ease, and she discovered that before long she was telling them all about her family and her work at Channel 12. When Tyler returned carrying her coat, his mother instructed him to put it down and join them.

"I imagine it's been difficult being away from your job and your fiancé," Millie remarked.

"You have a fiancé?" Renee looked not only surprised, but disappointed.

Kristen glanced down at her ringless finger. Before she could say anything, Tyler spoke up.

"She's engaged to the other anchor on Channel 12. They're the 'Amorous Anchors.'"

Kristen didn't appreciate the hint of sarcasm in his tone. Nor did she need him to speak for her. "That's how a local gossip columnist refers to us," she explained.

"I never pay any attention to KC's column. You and Keith make a lovely couple," Millie said with a smile. As if she sensed the tension the subject had created, she steered their conversation in a different direction. "So tell us when we can look forward to seeing you on the Channel 12 news again?"

Little did Millie know that Kristen wanted to talk about returning to work even less than she wanted to talk about Keith. "I'm not sure. It's taking me longer to get my strength back than I expected."

Millie reached across the breakfast bar and patted her hand. "Of course, and you must take your time. It does no good to rush these things. That's what I told Tyler, but he wouldn't take any time off after the crash."

"Because I didn't need any time, Mother," he said stiffly.

"Maybe his injuries weren't as bad as mine," Kristen said in his defense, which was ridiculous since she knew he needed no one to defend him.

"It must have been a terrifying ordeal," Renee said consolingly. "I mean, when I think about what might have happened..." She shuddered, her voice trembling with emotion.

"There's no point in dwelling on what might have happened," Tyler countered in a flat, emotionless tone. "And I think we should change the subject."

"I'm sorry, Kristen. I shouldn't have brought it up," Renee said.

"No, it's all right," Kristen assured her, ignoring

the glower Tyler gave her. "I don't really mind discussing the crash. Actually, I find it helpful to talk about it. It's easier to deal with something like this if you get it out in the open."

She didn't miss the way Tyler stiffened at her remarks. Any warmth that had been in his eyes when they were playing charades was gone.

"I wanted to come home and spend some time with Tyler after the accident," Renee continued, either unaware of her brother's uneasiness or else ignoring it. "He wouldn't let me. Said he was fine and that the media had sensationalized what had happened."

Kristen knew Tyler didn't want to be called a hero, but she felt she couldn't let the opportunity pass without telling his sister just what he had done for her.

"It was a horrible accident, Renee. And the truth is I wouldn't be sitting here today if weren't for your brother," she said.

"Thank goodness you're both here," Millie said, placing a hand on each of their shoulders.

To Renee Kristen said, "If you have any questions you want me to answer, I'd be happy to do that."

"Sure. Just ask the reporter. You'll get a story," Tyler interjected with a sardonic smile.

Kristen didn't miss the look that passed between mother and daughter. They didn't understand his attitude, that much was certain.

Uncomfortable with the tension in the room, Kristen glanced at her watch. "Oh, my, it is late now. I really need to go."

Renee and Millie tried to get her to change her mind, but Kristen was adamant. After thanking them both, she pulled on her coat and followed Tyler outside to his car.

They were silent on the way back to her apartment, but this time her silence was not caused by her falling asleep. She was angry. When he parked out front and came around to open her door, she said coolly, "You don't need to come in. I'll be fine." The sooner she was away from him, the better.

"I'm not dropping you off at the curb," he said stiffly and walked her up the front walk and into the lobby.

As she dug in her purse for her keys, she said, "You can go now."

He made no move to leave. When she found the keys, he took them from her and opened the door. As soon as she was inside, she held out her hand for the keys. He didn't give them to her.

"You don't need to take me to my door."

"Yes, I do. I left my gloves in there."

She shrugged, then turned and started for the stairs. He followed. Once they reached her apartment, he unlocked the door, then dropped her keys onto her open palm.

"I think I left them on the sofa," he told her as he stepped into the entryway.

She didn't invite him in, but walked into the living room alone. There on the sofa was a pair of black leather gloves. She picked them up and returned to the entry. "Here."

He took them from her. "You're angry."

"I'm tired." She wasn't about to get into a war of words with him. "I told you that this morning. That's why I fell asleep in your car. That's why I slept all day. Now why don't you just leave?"

"I want to know why you're so upset."

She stared at him in disbelief. "I'm angry because of the way you react every time the subject of the plane crash comes up. I enjoyed meeting your family. And everything was nice until Renee brought up the subject of the crash and you had to make that crack about me being good at telling stories…insinuating that because I'm a reporter I'm going to embellish the facts." She took a deep breath to calm her emotions.

"You've seen the way the media covered this whole mess. Admit it. They sensationalized the whole thing and what they reported hasn't always been accurate," he said, his voice rising in anger.

"So because there are few bad reporters out there, I'm tarred with the same brush?"

He raked a hand through his hair. "You seem to take pleasure in talking about what happened."

"Pleasure?" She made a sound of disbelief. "Believe me, Tyler, I don't for one minute *enjoy* talking about that disaster. If I could erase it from my memory, I would. But I can't. It's hanging in there like a toothache, throbbing in my brain. It won't let me eat or sleep in peace."

His stern face softened. "Is that why you took pills today?"

"It's medication prescribed by my doctor," she

said defensively. "And there didn't seem much point in being awake today."

He didn't speak for several moments, then said quietly, "You're letting this thing get the better of you, and I don't understand why. You're not a weak woman, Kristen."

That brought her head up. "And how would you know?"

"Because a weak woman would have given in to the cold and the rain and the hopelessness that stared us in the face as we fought to survive that day."

"I didn't fight, Tyler. You did."

"We both did. And now it's all behind us."

"Is it?"

"Yes, and that's where it has to be."

There was such strength and conviction in his eyes she wanted to believe him. Yet she knew differently. "That's easy for you to say. You seem to have no feelings about the crash."

"I can't afford to have feelings about something I can't change. I did what I had to do and now you have to do the same," he told her. "Be the strong woman I know you can be."

She wrapped her arms across her chest, turning her back to him. "Fine. I'll be strong. You can go now."

He didn't move. Even though her back was to him, she knew he made no attempt to leave. There was silence until he asked, "Are you sure you'll be all right?"

"Yes. Go home to your family." Still, he didn't leave. Finally, she said, "Look, if you're waiting for me to thank you for dragging me over to your house for dinner, I'm not going to do it. I didn't want to go in the first place and you didn't want me there.''

"I'm sorry, Kristen. Tonight, when my family started asking you all those questions, I realized I'd made a mistake. I shouldn't have made you spend the day with us.'' He placed his hands on her shoulders and turned her around to face him. "But you're wrong if you think I didn't want you there.''

"I don't believe you. You came over here because you have some misguided sense of obligation toward me and…and because you pity me. Well, I don't need any man's pity and I'm not your responsibility. You said you don't want to be a hero, so don't be one.''

"I'm not a hero.'' The words sounded almost tortured as he said them.

"Maybe you should just leave and forget we ever met. You'd be doing both of us a favor.''

His eyes darkened then. "That's the problem. I can't forget you.''

Every nerve in Kristen's body pulsated. "You told me you had put the crash behind you.''

"The crash, yes. You, no.''

She looked into those dark eyes that had been such a comfort to her when she'd been cold, wet, in pain and close to giving up hope. This time, she saw no compassion there, but another emotion instead. Desire.

Those eyes studied every inch of her face. Automatically, she tossed her head so that her hair would cover the scars she knew were once again visible.

His hand reached up to push the blond strands away from her cheek.

He leaned closer to her. Kristen knew he was going to kiss her. He knew she knew. He paused, giving her time to turn away. She didn't. Her lips parted slightly in anticipation.

Yet it wasn't her mouth he covered with his lips. It was her cheek. Her scarred cheek. He kissed the imperfect flesh, softly murmuring, "You're so beautiful, Kristen."

Then he placed his mouth on hers and Kristen felt as if someone was pouring water on her parched soul. It was the kind of kiss that should have been given to her by her fiancé. Hungry, exciting, intimate. For weeks she had wanted Keith to take her in his arms and kiss her the way Tyler was kissing her now. To make her feel as if she was the most important woman on the earth.

Instead it was a man she barely knew making her come alive. She clung to those broad shoulders, returning his kiss with a passion that had been buried beneath pain. It felt so good, so right to be in his arms, she held back nothing.

Then suddenly it was over. The desire that had burned in his eyes was quickly masked by an aloof glare. She wanted to ask him why he had kissed her, but nothing came out of her mouth. She just stood staring at him. Confused by his behavior. Confused by her own reaction to him.

He obviously had no intention of staying even a minute longer. He reached for the doorknob saying,

"Take care of yourself, Kristen."

And then he was gone.

ONCE AGAIN, TYLER had difficulty falling asleep that night, tossing and turning as the digits on the clock relentlessly turned over. He glanced at it for the hundredth time and closed his eyes, trying to think about the problems at work that he needed to solve. Machines, blueprints, computer chips. Anything to keep his mind off Kristen and all the memories she triggered.

Nothing helped. The image of Kristen lying on Brittany's bed kept appearing. She'd looked so vulnerable. Soft. Sexy.

It was that last adjective that bothered him more than anything. If he was simply reacting to her frail physical condition, he would know what to do. He'd regard her in the same protective way he regarded the other women in his life. But he felt much more than protective of her. With no visible effort on her part, she sent the blood rushing through his body in a most unsettling way.

He didn't want to feel like this. He didn't want or need a woman in his life. All that mattered was Brittany. Taking care of her. Making up for what she had lost—for what he had taken away from her. Her mother.

He buried his head in the pillow at the thought of Susan. For almost five years he had lived with the knowledge that he hadn't been able to be a hero when it would have counted most to Brittany. And now he didn't deserve a woman in his life. How he could have forgotten that and kissed Kristen was beyond his comprehension. But what good did it do to chastise himself now? It was over and done with. The important thing was not to do it again.

He wouldn't see her anymore. There was no point, no necessity, to see her. Any problems she was having because of the crash—well, she'd have to deal with them on her own.

With that resolution, he finally fell asleep. When he awoke the following morning, he felt just as uneasy and out of sorts as he had the night before. After a quick shower and shave, he decided there was only one way to get his mind back on track.

If he were lucky, Brittany would still be asleep when he went downstairs for breakfast and he could go to the office for a couple of hours. Luck was not on his side; however, Brittany, dressed in a purple dress with white tights, sat at the breakfast bar eating a pancake. Renee and Millie were there, as well.

"Hi, Daddy, like my hair? Auntie Renee braided it for me," she said when he entered the kitchen.

"It looks very nice," he replied, feeling a lump of guilt the size of a bowling ball in his stomach. "You're up bright and early. I thought you'd be sleeping in after staying up so late last night."

"Uh-uh. Not when we're going downtown. I can't wait to see the little people."

The "little people" was Brittany's description of the miniature town one of the department stores constructed each holiday season depicting an old-fashioned Christmas scene with animated figures and electric lights. It was unveiled each year on the day following Thanksgiving, and this year Tyler had promised his daughter they'd be there on opening day.

And he'd keep his word. But first he needed to regroup. And a few hours at the office would help.

"Hurry up and eat, Daddy, so we can go," Brittany urged him.

"I'm afraid our plans have changed," he said, wishing he didn't feel like such a heel.

"You're not going in to work?" It was his mother who asked the question.

"Just for a couple of hours," he answered.

"I thought you said you didn't have to work today." Brittany crossed her arms accusingly.

"You know I wouldn't go in if it wasn't important," Tyler responded, grabbing a cup of coffee before taking a seat at the breakfast bar.

"But I thought we were going downtown to see the little people."

"We are. We're going this afternoon," Tyler stated evenly.

"You might want to reconsider that one," Renee piped up. "Traffic will be horrible by midday. If you don't go early, you might as well not go at all."

"There won't be any parking, either," Millie added as she set a stack of pancakes in front of her son.

Tyler unfolded his napkin and spread it across his lap. "Then maybe we'll wait and go after dinner. If we do that, all the outdoor lights will be on."

"Sounds as if you're planning to work more than a couple of hours." Millie arched one eyebrow in sharp criticism of her son.

Tyler held her gaze but spoke to his daughter. "Brittany, you don't mind waiting, do you?"

"We're not going till tonight?" The look on her face moved the lump of guilt from his stomach to his chest.

"I can take her this morning," Renee volunteered, then turned to Brittany. "Want to go with your auntie Renee?"

With a dejected face Brittany said, "I'll wait for Daddy."

The words should have given Tyler pleasure. They didn't. It only made him feel worse for the look on her face was hardly of understanding. She poked at her pancakes with her fork, not looking very happy at all.

"Why are you working? I thought you gave your employees a long weekend," Renee commented, sipping her tea.

His mother answered for him. "Your brother is very good to his employees. It would be nice if he treated himself as well as he does them."

"You should've mentioned this yesterday. I know Marsh and Lynn were going downtown this morning. I bet they would've been happy to have some company," Renee pointed out.

"I'm planning to take Brittany downtown," Tyler snapped a bit impatiently. "I just can't go this morning. I'm sure she can find something to do for a couple of hours."

"I'll play with Walter," Brittany said with a half-hearted enthusiasm.

Tyler didn't appreciate the looks his mother and sister gave him.

"I can take Brittany over to the mall with me this morning. We need to spend some time together anyway, don't we?" Renee gave Brittany an affectionate hug.

"If I go with Renee, will I still get to go downtown later?"

"Of course," Renee answered.

Then Brittany looked at Tyler and asked, "You won't be gone all day, will you?"

"No. Four hours max. I promise," he said, holding up four fingers for emphasis. Then he turned to Renee. "Thanks for the offer. You sure you don't mind?"

Renee gave her niece another hug. "Are you kidding? That's why I came all the way from California. You didn't think I came to see you, did you?" she teased, and Brittany giggled.

"I wish you'd stay forever, Auntie Renee. If you lived here, then we could play all sorts of games." Brittany clung to her aunt's arm affectionately. "I had fun last night."

"Me, too," Renee told her.

"Don't you think Kristen is pretty?"

Renee exchanged glances with her brother. "Very. Maybe she'll come visit after I've gone back to California."

Brittany looked at her father. "Will she?"

"I'm not sure," he said evasively. "She's a busy lady."

"She's a lot like you, Auntie Renee. She's fun to be with."

Fun? It wasn't an adjective Tyler would use to describe any aspect of Kristen's personality. Except for the time when they'd played charades. For a short while her eyes had lost their haunted look.

"Why, thanks for the compliment, Brit. You know what? I liked Kristen, too," Renee added, giving her brother a look he knew all too well. She was waiting for him to say exactly what he thought about Kristen.

Well, he didn't intend to satisfy her curiosity. Because he didn't want to talk about Kristen Kellar. Hell, he didn't want to even think about her.

"ARE YOU ALL RIGHT?"

"Why wouldn't I be?" Kristen asked Gayle when she turned up at her place with a bag of bagels the following morning.

Gayle shrugged and took off her coat. "I tried calling all day yesterday and you never answered. I was worried."

Kristen gave her hand a gentle squeeze. "I appreciate your concern, but I'm fine. Really."

Gayle sat down at the kitchen table and eyed her curiously. "So where were you yesterday?"

Kristen poured them each a cup of coffee. "Tyler came over and insisted I have dinner with his family."

"Well, well, well."

"You can take that smug look off your face. It's not what you think."

"And what is it that I think?"

"That he's interested in me, but I can tell you he's not. He only feels sorry for me." She emphasized the last word.

"Uh-huh."

"Because he saved my life, he feels this…this responsibility for me," she said, her skin warming as she remembered the way his lips had felt on hers.

"So you had dinner at his home and stayed there until midnight? That's a lot of responsibility," Gayle said with a wicked grin.

Kristen spread cream cheese on a wheat-and-honey bagel. "I hate to burst your fantasy bubble, but I spent most of the day asleep in his daughter's bedroom."

"What?"

"You know how restless I've been lately. Well, I had had an awful night, so I decided to take a couple of sleeping pills my doctor prescribed."

"How bad was it? You didn't fall asleep in a chair, did you?"

"No, in his car on the way there." She took a bite of the bagel. "When I didn't wake up, he carried me into the house and put me in Brittany's bed. I slept right through dinner, which I'm not sorry about. I really didn't want to crash their family time."

"So what time did you finally wake up?"

"Eight. I would've left then if I could have crept out without anyone seeing me. Instead, I ended up eating leftovers in the kitchen."

"So you didn't have to meet his family."

"Only his mother and his sister. They were charming. That's why I stayed until midnight." She didn't volunteer any information on what had happened when Tyler brought her home.

"I see you're not wearing your ring again," Gayle commented.

Kristen looked down at her finger. "Doesn't seem to be much point, does there?"

"Did you wear it yesterday?"

Kristen shook her head. "Don't jump to any conclusions. It has nothing to do with Tyler Brant."

Gayle held up her hands defensively. "I didn't say it did."

"Good, because with everything that's been going on, I don't need to complicate my life any further." Gayle shifted uncomfortably and Kristen could see by the look on her face that she was keeping something from her. "All right. What's going on?" she asked.

Gayle avoided her eyes. "Nothing," she replied.

"Yeah, right," Kristen drawled sarcastically. "You didn't just come over here to check on me, did you? What is it?"

Gayle nervously cleared her throat. "There's no easy way to tell you this."

"Tell me what?" Kristen asked impatiently.

"When I called the station yesterday to find out if I could get Sunday off, Angela told me Bob was in a bad mood because so many people wanted time off this weekend. Apparently, Janey was one of them."

Kristen shot her a quizzical look. "Meaning what?"

"She went out of town for turkey—or maybe I should say *with* a turkey."

Kristen swallowed hard before asking, "Where did she go?"

Gayle hesitated a moment, then finally said, "The Bahamas."

Kristen squeezed her eyes shut. "Damn him," she said quietly.

"I didn't want to be the one to tell you, but I didn't want you to read about it in KC's column, either." Gayle reached across the kitchen table and placed her hand over Kristen's clenched fist. "I'm sorry." To Kristen's dismay, she felt tears begin to roll down her cheeks, prompting Gayle to say, "He's not worth crying over."

But Kristen couldn't stop the flow, no matter how hard she tried. She dropped her head in her hands and cried. Not just for Keith, but for all the hurt she had suffered since the crash. Gayle brought a box of tissues from the bathroom and set it beside her.

When the tears were spent, Kristen insisted, "I'm not crying over him. I've known for a while now that our relationship was over. Things haven't been right between us since the crash—you know that—but I never expected he'd cheat on me."

"The guy's pond scum," Gayle said derisively.

"He's shallow is what he is. I never realized how self-centered he was. Do you know he can't even look at my face if I don't have makeup on to cover the scars?"

"He's lower than pond scum," Gayle derided him. "The guy doesn't deserve you."

Kristen could only shake her head. "How could I ever think I was in love with him? The man's always

got one eye on the mirror. Janey's welcome to him.
He probably gave her my plane ticket.''

"She wouldn't have paid her own way. My bet is
that she'll take him for everything she can get. They
deserve each other,'' Gayle said vindictively.
"You're lucky to be rid of him. But I'm worried
about your job...''

"Janey already has my job, Gayle.'' Kristen blew
her nose, then exhaled a long breath. "Not that I
care. I probably won't go back to work there anyway.''

"Kristen, don't say that. You love your work.''

"Maybe I did at one time, but—''

"You've been through an awful lot in a very short
time, both emotionally and physically. And now the
news about Keith. You shouldn't make any decisions
based on how you feel today.''

"And what if I don't feel any differently next
week or next month? It's been almost two months
since the crash.'' She rubbed her temples with her
fingertips. "I don't know, Gayle. I've been telling
myself to take it one day at a time, but I have to tell
you, the future's looking a bit scary.''

"Change is never easy,'' Gayle said sympatheti-
cally. "And you've had several big changes recently.''

"Yeah.'' Kristen noticed a copy of *Bride* maga-
zine on the coffee table. She picked it up, stared at
it briefly, then tossed it aside. "I won't be needing
that, will I?'' She couldn't keep the bitterness from
her voice.

"Don't think about him. He's not worth another moment of your time."

"Actually, I'm relieved something's finally happened. The way Keith and I were pretending to be this happy couple...well, it was ridiculous."

"That was a lot of tears for something you thought was ridiculous," Gayle noted.

"They weren't all for him," she admitted.

Gayle gave her arm a gentle squeeze. "Is there anything I can do?"

Kristen gave her a smile. "Thanks for telling me. I know it wasn't easy for you, was it?"

Gayle only shook her head. "Better to hear it from a friend than someone else, right?"

Kristen agreed. "I suppose next week it'll be in KC's column." The thought of his infidelity being printed for the whole world to see sent another pain through her heart. And anger. Why did Keith have to do this to her? Humiliate her in front of her audience.

"Maybe it doesn't have to be," Gayle reflected thoughtfully.

"And how do you plan to stop KC from printing such a hot news item?" Kristen wanted to know.

"The woman has to have some emotions buried somewhere behind her wagging tongue. I'll appeal to her sense of loyalty to the sisterhood of women who've been treated badly by men."

"Lots of luck. I think KC sprang forth from a rock and still lives beneath it," Kristen said bitterly.

Gayle threw up her hands. "There's no harm in trying, is there?"

"I guess not."

UNFORTUNATELY, KC DIDN'T consider herself a member of any sisterhood. When Kristen opened the paper on Sunday morning, before Keith and Janey had even returned from their tryst in the Bahamas, the story was there in bold print.

Kristen paced back and forth in her apartment. She couldn't sit still and pacing was the only thing that came close to calming her frazzled nerves. When she realized, however, that if she kept doing that until Keith's return, she would wear holes in the carpet, she knew what she had to do.

She picked up the phone and called him at his hotel in the Bahamas. Their conversation was brief.

"Kristen, it's not what you think," he tried to explain, but she cut him off.

"You don't know what I think, Keith. That's the whole problem with our relationship. You've never taken the time to find out what's going on in my head. It's always been what *you* need, what *you* want. Well, I'm going to tell you something and I'm only going to say it once. I don't want you and I don't need you. So just stay the hell out of my life."

And with that, she hung up on him. She picked up the newspaper, crumpled it into a ball and tossed it in the trash. Then she did what any other woman would have done in her situation. She started getting rid of his stuff.

NORMALLY, TYLER would have read the Sunday paper first thing in the morning, but with a house full of company, life was not normal at the Brant home. When the weather bureau announced a winter storm warning for the area, Marshall and Lynn decided to get an early start on their trip back home. Then shortly after breakfast, Tyler found himself on the way to the airport with an anxious Renee hoping her flight wouldn't be delayed.

Unfortunately, she didn't get her wish. However, it wasn't snow that delayed the departure of flight 1217 to Los Angeles, but mechanical problems. Tyler and Brittany spent most of the day waiting with her at the airport.

By the time her flight finally took off, the snow had started to fall. All the way home, Brittany watched gleefully as the windshield wipers swiped at the big white flakes and she begged her father to let her play outside when they got home.

However, it was dark as they pulled into the driveway and there was only time for dinner before Brittany had to go to bed. It wasn't until after he'd read her a bedtime story and tucked her in that Tyler had a chance to read the newspaper.

Seeing him with the business section of the Sunday paper in his hands, Millie asked, "Did you see KC's column?"

"You know I don't pay any attention to gossip," he answered.

She dug through the stack of papers beside him. "Not even when it concerns Kristen Kellar?" she demanded, shoving a section of the paper under his nose.

"She's a media celebrity. There's bound to be

something printed about her." He tried to sound dis-
interested even though his fingers were itching to
grab the paper out of his mother's hands.

"Well, this isn't just *something,* Tyler," his
mother said with a hint of admonishment in her tone.
"Aren't you the least bit curious?"

Tyler wanted to say no. He'd made a vow that he
wouldn't get sucked into Kristen Kellar's world. Cir-
cumstances had caused their paths to cross, but he
was determined to forget her. To get further involved
in her life was not something he could afford to do.

Besides, she drew attention wherever she went.
Even if he had wanted a relationship with a
woman—which he didn't—he preferred someone
who wouldn't jeopardize his privacy.

"I guess it doesn't matter," his mother said. "You
probably already know what's printed here anyway."

Unable to resist, he grabbed the newspaper and
quickly scanned the column until he found what had
caught his mother's attention. There in black and
white was KC's latest bit of gossip.

"Weekend anchor, Janey Samuels, hasn't only
taken Kristen's chair on the six o'clock news, she's
taken her fiancé, as well. Word is that Keith Jaxson
and Janey spent a romantic Thanksgiving in a very
secluded setting on a tropical island."

Tyler slapped the paper down, his blood pounding
in his temples. "Damn, that narcissistic jerk," he
grumbled to himself.

"Then you think it's true?"

Tyler knew that more than likely it was. If Jaxson
had risked meeting a woman at a local hotel, he cer-

tainly wouldn't hesitate to have a rendezvous thousands of miles from home.

"As much as I'd like to say it isn't, it probably is," he said grimly.

"You know, when I read it, I wondered if this was the reason you went rushing out of here on Thanksgiving Day to see if Kristen was all right."

"No, I didn't know about this," he said, waving the paper in midair.

"It must be awful to have such a story in the newspapers, and if this is how she learned the news, well...that poor girl." His mother shook her head.

Tyler listened, but he only heard snatches of what his mother was saying. He kept seeing the haunted look on Kristen's face. Was she okay?

There was only one way to find out. Go see for himself. "I'm going out for a while," he said as he jumped to his feet.

"Out? In this weather?" Millie followed him as he made his way to the hall closet.

"A little snow never stopped me before. I'll take the Jeep."

"But this isn't a little snow. There's a travel advisory," she reminded him, her face creasing with worry. "You heard it yourself on the television. They're advising no travel anywhere in the Twin Cities."

"I've lived here thirty-one years, Mom. I can drive through snow."

She looked as if she wanted to argue, but changed her mind. "If anyone calls, what should I tell them?"

"That I'm out," was all he said, and left.

CHAPTER SEVEN

AS SOON AS TYLER PULLED out of the garage and onto the side street, he knew why the weather bureau had issued the warnings. Snow appeared to be coming down from every direction, creating a swirling mass of white. Because it was Sunday, none of the streets had been plowed, which meant he had only the narrow tire tracks left by drivers like himself who had ignored the travel advisories.

When Tyler slid through an intersection and nearly smashed into a parked car, he thought about turning around and going home. He dismissed the idea quickly. He had to make sure Kristen was okay.

The trip seemed to take forever, especially since he stopped twice to help other drivers stuck in the snow. When he finally pulled up outside her building, he saw that a light was on in her apartment. Now that he was at her place, he wished he had called before driving over to see her.

He lifted his car phone and dialed her number. She answered after only two rings.

"Hi. It's Tyler," he said, wondering if she was curled up on the sofa in front of the fire.

"Hi." It was softly spoken.

"Are you all right?"

"Why are you always asking me that?"

He ignored the question.

"Feel like company?"

"Tonight? In case you haven't noticed, we're in the middle of a blizzard."

He chuckled. "I've noticed."

"You'd have to be nuts to go out on a night like tonight."

"I can tell you didn't grow up here."

"I grew up in Wisconsin. Same difference."

He smiled. "Hardly. You got any coffee?"

"You're not thinking of driving all the way over here for a cup of coffee?"

"I could use one. My feet are cold and my gloves are wet."

"What have you been doing?"

"Helping people who were stuck, which, by the way, may be my problem right now. I'm not sure I'll be able to get out of this parking spot I just pulled into."

"You're in your car?"

"Mmm-hmm. Look out your front window."

He saw the curtain move and there she was, standing with the cordless phone pressed to her ear. He thought he heard her gasp.

"So, do I get that cup of coffee?"

She let the curtain fall. "I can't believe you came over here in this weather."

"Is that a yes?"

"Yes." It came out on a sigh of exasperation.

By the time he reached the lobby, Kristen was buzzing the door open. As he climbed the stairs to the second floor, he realized just how wet his clothes were. He left a trail of snow and water in his wake.

She was waiting for him, wearing a soft pink sweater over a pair of black slacks. Her hair was pulled away from her face, secured with a headband. He experienced the familiar rush of excitement at seeing her.

"You're wet," she said.

"It's snowing," he responded, trying to shrug out of his jacket without dripping water on her carpet.

As soon as he removed his boots, she led him into the living room. "Come sit in front of the fireplace. I'll make some coffee."

"A brandy would warm me up faster—if you have one," he told her.

"I have one." She disappeared into the kitchen. While she was gone, he noticed the television was on, a continual weather warning scrolling across the lower portion of the screen. He glanced toward the dining room and saw boxes spread out across the table as if she'd been packing.

"Are you moving?" he asked when she returned with a small glass of brandy.

"No, just getting rid of stuff I don't want," she answered, wrapping her arms around her waist.

"Aren't you going to join me?" he asked before taking a sip of the brandy.

"In a minute. I'm heating water for tea," she answered. "I can't believe you're out driving around on a night like this. It's so bad they've even pulled the plows from the interstate."

"I wasn't just driving around. I came to see you."

His words caused her to shift from one foot to the other. Their eyes locked and the atmosphere became charged with tension.

Then the teakettle whistled, and he could see the relief in her eyes as she excused herself. While he waited, he idly surveyed the stuff on the dining room table. A stadium blanket with the Minnesota Vikings logo stitched across it, a foam-rubber brick with the same logo, a windbreaker, a pair of running shoes, a sweat suit, an empty wine bottle, several cans of caviar, a box of imported cigars.

"See anything you want?" she asked when she returned carrying a mug emblazoned with the Channel 12 logo.

He held up a bottle of Ann Taylor perfume. "I don't think this is my scent."

She didn't so much as crack a smile. She reached into a box and pulled out a pair of men's sandals. "What about these?"

He shook his head. "I'm not flying off to the Caribbean in the near future. And I don't think they're my size."

"You saw KC's column, didn't you?" she stated soberly.

He waved his arm over the pile of things on the table. "I guess this means KC has a reliable source."

She nodded, then sipped her tea, her fingers clenched around the dark blue mug. "Those hugging bears—" she pointed to a couple of stuffed animals, one pink, one blue, with their arms entwined "—KC sent them to me when she heard Keith and I were engaged."

"I'm sorry he hurt you, Kristen," Tyler told her.

She wandered back into the living room and sat down, setting her cup on the coffee table. "It's why you came, isn't it?"

"Did you know he wasn't going alone to the Bahamas?"

She shook her head. "No, but I guess it shouldn't have surprised me. Keith likes to surround himself with people who constantly make him feel good. Janey's a beautiful woman."

He wanted to say, "She can't hold a candle to you," but he knew she'd interpret his compliment as a gesture of pity.

She took a sip of tea, then said, "If you were worried I'd do something foolish because my fiancé dumped me, you've wasted your time coming here."

"That wasn't why I came."

"Well, good, because I don't need pity. I've told you that before."

He raised his glass in salute to her. "Good." He downed the remainder of brandy, then slammed his glass down on the table. "Because I'm not in a pitying mood."

"Then why are you here?"

If she wasn't so defensive, he would've told her the truth. That he couldn't stand to think of her being hurt by a man like Keith Jaxson. That if she needed a shoulder to cry on, he wanted it to be his. That he simply wanted to be with her.

But with the mood she was in, there was no point in saying any of that. She thought he had come to rescue her. To play the knight in shining armor. A role he didn't want and one she certainly wouldn't appreciate, at least not tonight.

"I was concerned about you, but it's obvious you don't want or need my concern, so I think it would be better if I left," he said as he got to his feet.

She didn't try to stop him but simply watched as he pulled his boots back on and slipped his arms back into his still-wet jacket.

"Good night, Kristen," he said to her on his way out.

"Good night." He was halfway down the hall when she called out to him from the doorway. "Tyler, wait! I do appreciate your concern…it's just that I need to be alone tonight."

"I understand," he said, although he really didn't.

So he headed back out into the storm. Only when he stepped outside did he realize just how bad things had become. In the short time he had been in Kristen's apartment, the snow had piled up over the rims of his tires. Getting home was certain to be even more of an adventure.

After doing his best to clear off the car, he slipped his key in the ignition but discovered that when he shifted the vehicle into gear, his tires spun, the engine revved, but the Jeep didn't move. He climbed out to look at his wheels. They were barely visible in the snow. Keeping the door open, he tried to rock the car out of its spot, but as he did, his foot slipped on a patch of ice and he lost control, bumping his head on the door as he fell forward.

It didn't take long for him to realize he wasn't

going to get the sports utility vehicle back on the road without help.

After being laughed off the phone by numerous service station attendants, he finally climbed out of the car and back up the apartment steps.

KRISTEN DIDN'T SAY A WORD as she opened her door to a snow-covered Tyler. She'd been feeling guilty about letting him go out into the storm. But now she was too embarrassed to apologize. So she simply stood there with a towel dangling from her finger.

Careful not to drip water on her carpet, he removed his jacket. She traded him the towel for the jacket, then carried it into the kitchen where she draped it over the back of one of the kitchen chairs.

He ran the towel over his head and his face, then slung it around his neck. "So go ahead. Say it."

"Say what?"

"Anyone who's out driving on a night like this deserves to be stuck." There was self-derision in his tone. "It's what you're thinking, isn't it?"

"Actually, I was wondering how you got that goose egg over your left eye."

He lifted his fingers to the lump. "I bumped it," he said glumly.

"It looks nasty. Maybe I should get you an ice pack for it."

He held up his hands. "No. Nothing cold. Please. It'll be fine."

She could see he was shivering. Noticing his socks and the lower portion of his pants legs were soaking wet, she said, "You should probably get out of those wet clothes. I could put them in the dryer for you."

"And what do you suggest I put on while you dry them?" he asked with a lift of an eyebrow.

She walked over to the dining-room table and pulled a pair of sweatpants from one of the boxes. "You can have these."

Tyler took them from her and held them up in midair, examining them with a wary eye. "You want me to wear something of his?"

"Would you prefer something of mine?" she quipped.

He didn't crack a smile but took them from her and said, "I guess they'll have to do."

She pointed out the bathroom, then went back into the kitchen to fill the coffeemaker. When he returned, she had to stifle a giggle. The pants stopped about an inch above his ankles and looked more like tights than sweats.

"Go ahead. Laugh. I know I look ridiculous," he said in a dour tone.

"That's not why I'm smiling. It's just that seeing you in his clothes makes me realize what a small man Keith really was—in more ways than one."

That brought a glimmer of amusement to Tyler's eyes. "What should I do with these?" He held up his wet clothing.

She swung open a bifold door to reveal a washer and dryer. "Toss them in here," she instructed, opening the dryer.

Looking extremely uncomfortable, he did as she

instructed. She closed the door and turned on the machine.

"I can make some coffee. Or if you're hungry, I can fix you a sandwich and heat up some soup," she offered, trying not to notice Tyler's bulging muscles.

"Coffee would be nice," he said, taking a chair at the table.

On her way to get a mug, she switched on the five-inch TV on the counter. "They're advising no travel until tomorrow," she said as weather reports filled the tiny screen.

"I tried at least a dozen towing services and all of them laughed in my ear when I asked how long it would be before they got here."

"How long will it be?"

"The best I could do was to get one guy to say he might be here around sunrise."

Suddenly, Kristen realized that Tyler was here for the entire night. Not only was she going to have to dry his clothes and give him something to eat, she was going to have to find him a place to sleep. It would be just the two of them alone in her apartment.

Some of her anxiety must have shown on her face for he said, "I'm not looking for a bed, just a warm, dry place to wait until the tow truck arrives. I'm sorry to have to impose on you. I know you wanted to be alone tonight, but I really have no choice."

"It's not an imposition," she told him, pulling a spoon from the drawer. "Considering you gave me a bed and a meal on Thanksgiving, I can certainly reciprocate and offer you the same in a blizzard."

"Thank you. I need to use your phone to make a couple of calls."

She nodded. "The cordless is in the living room. It'll be less noisy in there," she told him as the sound of his clothes tumbling in the dryer echoed in the kitchen.

Kristen watched him walk into the living room, the sweatpants showing every curve on his legs and buttocks. *Nice butt.* She almost spoke the words aloud. She closed her eyes and shook her head as if she could change the direction her thoughts had taken. She needed a distraction. While he made his calls, she listened to the latest weather updates on the small television.

"It's not good, is it?" Tyler stated when he returned and saw her gazing intently at the screen.

"No. There've been quite a few accidents. Nobody should be out on the roads tonight."

"Apparently, they've already canceled school for tomorrow."

She filled his mug with coffee. "What about Brant Electronics? Will it be open for business?" she asked.

He rubbed the back of his neck. "I'll make a final decision tomorrow, but I have a feeling we'll be closed."

She set the coffee in front of him and was relieved when he sat down. As long as he was standing, the tight sweatpants kept fueling her imagination.

He took a sip of coffee, then asked, "You don't have to go in to work, do you?"

She sat down at the table across from him. "No."

"You're still on a medical leave?"

"Yes."

He didn't pursue the subject any further, but Kristen found she needed to explain to him why she hadn't gone back to work. She didn't want him thinking she was avoiding being on camera because of her scars.

"I want to go back to work," she lied. "The problem is I'm just not ready. I still get these moments of weakness."

"I understand."

"Do you?"

He shrugged. "Sure. Why would you think I wouldn't?"

"Because Keith didn't. He said I had a bad attitude, that I needed to get on with my life and stop feeling sorry for myself," she admitted.

"I think there's a difference between someone with a bad attitude and someone struggling to come to terms with a difficult situation. I don't think you're wallowing in self-pity." The sincerity in his eyes gave her the courage to be honest with him.

"No, you're right. I'm not," she said with more confidence. "I don't feel sorry for myself. I just feel confused at times."

"Confused how?"

She looked down at the finger that at one time had worn a diamond solitaire but now was bare. "Ever since the crash I feel as if I'm searching for my identity. It's like I don't know who I'm supposed to be."

"Can't you just be yourself?"

"I'm not sure I know how," she acknowledged

candidly, meeting his gaze once more. "I know when a person survives something as traumatic as a plane crash, it's not uncommon to feel a need to reassess one's life and change priorities, but..." She hesitated, suddenly feeling self-conscious about confiding in him. "I shouldn't be telling you this. You don't want to hear my problems."

"What makes you say that?"

"Because you're coping just fine. You act as if that plane crash never happened."

"I don't act as if it never happened," he denied.

"Yes, you do. You won't talk about it, and if I mention the word 'hero' and your name in the same breath, you look as if you've been given a life sentence of hard labor."

"Because I'm not a hero," he stated in no uncertain terms. "And unlike you, I don't feel a need to talk about it, Kristen. It's over."

"For you, maybe, but not for me. Which is why I don't understand why you came over here. It seems like every time we're together, the subject of the crash comes up and you get uncomfortable."

He reached for her hand and covered it with his. "I'm not uncomfortable around you. If I was, I wouldn't have brought you to spend Thanksgiving with my family."

She struggled to ignore the warmth that spread through her at the contact. "You only did it because you were worried about me and because you feel responsible for me."

"Do you think that's why I came over here?"

"What other reason could there be?"

He looked as if he was about to deny her accusation, but he stopped himself. "You're right. I do worry about you. I don't know why, but I do."

Her shoulders sagged. What had she expected? That he'd tell her the reason he kept coming over was because he liked being with her? She swallowed back her disappointment and pushed herself away from the table.

"It's getting late. I'll get you some blankets for the sofa," she said as she cleared away the dishes. "If no one's coming before morning, you might as well get some sleep, too."

"Do you think my pants are dry by now?" he asked, gesturing toward the silent dryer.

"I'm sure they are. Go ahead and use the bathroom while I make up the sofa."

She expected him to protest. When he didn't, she went to the linen closet, pulled out a set of sheets and a blanket, which she spread out over the sofa. She was plumping a pillow when he returned, dressed once more in his own clothes.

"If there's anything else I can get you, just let me know."

"No, this should be fine. I'm sorry to have to inconvenience you this way," he told her.

"And I've said it's no imposition." Although that really wasn't the truth. Having Tyler spend the night sent her emotions swirling. When she was with him, she felt a sense of security and at the same time a feeling of uneasiness. He *was* her hero whether he wanted to be or not.

But he wasn't simply someone who had saved her

life. Each time she saw him, he revealed a little bit more of himself, and she was discovering that she liked Tyler Brant the man. And then there was the memory of his kiss.

She couldn't forget what it had been like in his arms. The way her heart had nearly stopped beating when he'd planted tiny kisses on her scarred cheek. The way he'd taken her breath away just by holding her.

"I won't wake you when I leave," he added, interrupting her musings. "In case I'm gone by the time you get up, I'll say my thank-you tonight."

He was so impersonal he might have been a perfect stranger who had never laid eyes on her before.

"You're welcome," she replied, then padded off to her bedroom. As she prepared for bed she wondered what had happened to the man who'd kissed her so tenderly only a few nights ago. Tonight she had seen nothing to indicate he wanted to repeat that kiss.

Then she chastised herself. Until this morning, she'd been engaged to be married and now she was lying in bed thinking about kissing another man. If she were smart, she'd banish any thoughts of a romance with Tyler from her mind.

The last thing she needed in her life right now was to fall in love.

CHAPTER EIGHT

THE TELEPHONE WOKE Kristen the following morning. A quick look at the clock told her it was after eight.

Shoving herself up into a sitting position, she answered the phone. Millie Brant asked to speak to Tyler.

"I think he may have already left, but if you wait just a minute, I'll check." She set the receiver down, then scurried out to the living room where she saw the blankets neatly folded on the sofa. She peeked through the curtains and saw that Tyler's Jeep was indeed gone. "He must be on his way home, Mrs. Brant," she told the older woman.

"I had hoped to catch him before he left your place."

Kristen could hear the anxiety in her voice. "He'll probably be home shortly."

"I need to speak to him as soon as possible. I'd better try to reach him on his car phone."

Kristen noticed the urgency in her tone. "Is there anything I can do, Mrs. Brant?"

"Oh…no…" she said uncertainly. "I need to talk to Tyler. You see, I've had a bit of bad news. My sister had to have emergency heart surgery last night.''

"Oh, I'm so sorry to hear that.''

"She's going to be all right, but there's no one to care for her. She lives in Kentucky and normally I'd just get on a plane and go to her, but there's Brittany. Tyler refuses to leave her with anyone but me. The last time he hired a temporary nanny he was not happy...'' she broke off, as if suddenly embarrassed. ''I'm sorry, Kristen. You don't need to listen to my troubles.''

"No, it's all right, Mrs. Brant. I just wish there was something I could do to help out.'' As she spoke the words, she realized there was something she could do. Without even considering the consequences of such an offer, Kristen said, ''Mrs. Brant, why don't you let me help you with Brittany?''

"Oh, I couldn't ask you to do that,'' Millie protested.

"You're not asking me. I'm volunteering my services. Your family was kind enough to entertain me on Thanksgiving, and Tyler—well, I owe him my life. I certainly can watch Brittany while you're away.''

"It's very generous of you to offer, but you have too many important things to do and I can't expect you to be a live-in nanny for my granddaughter.''

"Live-in?'' A warning flashed in Kristen's mind. "You'd need me to stay at the house?''

"She's only six, and with the long hours Tyler works, we really need someone to sleep over. At least during the school week,'' Millie explained.

Having heard the hesitation in Kristen's voice, she added, "So you see, I can't let you do it, Kristen. You're still recovering from the crash. You don't need the responsibility of being a live-in nanny."

Kristen knew she was being given the opportunity to reconsider her offer. And she should have. What she didn't need was to stay under the same roof as Tyler. But then she thought about little Brittany.

She was such a sweet little thing. And Mrs. Brant had been so warm and welcoming on Thanksgiving Day. "It's true I'm not quite ready to return to work, but I feel fine. I've been looking for something to do during my absence from the station, so I don't want you to think this is an imposition on my time. Brittany's a lovely child and I would really like to do this favor for you."

"It's such a generous offer, I don't know what to say," Millie replied emotionally.

"Just tell me what time you want me there."

"Thank you, Kristen. I'll call the airline and see what time I can get a flight."

"Great. I'll pack a few things and be over as soon as the roads have been cleared."

"This is so kind of you, Kristen. Tyler will be so relieved not to have to find help through an agency," Millie gushed gratefully.

Only Tyler didn't look relieved at all when Kristen showed up on his doorstep with her suitcase later that day.

"I guess your mother told you about my coming," she said smoothly, trying not to let the look on his face intimidate her. When he didn't step aside, she said, "Aren't you going to let me in?"

"I tried calling you to let you know you didn't need to come, but there was no answer. I'm sorry, but you've made an unnecessary trip. "

"Your mother isn't going to Kentucky?"

"Yes, she is, but you don't need to care for Brittany. I'll adjust my hours so that she's not home alone."

"And that's a ridiculous idea if I ever heard one," Millie Brant said behind his back. She gave Kristen a welcome hug, saying, "Come on in. Brittany's been waiting for you."

Tyler faced his mother. "You told her Kristen was coming over?"

"Of course. And she was delighted. As I am." She led Kristen into the house, reciting a litany of instructions, all of which were written down on a tablet in the kitchen.

When she had finished, Kristen said, "I don't think Tyler wants me here, Mrs. Brant."

"It's Millie," the older woman corrected her. "And Tyler doesn't like the idea of anyone moving in to take care of Brittany. He's a bit overprotective when it comes to his daughter. You've probably noticed?"

"He's a typical father, I guess," Kristen said, not wanting to criticize her temporary boss. "Look, don't you worry about a thing. I'm sure we'll get along just fine. You just focus on taking care of your sister."

"Thank you, Kristen. Your being here makes it so

much easier to leave. Now come upstairs with me and we'll tell Brittany the good news.''

Any reservations Kristen had regarding her offer to be a nanny dissolved when she saw the little girl sitting by herself in her pup tent. She was playing school with Walter and a couple of her dolls, engrossed in her make-believe world.

''Knock, knock. Anybody home?'' Millie called out.

Brittany scrambled to the opening in the tent and stuck her head out, her eyes widening at the sight of Kristen. ''You're here! Gram told me you were coming over,'' she said excitedly.

''She's come to stay for a while,'' Millie said calmly, her arm around her granddaughter. ''Remember how I told you that your great-aunt Bernice had to have an operation and I wanted to visit her? Well, Kristen's offered to stay with you so I can go.''

''Really?'' She jumped to her feet, her eyes lighting at the thought. ''You mean you didn't just come to visit? You're going to be my nanny?''

''If that's okay with you,'' Kristen told her.

''It is. I told my dad I wanted you to come over again, but he said you were too busy.''

''Busy'' seemed like a word from another lifetime. ''My schedule does get a little hectic when I'm working at the station, but right now I have plenty of time to spend with you. I think we're going to get along just fine, don't you?''

''Uh-huh. I have lots and lots of stuff to show you.'' She grabbed Kristen's hand and held on to it.

''Brittany, I've made a list of reminders for Kristen, but I'm counting on you to help her find her way around the house,'' Millie said to her granddaughter. To Kristen, she said, ''You'll quickly discover that Brittany is much older than her six years. She'll be able to show you just about everything you need to know.''

''I like to cook, too,'' the child boasted to Kristen.

''Well, that's good,'' Kristen responded, suddenly realizing she'd be more than Brittany's baby-sitter. She was going to be the housekeeper as well which meant making meals for Tyler and his daughter.

''And you can always call me in Kentucky. I've left the number next to the phone in the kitchen,'' Millie told her. ''If you follow me, I'll show you to the guest room.''

With Brittany leading her by the hand, Kristen followed Millie down the hallway, listening as the older woman explained who slept where. Brittany's grandmother's room was right next to Brittany's. The next bedroom was vacant, but Millie marched right past it to another room that was decorated in lemon yellow, from the plush carpet beneath her feet to the voile curtains on the windows.

''This isn't the closest room to Brittany's, but I'm going to put you in here so you can have a private bath.'' She pushed open a second door that led to a bathroom also decorated in the same shade of yellow. ''I wanted to have fresh flowers in here but because of the snow I couldn't get out.''

''I don't want you to fuss over me, Millie. This room is lovely.''

"I'm sure you're used to having nice things..." the older woman said with an apologetic smile.

"I live the same way you do. I take out my own garbage, I make my own bed, and to be perfectly honest, since the crash I've had so many flowers it's rather refreshing not to have them."

"That's sweet of you to say, but I'd feel much better if there was at least a small vase of daisies to brighten the room. Flowers add something special, don't you think?" Not waiting for an answer, she explained Brittany's schedule once more as they headed back down the stairs to the main floor. When they ran into Tyler in the hallway, Millie said, "Tyler, would you take her bag up to the guest room...the one with the bath?"

Tyler did as he was asked without saying a word to Kristen.

Millie seemed oblivious to the undercurrents in the house. Her mind undoubtedly was on her sister's health. As she left for the airport with Tyler, Kristen felt a sudden knot of anxiety in her stomach. Taking care of a precocious six-year-old was one thing, but putting up with her father was another matter altogether.

Shortly after Tyler and Millie left, a classmate of Brittany's called to invite her to go sledding after school the following day. Brittany asked Kristen if it would be all right. When Kristen hesitated to give her permission, the child assured her that Melissa's mother was the one taking them to the park where they would be sledding.

Kristen could see how excited Brittany was at the

prospect and told her she could go on one condition. That Kristen accompany them, too. This brought a screech of glee out of the girl's mouth as she wasted no time telling Angela that the Channel 12 newslady was going sledding with them.

Tyler, however, didn't share his daughter's enthusiasm.

"Guess what, Daddy. Kristen's letting me go sledding tomorrow after school," Brittany boasted over dinner that evening.

Tyler's fork stopped in midair. "What do you mean, sledding?" He fixed Kristen with a glare.

"Her friend Angela invited her to go after school tomorrow." She tempered her explanation with a smile.

"And you gave her permission without asking me first?" he demanded, continuing to glower at her.

"Did I *need* to ask your permission?"

Before he could answer, Brittany intervened. "Daddy, you're not going to make me stay home, are you?" She flashed her big blue eyes in a most appealing manner. "I want to go, really bad. I never get to go sledding. You always say you're going to take me and then there's always work to do." The words were said in a very adultlike, reasonable manner, not in a childish whimper as Kristen would have expected from a six-year-old.

Kristen could see the range of emotions in Tyler's face. Guilt. Annoyance. Frustration.

"Please say I can go, Daddy?" Brittany begged.

Kristen held her breath, waiting to see what Tyler

would do. It shouldn't have come as a surprise to her that he had a solution that would let him off the hook.

"I would, but then what will I do with the tickets I have for the ice show?" he asked with a sly grin.

Brittany's eyes widened. "You got tickets for *Stars on Ice?*"

Tyler turned to Kristen and said, "That's why you needed to ask me first."

"I'm sorry. I didn't know. Your mother didn't have it on the calendar," she said in her own defense.

Tyler said to Brittany, "Tomorrow I want you to come home right after school lets out so we can go to dinner first and then to the ice show."

Throughout the rest of the meal, Brittany chatted about how much she loved ice skating and how beautiful the skaters were. And wouldn't it be neat to wear those sparkly costumes? From the way Tyler avoided her eyes, Kristen suspected that there were no tickets to the ice show.

Her suspicions were confirmed after dinner when she checked the schedule Millie had left for her. Everything from getting dressed for school to brushing teeth was accounted for on paper. There was no mention of any ice show.

When it came time for Brittany to get ready for bed, Kristen climbed the stairs to the second floor with her hand linked to the little girl's. "You'll have to help me along here. I've never been a nanny before."

"Don't you know how to take care of children?" Brittany asked as she turned on the light in her room.

"I used to baby-sit when I was in high school, but that was a long time ago."

Brittany went over to the dresser and pulled out a pair of pajamas. "I'm pretty easy to take care of. I'm not a baby, you know."

Kristen nodded. "I know."

"I take a bath by myself, but Gram likes to check to make sure the water's not too hot."

"All right. I can do that," Kristen told her, following her into the bathroom.

Brittany twisted the handles of the faucet and a stream of water flowed into the tub. Next she climbed up on a stool to reach a fluffy red towel on a wicker shelf.

"Do you like baths better or showers better?" she asked as she spread the bath mat on the floor.

"Shower in the summer, bath in winter," Kristen answered.

"I like showers, but Gram gets a little nervous when I take one. She's worried I'm going to slip and fall." She began to unbutton her flannel shirt. She kicked off her shoes and pulled off her socks. Then she turned off the water, dipped her right toe in and said, "It's a little cold. What do you think?"

Kristen dipped her left hand in the water. "A little more hot, I think."

So Brittany ran more hot water into the tub. After several more toe dips, she was finally satisfied that it was just right. Kristen tested it one more time and agreed.

Brittany unzipped her jeans and tugged them down over her hips. Until this evening, Kristen had only seen the little girl with her legs covered. Now, as she stood bare-legged before her, Kristen saw that both her legs were scarred as if they'd been burned.

Brittany didn't seem the least bit concerned, stripping off her clothes as if she didn't have a care in the world. When she had taken off everything except her underwear, she said, "Gram usually turns her back."

"Oh—of course." Kristen did as she requested.

"You can get a book if you want."

"Is that what your grandmother does? Read?"

"Uh-huh. She leaves the door open, then sits on my bed. That way if I need her, she can hear me," Brittany explained. "You can read one of my books if you want."

"All right," Kristen answered, then moved into the bedroom where she scanned the rows of books on the shelves. Some of the titles were familiar, some not. She grinned as she realized that *Curious George* was still a favorite of children. She removed several picture books from the shelf and took them over to the bed, then sat down to wait for Brittany.

Brittany took her time in the bath, which Kristen guessed was due to the fact that several rubber dolls, which Brittany called her water babies, went in the tub with her. By the time she was finished, Kristen had read half a dozen children's books.

Brittany was right about being independent. She picked up after herself in the bath, brushed her teeth and put her clothes in the hamper before coming into the bedroom. Kristen rolled back the covers and motioned for her to climb under them.

Brittany reached for the picture Kristen had seen on Thanksgiving and gave it a kiss. "Good night, Mommy," she said, then climbed into bed.

"You look a lot like your mother," Kristen told her as the little girl fussed with the stuffed animals surrounding her.

"Everybody says that," Brittany remarked. "She looks nice. What do you think?"

"She looks very nice. I'm sure she must have been if your father was in love with her, don't you think so?"

She nodded. "I wish I could see her and talk to her one time, but you can't leave heaven once you get there." It was said in a very matter-of-fact way, but it was enough to clog Kristen's throat with emotion. "You need to get my dad now. He always reads me a story and tucks me in," she informed Kristen.

"All right." She started for the door, unsure whether or not she should give the child a good-night hug. In the doorway, she paused and said, "I'll see you in the morning."

"Wait!" Brittany sat forward, her arms spread wide. "Aren't you going to give me a hug?"

"Of course." Kristen went back over to the bed and hugged her.

Her throat once more choked with emotion when the little girl said softly in her ear, "I'm so happy you're my nanny."

Then Kristen went downstairs in search of Tyler. She found him in his office, working. "Brittany's ready for you to tuck her in."

He punched several keys on his laptop, then rose

to his feet. "If you don't mind, I'd like you to wait here for me. We need to talk," he told her on his way out of the room.

She sat in one of two large, leather wing chairs, noting how very masculine everything looked. The dark leather chairs, impressive mahogany furniture and hunter-green wallpaper left no doubt that this was a man's study. She glanced at some of the titles on the bookshelves. It was apparent he loved mystery and intrigue. Tom Clancy. John Grisham. Tami Hoag. And several shelves of technical manuals.

In the very center of the bookcase was an aquarium with dozens of brightly colored tropical fish. On the floor was a tiny step stool that Kristen deduced was for Brittany's use.

Behind the desk was a stately-looking leather chair. Beside it was the twin to the chair Kristen was sitting in, positioned so that whoever sat in it would be at his right hand. Kristen guessed it was also there for Brittany.

For someone who'd been working, he'd left very little clutter on his desk. Just a laptop flashing a screen saver of neon fish swimming in a bright blue sea. There were two photographs on the massive desk. One was Brittany's school picture, the other the same photo Kristen had seen on Brittany's nightstand.

Suddenly feeling as if she were prying, she closed her eyes to wait for Tyler. It didn't take long for him to return.

"Everything all right?" she asked.

"Brittany's fine, if that's what you mean."

"It is."

He gave her an odd look, then sat in his chair, resting his elbows on the desk. "I think we need to get a few things straight," he began.

Kristen's stomach tightened. "Something's bothering you."

He didn't waste any time in telling her what it was. "I don't want you to encourage Brittany to do things that could be dangerous."

"Dangerous?" She gave him a puzzled frown. "Are you talking about the sledding?"

"Yes, I'm talking about the sledding," he repeated. "I don't want her flying down an icy slope on something that could easily go out of control."

"I don't intend to let her fly down any hill," Kristen insisted. "We're not talking about tobogganing down a kamikaze course, but a few trips down a gentle slope on a plastic sled."

"Accidents can occur on even the smallest of hills. It's not an activity I want Brittany to do and I would appreciate your not telling her she can do something without asking me first."

"Fine. I won't do it again, but I think you're overreacting to the whole thing. Didn't you go sledding as a kid?"

"Yes. Remember the broken arm I told you I had? That's how I got it."

"That doesn't mean Brittany's going to break her arm if she goes with her friends," Kristen argued.

"No, it doesn't, but I'm not willing to take that chance. She is *my* daughter, Kristen," he said pointedly.

And that's that, Kristen thought. "I understand. Is there anything else?"

"About your wages—" he began.

Kristen held up a hand in protest. "I told your mother I didn't want to be paid for staying with Brittany."

"Why?" When she didn't answer right away, he said, "I hope you don't think you owe me something because of what happened the day of the crash?"

"No, I don't," she lied. "Actually, I've been getting restless sitting at home, and when your mother told me she was in a bind, I thought it would be a good opportunity for me to do something constructive with my time."

"Good. Because I've already told you, I didn't do anything anyone else wouldn't have done." His tone was cool and impersonal. "I'd still like to pay—"

"I'm not doing this for money," she broke in. "But if you insist, then make a donation in my name to the new children's wing at the hospital."

"Very well, I'll do that." His tone was cool and impersonal.

She wished that those tight facial muscles would relax so she could get a glimpse of her hero—the man who could look at her with a tenderness that made her forget the suffering they'd been through. She wanted to see compassion in his eyes and hear him say that he cared about her.

It wasn't going to happen. So she said, "If that's all, I'll go upstairs."

He nodded. "Good night."

She started for the door, then stopped. "Tell me

something. Did you have tickets for the ice show or was that simply your way of not letting Brittany go sledding with her friends?''

"I phoned the ticket office while she was taking her bath,'' he admitted without any shame.

She didn't comment. She simply turned and walked away.

As she did, she heard him call out to her, "I told you I'm no hero.''

CHAPTER NINE

DURING THE FIRST WEEK of Millie's absence, Kristen found her job more challenging than she'd expected. Not because Brittany was a handful. On the contrary, she was a delightful child.

It was her father who was difficult. After only a few days in the Brant home, Kristen realized that he wasn't simply a strict father; he was overprotective to the point of not allowing Brittany to do many of the things normal kids do. The list of activities she couldn't participate in was longer than the list of acceptable ones.

And if it wasn't bad enough that *he* had a fear she was going to get hurt, he had instilled that fear in her. Many of Kristen's suggestions for activities were nixed by Brittany herself who sounded like a miniature version of her father at times.

It was no wonder that the little girl spent most of her time in a pup tent playing with an imaginary friend, Kristen thought. The child was bright, articulate and outgoing, yet she was practically a prisoner in her own home. Except for the time she spent at school, she had little interaction with kids her own age.

Kristen knew what it was like for a child to spend

most of her time by herself and decided to do something about it. If Tyler refused to let his daughter participate in activities away from home, Kristen would bring the activity to Brittany. So when Tyler announced he would be away overnight, Kristen asked the six-year-old if she'd like to invite some friends over after school the following afternoon.

"It's probably not a good idea," Brittany told her.

"Why do you say that?"

She heaved a long sigh, just as her father often did. "Because someone could get hurt."

"Playing in your room?"

"Well, I'm not sure Walter would want them in our room," she said.

"Maybe you should ask him. If he'd rather not have girls hanging around, we could always do something down here. Like bake cookies," Kristen suggested.

The child's eyes widened. "You'd let us bake cookies?"

"Sure. Would you like that?"

"Yes, but what if someone gets burned using the stove?"

Kristen put an arm around her. "I'll tell you what. I'll watch very carefully to make sure no one gets close to the oven. I'll be the baker and you and your friends can be the frosting makers."

"We get to frost the cookies?" Her eyes opened even wider.

"It's getting close to Christmas. Wouldn't it be fun if we made some cutouts? You know, trees, bells, wreaths. I like to frost them with different colors and sprinkle those sugary things on them. What do you think?''

Brittany danced with excitement. ''How many friends can I have over?''

''I think three might be a good number. That way we'll have enough room for everyone to work.''

''Okay. I'll have Leslie, Heather and Kaylin.''

She scrambled up the stairs with Kristen calling after her, ''Do you need me to help you make the calls?''

''No, thank you. I can do it. I have speed dial and Gram helped me put all of my friends from school on it,'' she called back over her shoulder as she raced into her room.

Which made Kristen wonder what Millie Brant thought of Tyler's overprotectiveness. Why would she put all of Brittany's friends' numbers in the phone index if she didn't want her granddaughter to use them?

Although Brittany did the telephoning, Kristen wasn't surprised when all three of the mothers wanted to talk to her to confirm plans. Kristen assured each of them that she would be supervising the girls as they baked the cookies. No one expressed any concerns about safety. Since Tyler wasn't scheduled to be back until late that evening, Kristen suggested the girls stay for supper and that their mothers pick them up afterward.

Kristen had little experience with six-year-olds. And even less with baking. The most she'd ever done with regard to cookie making was to cut a slice off a roll of refrigerated dough and plop it on a baking sheet. Although she'd watched her mother bake Christmas cookies, she had the feeling she was way out of her depth.

She was right. Chaos was an understatement when it came to describing the state of the kitchen during the project. Thanks to Millie's organizational skills, she had no trouble locating ingredients. And utensils. Deciphering the handwritten recipe was a challenge. Kristen was grateful that she was the only adult in the house, for she would have been embarrassed for anyone else to see the mess. Fortunately, the food coloring washed off the girls' hands and clothing. As for the kitchen, Kristen pulled the door shut and kept the children in the television room while they waited for their rides home. By the time the mothers arrived, each of the six-year-olds had a smile on her face and a bag of cookies in her hand and no one saw the disaster that was the kitchen.

Except Tyler, that is. Just as Kaylin was walking out the front door waving goodbye to Brittany, he arrived home. To Kristen's dismay, Kaylin's mother expressed her thanks by telling him what a wonderful idea it was to have a cookie-making party for the girls.

Although Tyler had a smile on his face while he spoke to Kaylin's mother, the minute the door closed and they were alone, Kristen could see he wasn't pleased.

"What cookie party?" he asked as Brittany plowed into him for her hug.

"We had so much fun!" the little girl said in a rush. "Kristen let us bake cookies and frost them with real frosting. I made a Santa with a red suit and Christmas trees with green frosting and little red cinnamon candies on them.''

She rambled on, telling him as much as she could remember from the afternoon with her friends. All the while, Tyler said nothing, but the looks he flashed at Kristen told her she needed to rehearse her defense.

Finally, Kristen said, ''Brittany, I bet your dad would like to sit down.''

''What I would like is something to eat,'' he answered.

''You haven't eaten?'' she asked, a note of panic in her voice at the thought of the chaos in the kitchen. ''I can make you something. Just tell me what,'' she said with a false cheerfulness.

''I'll just have whatever leftovers there are from whatever you two ate.''

''We had pizza,'' Brittany boasted.

Kristen gave him an apologetic smile. ''Sorry, no leftovers. I could make you a sandwich.''

''It's not necessary. I'll get myself something.'' He started walking toward the kitchen, but she intercepted him.

''No, you go sit with Brittany. I know how much she missed you, and she's eager to talk to you.''

Brittany took him by the hand and said, ''Come on, Daddy. I made a poem in school today and I want to show it to you.''

Kristen gestured for him to go. ''I'll bring your sandwich into the family room,'' she said.

He looked as if he wanted to protest, but Brittany was dragging him by the hand.

Kristen hurried into the kitchen, thinking she could make Tyler the sandwich, then clean up while he ate it in the other room. He'd never have to see what a mess the kids had made. It was a plan that would have worked had Brittany not gone upstairs to get her school papers. While Kristen piled pastrami and cheese onto rye bread, Tyler strode into the kitchen.

"What on earth happened in here?" he asked, surveying the mess.

"Making cookies can be a little messy at times," she told him with a false smile.

He just stood there, slowly turning around as if in total disbelief. "I think there's some frosting on the wall," he observed with a grimace.

Kristen grabbed a paper towel and swiped at the green and red blobs on what had been pristine white walls. "It's washable. See?" She gave him another forced smile. "I know that the kitchen is a little messy—"

"A *little* messy?" he interrupted her.

"All right. It's a big mess, but the girls really had a good time and that's what's important. All of this can be cleaned up," she said with a sweep of her arm.

Before he could argue with her, Brittany entered carrying her papers. "Come on, Daddy. I have to show you this stuff and it's too messy in here." She lifted her nose in disdain.

"I'd like to talk to you later," was all Tyler said before he left.

Kristen had a pretty good idea what he was going to say. She hadn't followed the rules of the house, which meant he'd have a frown on his face. And after being lectured about the rules, he would repeat them for her again. Not that he needed to. Brittany had recited them so often that there was no chance she would forget one.

As she expected, after Brittany was asleep, Tyler called her into his office. Before she could take a seat, he said, "This isn't working out the way I hoped it would."

Kristen bit her lip. "You want me to leave?" she blurted out.

"No. Why would I want you to leave?"

"Because of the cookie party?"

He grinned then—the first real smile she had seen in a long time. At least the first directed at her. "I don't think frosting on the wall is going to put my daughter's life in jeopardy."

She returned the smile. "At least the girls had fun. You said something isn't working…what?"

"My schedule. I know I originally told you we wouldn't need you on Saturdays or Sundays, but something's come up and I'm going to have to spend most of the weekend at the plant."

"No problem. I can stay with Brittany."

"Everyone needs a break. You deserve some time for yourself."

She crossed her arms. "I've had enough time to myself to last me quite a while. I like being with your daughter, Tyler."

"I thought about calling my sister-in-law and asking her to come and stay for the weekend, but when I told Brittany, she begged me not to. She said I should pay you a lot of money to stay because you're the best person in the world to baby-sit her.''

"I'll stay with her and you don't have to pay me any money.''

"Let's not argue over that one again. Besides, after seeing that kitchen, I'd say you've earned a bonus.'' Once more, his lips twitched into a grin. He reached for a checkbook and pen. "Still want this to go to the hospital?''

"Yes.''

"All right. Then it's settled. You'll stay the weekend.''

ON SATURDAY, KRISTEN took Brittany shopping at the mall and out for lunch at the Rainforest Café. Since Tyler had told her not to expect him home for dinner, she ordered a pizza for supper and they watched one of Brittany's favorite videos that evening—*The Wizard of Oz*.

Tyler didn't return home until after they had both gone to bed. Kristen stirred when she heard his car pull into the garage, automatically glancing at the clock on the bedside table. It was after midnight. No wonder his footsteps sounded weary as he climbed the stairs. Although he'd called Brittany to say goodnight, Kristen hadn't expected that he'd actually miss tucking her into bed.

As she listened to the faint sounds of Tyler moving through the house, her mind drifted to thoughts of the past week. She'd managed to fit into their routine with surprising ease. Any trepidation she had had regarding meals had been pushed aside when she had discovered that Millie Brant had a cook who came in bimonthly to prepare meals to be stored in the freezer.

Her other concern—that it would be awkward being around Tyler—was as easily dismissed. Not only did he work long hours, which meant he was seldom home, but when he was there, they were infrequently alone. And Brittany's joy at her presence made up for Tyler's aloofness.

Looking after Brittany had been good for Kristen and she wasn't looking forward to returning to her lonely apartment when Millie came home. She envied Tyler his ability to go back to work so soon after the crash and resume his life as if nothing had happened. If he was troubled by the disaster, he didn't show it. Except for his affection for Brittany, he revealed little of his feelings.

Kristen sensed that he didn't want her to know what made him tick. He deliberately put a distance between them, reluctant to let her discover who he was. But with or without his consent, she had learned a lot about Tyler Brant. One didn't live under the same roof with another person and not learn some things.

Such as the fact that he liked everything to be in order. Boots had to be lined up evenly in the mudroom. Chairs were always pushed all the way back in. Newspapers were stacked in a neat pile.

He used a straight-edge razor and shaving cream with a touch of lime in it. He used a stick deodorant, mint-flavored toothpaste and cinnamon dental floss. Judging by the way his bed looked in the morning, Kristen surmised he was a restless sleeper. The covers were twisted and strewn about the king-size bed.

If it hadn't been for Brittany, she wouldn't have seen what Tyler's room looked like. From day one, he had told her she need only be concerned with the kitchen. While Millie was responsible for meals and taking care of Brittany, a cleaning lady came on a regular basis and took care of the rest.

However, one morning after Tyler had left for work, Brittany couldn't find a permission slip she needed for a class field trip. She had insisted Kristen help her look and one of the places they searched was Tyler's bedroom.

Although there were three large windows on one wall, dark blue draperies kept out the sunlight. Everything in the room was dark—from the mahogany furniture to the bedspread and carpet. Nothing was out of place. No clutter on the dressers, no clothes on the floor. Over the bed was a print of a tiger and her cubs. Except for a picture of Brittany and her grandmother, there was nothing on the nightstand but a lamp.

"Daddy must have been in a hurry this morning. He forgot to make his bed," Brittany had remarked as she marched into his room in search of the missing slip of paper. Kristen had looked at the crumpled bedclothes and wondered if he was always such a restless sleeper or if something had been bothering him the previous night. Brittany answered her silent inquiry, stepping over a crumpled, dark blue duvet and saying, "Daddy throws his covers on the floor. I think he gets hot or something."

Or something. Kristen thought it was more likely the latter. She'd felt odd being in Tyler's bedroom, especially since she was with a six-year-old who kept up a nonstop monologue on her father's habits.

Now listening to Tyler get ready for bed, she could picture him in that room, unbuttoning his shirt. Unzipping his trousers. She closed her eyes and buried her face in the pillow, trying to banish the images flashing in her mind. If he hadn't kissed her, she wouldn't even be thinking about him in such a way.

Or would she?

She punched her pillow and tried to think about the day ahead. She'd take Brittany to Sunday school, then maybe they'd go over to the arena to watch the skating club perform. She mentally made a list of things she wanted to accomplish before Christmas. Cards to be addressed, gifts to be purchased, people to visit.

For the next hour, she lay awake thinking of everything and anything, hoping to fall asleep. She didn't. Just when she thought she might doze off, she heard Tyler's voice. At least she thought she heard it.

She sat up and listened. The sound was muffled, but it was definitely a man's voice. Gingerly, she climbed out of bed, pulled on her robe and padded toward the door. She poked her head into the hallway and listened.

It was definitely Tyler's voice, but it impossible to

figure out what he was saying. One thing was certain—he was in distress. She crept toward his door and bent her head toward it.

"Get out! Get out!"

Startled, she flinched back. Then she realized that the words weren't directed at her. Once more, she put her ear to the door and heard him uttering garbled sentences.

Suddenly, she heard a thump. Then the door flew open and she gasped. The look on Tyler's face was of sheer panic. He reached out and grabbed her, pulling her close to him and hugging her so tightly she thought he might squeeze the air right out of her lungs.

His naked chest was warm, his arms strong. And he smelled good. Like a fragrant soap. Musk.

Before she had time to notice anything else, he released her. He heaved a long sigh, then closed his eyes and stumbled back until he was leaning against the wall.

"Are you all right?" she asked, trying not to notice that he wore nothing but a pair of Joe Boxer pajama bottoms that had ducks all over them. Barefoot and bare-chested, he stood before her. His hair was mussed, his jaw darkened by the beginning of stubble. He gazed at her blankly. "Tyler?"

"What are you doing here?"

"I heard a noise and wondered if something was wrong," she said, missing the warmth that only seconds ago had enveloped her.

His broad shoulders sagged, his face paled, making him look completely disoriented. Kristen had to fight the urge to put her arm around him and comfort him.

"No, nothing's wrong," he muttered.

"You're sweating," she noted. "Are you ill?"

"No. I just…" He paused and stared at her. What she saw in his eyes made Kristen shudder.

"You were having a nightmare about the crash, weren't you?"

He squeezed his eyes shut and leaned back against the wall. "Go back to bed, Kristen. It doesn't concern you."

"Of course it concerns me. I was in it, too. I know what you're going through."

"I'm not *going* through anything," he retorted, lifting his head and piercing her with a stare that dared her to challenge his response.

"You think a nightmare about something that happened over two months ago is nothing?"

"I don't want to talk about this," he told her, then staggered back into his room.

She followed him. When he dropped down onto the bed with his head in his hands, she sat down beside him.

"Tyler, please talk to me."

"I told you. There's nothing to talk about," he said without lifting his head.

"You had a nightmare that was so frightening it woke you up and sent you out into the hallway in a panic."

He looked at her then. "So?"

"So you told me you didn't have any aftereffects

from the crash. That you had tucked it all away neatly into the past."

"All right, I lied. I do have dreams about the crash. I've had them ever since you sent me that letter thanking me for being a hero." There was such derision in his voice Kristen winced.

He blamed her for his nightmares. A sick feeling in her stomach caused her to wrap her arms around her middle. No wonder he had such an impersonal look in his eye whenever she was in the same room as him. Looking at her made him remember something he was trying to forget.

"I'm sorry. I didn't know I was..." She left her apology unfinished, having to swallow back the emotion clogging her throat. Then she sprang to her feet. "You should have told me."

She wanted to be angry with him, but all she could feel was humiliation. How naive she had been to think that he'd pour his heart out to her, that together they would be able to find peace and finally forget about the crash.

She needed to get away from him. "I just didn't realize. I'll try to stay out of your face as much as possible," she told him, hating the way her voice quivered when she spoke.

Before she could rush out of the room, he grabbed her hand and pulled her back to him. In one smooth movement, she was on his lap, her hands pressed against his bare chest. His skin was warm beneath her fingertips, his heart beating strong and steady beneath her palm.

"I don't want you out of my face," he said, looking at her with eyes that were anything but distant.

Something stirred deep inside her. "But you said—"

"Forget what I said." He studied her face intently. "It's not what you think."

"And what am I supposed to think, Tyler?" she asked, her breathing becoming irregular as he traced the curve of her jaw with his fingers. Next his fingers outlined her lips in a seductive caress that sent a flush through her body. Then she felt a warm breath in her ear.

"Maybe it would be better if neither one of us did much thinking," he whispered.

She wrapped her arms around his neck, wanting to be closer to him. "I'm sorry every time you look at me you think about the—"

"Shhh." He stopped her words with a finger pressed to her lips. "When I look at you, there's only one thing I think about," he said huskily.

There were certain things in life a woman didn't need to be told. One of them was when a man wanted to make love. Tyler had that look in his eyes that very moment. He wanted her. It should have frightened her. She was in his bedroom, in her nightgown, on his lap.

And when he bent his head to plant tiny kisses on her neck, she should have pulled away from him. But she couldn't. Because the same longing she saw in his eyes was creating an ache deep inside her.

She arched her head back, loving the feel of his lips on her skin. "I should go back to my room," she murmured, struggling to control emotions that could easily be unleashed.

"I don't want you to go, Kristen." He pulled her with him as he fell back against the mattress. For a brief moment, she was on top of him, but then he turned on his side so that his body was half covering hers. "Do you know how many nights I've lain here and imagined what it would be like to have you in my bed?"

The words had the same effect as any physical caress. Kristen felt a tingling all through her body. When he covered her mouth with his, she held nothing back, returning his kisses with a passion that matched his.

Any thoughts Kristen might have had about the wisdom of being in his bed were quickly dismissed as he pressed every inch of his body against her and she felt the urgency of his desire. When his hand slid under her nightgown, she moaned in pleasure, and her own fingers set off on an exploration of their own.

She could tell by the way his breathing changed that he was as affected by her touch as she was by his. They were like two starving lovers, hungrily devouring each other, clinging and touching as if they couldn't get enough of each other.

"You make me feel so alive," she whispered between kisses, expecting him to express the same emotion.

He didn't. Her words had put a halt to their lovemaking.

"We can't do this." He rolled onto his back and

covered his eyes with his forearm. "My daughter's bedroom is just down the hall."

Reality. It had intruded with a cold abruptness. "I wasn't thinking…" she began, realizing just how little thinking she had done. She should never have come into his room wearing nothing but her nightgown. Or allowed him to pull her onto his bed. Or encouraged him to touch her.

The thought of Brittany had her scrambling off the bed. Without another word, she hurried out the door. This time, he didn't try to stop her.

To KRISTEN'S DISMAY, she overslept the following morning. By the time she came downstairs, Brittany was at the breakfast counter eating cold cereal. Tyler was nowhere in sight.

"I'm sorry, Brittany. I didn't hear my alarm this morning," Kristen said. "Why didn't you wake me?"

"It's okay," the little girl said between spoonfuls. "Daddy told me you were probably really tired and needed your sleep."

That brought a flush of heat to Kristen's cheeks. "Has he gone already?" she asked.

"Uh-huh. He had to leave early today 'cause he had an important business meeting out of town. He left a note for you on the counter."

Kristen spotted a slip of paper near the toaster and picked it up. It read, "Called out of town unexpectedly. Will be back tomorrow evening. If you need me, you can reach me on my cell phone. Tyler."

Disappointment chased away the warmth she had

been feeling ever since she'd awoken. The message was all business. But then, what did she expect? Just because they had nearly made love last night didn't mean he would suddenly get romantic in a note.

She wondered if what had happened in his bedroom was the reason for his early departure. Maybe he didn't want to face her after last night.

"Do you know how to ice-skate?" Brittany asked, forcing her mind from the subject.

"Mmm-hmm. There was a skating pond near my home when I was a little girl and I went nearly every day during the winter. Why do you ask?"

"Shannon Crawford is having a birthday party and everyone's going ice-skating, but I can't go because I don't know how," she stated matter-of-factly. "I thought you could teach me."

Immediately, Kristen thought about Tyler. He would expect to be notified before Brittany laced up a pair of skates. And no matter how often Brittany batted those blue eyes at him, Kristen was almost a hundred percent certain that he would object on the grounds that she might get hurt.

"Have you talked to your dad about it?"

Brittany rolled her eyes. "Yes. He told me to just stay home. He doesn't know how to skate, either. He's got weak ankles."

Kristen guessed that if that were true, ankles were probably the only things that were weak on his entire body. "I'd be glad to teach you to skate, but I think we really need to talk to your dad about it first."

Brittany's tiny shoulders sagged. "Just forget it. I don't need to go to Shannon's party."

Seeing her so dejected pulled at Kristen's heart-strings. "Don't you want to go?"

"Yes, but..." She put her hands on her waist and sat with her lips squeezed together. "What if I fall and get hurt? I probably got weak ankles, too, just like my dad."

"Are you skating indoors or outdoors?"

"Outside on the skating pond her dad made for her in their yard."

"Then you can wear extra clothes to stay warm, and if you do fall, they'll cushion you."

Brittany seemed to be thinking it over. "I don't have any skates."

"We can go and get a pair after Sunday school. In fact, since your dad isn't going to be home tonight, we'll go to the arena and have our first lesson."

Her eyes widened. "Really?"

"Sure. I'll call this morning and see what's open. Then I'll swing by my apartment and get my skates. Okay?"

"Okay."

Kristen knew she should have called Tyler and asked him about taking Brittany skating, but she had a pretty good idea that he would nix the idea. Later, any doubts Kristen had about going against his wishes were erased when she took Brittany to buy a pair of skates. The excitement in the six-year-old's face when she laced up the boots was worth the risk of Tyler's anger.

As soon as they'd paid for the skates, Kristen drove over to the arena. Inside, she patiently worked with Brittany until the little girl could glide across the ice without any help from Kristen. Although the lessons hadn't been accomplished without a few spills, Brittany never once complained. She'd fall down, pick herself up and keep going. The joy on her face at the accomplishment warmed Kristen's heart.

Kristen let her practice until she was as proficient as any six-year-old. Confident that Brittany could attend the party and not feel like an odd duck, Kristen suggested they go home. On the way they stopped to pick up a birthday gift, which Kristen allowed Brittany to wrap all by herself once they were home.

Before they went to bed that night, Kristen showed Brittany how to make yarn pom-poms for her skates. Together they threaded red yarn around a cardboard circle, then snipped with scissors and tied the strands together. The following morning, Brittany's new skates sat in the hallway with the pom-poms laced at the toe. As soon as she returned from school, Kristen would drive her over to Shannon's for the party.

Only minutes before the bus dropped Brittany off at home, Tyler arrived. It had been nearly two days since Kristen had seen him. Nearly two days since they had almost made love. When he walked through the door, she wished she could have greeted him with a kiss, but she wasn't sure he would welcome her into his arms.

"I thought you weren't coming back until after dinner," she said as he set his bag down in the entry.

"The meeting ended early."

No "Hello, how are you?" No "I've missed you." No hug, not even a smile. As he walked toward the closet, butterflies danced in Kristen's stomach.

"What are those?"

Kristen gulped. She had forgotten about Brittany's skates sitting next to the door. Tyler had seen them and was now glaring at her. "Ice skates."

"I can see that. But whose are they?"

"They're Brittany's. I bought them for her yesterday so she could go to Shannon's birthday party today," she said bravely.

"She's not going ice-skating," he said firmly as he hung his coat in the closet. His tone was dismissive as if that was the end of the discussion.

"She's going to feel like an outsider if all the other girls are skating and she's just sitting there watching," Kristen pointed out.

"No, she's not, because she's not going to the party."

"Why? Because there's an ice rink there?"

Just then, Brittany burst through the door. "Hi, Daddy!" She dropped her backpack and threw herself into her father's arms. "I missed you. Did you bring me something?"

He reached into his pocket and pulled out a set of barrettes that had tiny Christmas trees on them. "For you."

She cried out in delight, waving them in Kristen's face. "Can I wear them to the party?"

Kristen exchanged looks with Tyler. His was thunderous, hers pleading.

"About the party..." Tyler began. Kristen could see he was searching for a gentle way to break the news that she wasn't going. He stooped down beside his daughter. "We already talked about this party, Brittany. We agreed it wasn't a good idea because you don't know how to skate."

"Yes, I do. Kristen taught me and I did really good. Didn't I, Kristen?"

"She's a natural. No weak ankles," she concurred.

"See, Daddy?" She picked up the ice skates and slung them over her shoulder. "It's time to go, isn't it, Kristen? It starts right after school." She wiggled excitedly in the hallway.

Kristen turned to Tyler. "Shall I drive her over?"

He stood there silently fuming.

"We're having pizza for supper and Shannon's mom made a cake in the shape of a Christmas tree. It's going to be really fun," Brittany rambled on while her father gave Kristen all sorts of evil looks. Suddenly aware of the tension between the two of them, Brittany lost her smile. "I can go to the party, can't I, Daddy?"

He hesitated only briefly before saying, "Yes, you can go."

The smile was back. She flung her arms around him one more time, then scrambled up the stairs. "I got to get my present," she called out over her shoulder. "And go to the bathroom."

Kristen started up the stairs after her. "I'll come help you with your new barrettes," she said, eager to escape the glowering looks Tyler was giving her. She expected him to tell her to stay right where she was, that he wanted to talk to her. To her surprise, he didn't say another word.

She knew it was only a temporary reprieve. There was no way Tyler was going to let this whole incident pass without saying something to her. She had broken another of his rules and she would pay the price.

She just wondered what that price would be.

CHAPTER TEN

KRISTEN DECIDED the best way to avoid a confrontation with Tyler was not to return to the Brant home until she could go back with Brittany. So on her way out the door, she muttered something to Tyler about running errands while Brittany was at the party.

She spent the next few hours at the mall where she shopped and grabbed a quick bite at one of the fast-food restaurants. Although she had a small twinge of guilt that she wasn't making dinner for Tyler, she told herself that her job wasn't to feed him. It was to take care of Brittany.

That didn't stop her from wondering what Tyler was eating for dinner. Or even if he was eating.

When she went to pick up Brittany, she found her tired but happy, her ice skates slung over her shoulder and a goody bag in her hand. All the way home she regaled Kristen with stories from the birthday party, convincing Kristen that she had made the right decision concerning the skating.

It was obvious that Brittany was exhausted, however, by the way her voice took on a whining quality the closer they got to home. When she stepped through the front door and saw her father, she resorted to behavior that was more typical of a younger child.

"Did you have fun?" Tyler asked.

"Yes, but my legs hurt," she said on a whimper.

Tyler shot Kristen an accusatory look. "What happened? You didn't get someone else's blade in your leg?"

"Uh-uh. They just hurt." The usually adultlike voice suddenly became very childlike—almost babyish.

"That's normal. Skating is exercise," Kristen interjected.

Again Tyler gave her a look of reproach. He swooped Brittany up in his arms. "Let's go upstairs and you can show Daddy where it hurts, okay?"

"All right," she said in a tiny voice, laying her head against his shoulder. "Are you coming upstairs, too, Kristen?"

"I think I'll wait down here since you and your dad haven't had much time together the past two days," she answered.

Neither father nor daughter protested. Kristen went into the kitchen where she saw that nothing was out of place. Nor was there any indication that Tyler had fed himself. She didn't see a single dirty glass or cup. She pulled open the dishwasher and saw that it was empty—just as she'd left it.

Kristen put a kettle of water on the stove for tea, then waited for Tyler to come back down. When he did finally enter the kitchen, he had fixed a stern look in place.

"Brittany all right?" she automatically asked.

"She's in bed. She'd like you to come up and say good-night."

The words were said grudgingly, as if it annoyed him that his daughter had asked for her.

"Of course." She turned off the burner that was heating the water and left the kitchen with a sigh of relief.

By the time Kristen reached Brittany's room, the little girl was asleep. Kristen turned off the bedside lamp, her eyes catching a glimpse of the picture of Brittany and her mother.

Kristen would have liked to go directly to bed herself, but she knew there was no point in avoiding Tyler. Sooner or later, she'd have to speak to him. So she went back downstairs and found him in the kitchen. He had put the kettle back on the burner and had set two cups out for tea.

Feeling rather awkward, she said, "Brittany's asleep."

"That should come as no surprise. That kind of activity is quite rigorous."

The censure in his tone had her bristling. "It was only ice-skating."

"Yes, well, let's just hope she's able to go to school tomorrow," he said grimly.

"Why wouldn't she be able to?"

"You saw how sore her legs were. She could barely walk."

"She was tired and wanted you to carry her!"

"She didn't feel well, and if she's not better tomorrow, I may have to take her to the clinic. She was chilled to the bone. She sneezed several times while she was getting ready for bed. I hope she doesn't get a cold out of all of this.''

"Colds aren't caused by being outdoors," Kristen protested. "If she is coming down with one, it's because she was exposed to the virus at school, not because she spent some time ice-skating on a backyard rink."

He raked a hand through his hair. "You knew I didn't want her going to the party, yet you went out and bought her the skates. Why?" he asked on a note of exasperation.

"Because she wanted to go." The teakettle whistled and Kristen automatically went over to shut off the burner.

"Contrary to what you might think, I don't always give her what she wants," Tyler told her, following her as she moved about the kitchen. First to the stove, then to the table where the teapot and two cups sat.

"But she didn't get hurt. None of the children did because ice-skating is a fairly safe activity when it's supervised by parents." Kristen filled the teapot, then returned the kettle to the stove.

"You're missing the point. I don't want her ice-skating."

"What do you want her doing? Sitting in a pup tent in her room playing with an imaginary friend?"

"What are you trying to say? That you think there's something wrong with my daughter because she likes to read to an imaginary friend? Do you know what her IQ is?"

"This isn't about Brittany's intelligence, Tyler. She's a bright, wonderful, warm child who spends most of her time in her room or with adults. She likes being with kids her own age and she needs to be with them.''

''Since when did you become an authority on what children need?''

''I'm not, but I was a little girl once and I know what it's like to be left out—which is how she feels when you don't let her do the same things other kids do,'' she said, trying to reason with him.

''I don't intend to be one of those parents who's afraid to say no to my child simply because I don't want her to miss out on some fun. Brittany is my responsibility, Kristen, not yours, and my number-one priority is her safety. Having never been a parent, you probably don't understand that.''

They were interrupted by the unexpected appearance of his mother, who burst into the room with a look of horror on her face. ''Whatever are you two arguing about? I could hear you all the way outside.''

Tyler didn't look the least bit contrite. ''What are you doing here? You weren't supposed to come home until the end of the week.''

''Is that any way to greet your mother?'' she asked, offering him her cheek, which he dutifully kissed. ''The taxi driver needs to be paid.''

Tyler threw Kristen one last glance, then disappeared through the doorway.

Millie turned to Kristen and said, ''I thought I'd surprise you. Guess I did,'' she said ruefully, undoing the buttons on her coat.

''I'm sorry. Tyler is angry with me because I let

Brittany go to a birthday party where there was ice-skating.''

''She didn't get hurt, did she?'' Millie asked.

''Oh, no, but I'm afraid that doesn't count for anything with your son.''

Millie smiled in understanding. ''No, it wouldn't. I bet Brittany enjoyed the party, didn't she? Excuse me just a minute, Kristen. I'll hang up my coat and then we'll share a cup of tea. Looks like you just made a fresh pot.''

Kristen pulled another cup from the cupboard, not looking forward to the three of them having tea. When Millie returned, she was all smiles.

''It'll just be you and me for tea. Tyler has to make a phone call,'' she told Kristen as she noticed the three cups on the table. ''So tell me about this birthday party.''

''It was for Shannon.'' Kristen explained how they'd gone shopping for the present and that Brittany had wrapped it herself.

''And the ice-skating?''

''I taught her. We went to the arena to practice so that she'd be able to keep up with the others.''

Millie added a spoonful of sugar to her tea and stirred. ''So that's why Tyler's upset.''

''You think I was wrong?''

The older woman patted Kristen's hand. ''No. I'm sure it was good for Brittany to learn how to skate. It's just that Tyler can't bear the thought that she could possibly get hurt.''

''Why is that?''

Millie took a sip of tea before speaking. ''Has Tyler told you about the car accident that killed my daughter-in-law?" When Kristen shook her head, Millie said, "It happened when Brittany was a baby. All three of them were in the car."

"Oh, how awful. How painful it must have been for you," she said, placing her hand over Millie's.

"Yes, it was," the older woman said grimly. "Susan died and Brittany's legs were badly burned." She took a moment to compose herself. "They had to do extensive skin grafting."

"So that's why she has those scars," Kristen concluded.

"Mmm-hmm. She was just a little thing when it happened, which is probably good. She doesn't remember any of it."

Kristen sipped her tea thoughtfully. "Are her legs weaker than they should be?"

"No, they're fine. She can run and play like any other six-year-old," Millie answered.

"Tyler doesn't seem to think so."

Millie smiled indulgently. "Has he been giving you a hard time?"

Kristen shrugged. "We haven't exactly seen eye-to-eye when it comes to Brittany."

"Well, judging from the phone conversations I've had with my granddaughter, I'd say you've been very good for her," Millie said sincerely.

"Thank you. It's nice to hear you say that. And now that you're home, my job is done." She carried her cup over to the sink and rinsed it. "I think I'll get my things together."

"You're not leaving tonight?" Concern clouded the older woman's features.

"It's okay, Mrs. Brant. I'll be fine," Kristen assured her.

"Thank you for being here for Brittany."

"It was my pleasure," Kristen said honestly. "She's a lovely child."

"Who's going to miss you. You will visit, won't you?"

"Of course," she told her, thinking it would be best if she avoided those times when Tyler was at home.

Tyler was still in his office when she went upstairs to pack her things. Before leaving the yellow room, she wrote a goodbye note to Brittany, which she left on the child's nightstand. She thought she might be able to leave without seeing Tyler, but he was in the hallway when she went downstairs.

"Where are you going?" he asked.

"Home," she answered without pausing.

"I'll take you," he offered.

"I don't need you to take me. I have my car," she said, walking past him.

"Then I'll follow you to make sure you get home safely." He stepped in front of her, blocking her way.

"I'm an adult, Tyler. I can drive home without an escort. Now if you'll excuse me…"

He looked as if he wanted to say more, but to her disappointment, he simply stepped aside and let her go.

ONCE AGAIN, TYLER DIDN'T sleep well. When his alarm went off the following morning, he felt tired and grouchy. He blamed his lack of sleep and his disposition on Kristen.

It had been a long time since he'd felt such an overwhelming need for a woman. Too long, which was why he found it so difficult to control his desire for Kristen. From the moment he'd pulled her from the wreck of the airplane, he'd sensed a chemistry between them. How could any man not be attracted to such a woman?

She was beautiful. Sexy. Alluring. And she'd come into his room wearing nothing but a semitransparent nightgown. If he closed his eyes, he could still see her soft curves. And she had responded to his touch in a way no man would be able to resist.

He sighed, wishing he could make the desire go away. But as much as he tried not to think about Kristen and how she'd felt in his arms, the longing inside him simmered like some kind of magic potion—bubbling over when he least expected it. He had come so close to losing control that night in his bed....

But he hadn't lost control. They hadn't done anything foolish. And making love to Kristen would have been foolish. Theirs was not a match made in heaven. She saw him as some kind of hero. But she was dead wrong. He was no hero. In time, she would see that, too.

For five years he had managed to avoid becoming involved with any woman. He couldn't. Not after what happened to Susan. Guilt swamped him as he thought of his wife. Not once when he was in Kristen's arms had he thought about Susan. Not for a moment.

"Daddy, where's Kristen? I need her," Brittany said in a frightened little voice. She stood beside his bed in her pajamas.

"Why? What's wrong?" he asked, pushing aside the covers and swinging his legs over the side of the bed.

"I feel sick. Where is she?"

"She went home. Gram's back."

"But I don't want her to go home. I like having her here," she said, her lower lip trembling.

"But she doesn't live here, Brittany. She has her own place."

The child started to cry, her face flushed. It was only as he pulled her into his arms that he discovered why. She was hot to the touch.

"My head hurts, Daddy," she sobbed in his arms.

He lifted her onto the bed and settled her back against the pillows. "You stay in Daddy's bed and I'll be right back." He retrieved the thermometer from the medicine chest and took his daughter's temperature. It was a hundred and two.

"Do I have a fever?"

"A little one. What hurts—besides your head?"

"My throat. Am I gonna have to get a shot?" Fear widened her eyes.

"There's no point in worrying until we've seen the doctor." He wrapped her up in his blanket and carried her back to her room. He deposited her on the bed saying, "You wait here and I'll get Gram, okay?"

Tyler was relieved his mother was there to help. "Do you think we should take her to the emergency room at the hospital?" Tyler asked anxiously after his mother had examined Brittany.

"The clinic will be open at nine, Tyler," his mother said patiently. "It's probably a virus." She sat down beside her granddaughter and asked, "What about your ears? Are they okay?"

"This one feels kinda funny," Brittany said, tugging on her left lobe.

"Then we better have the doctor check it out. Gram will call as soon as the clinic opens, okay? In the meantime, you stay in bed and I'll bring you up something good to drink."

So while Tyler fretted, his mother calmly took charge. In her usual efficient manner, she called the clinic, bundled Brittany into her snowsuit and managed to keep things under control when Tyler drove them to the clinic later that morning.

To everyone's relief, the diagnosis was not strep throat but an ear infection—just as Millie suspected. Instead of a shot of penicillin, she returned home with a bottle of antibiotic liquid, which Millie assured Tyler she would administer in regular doses.

"You can go to work now," she told her son once they were back home and Brittany was resting in her bed. "She's going to be just fine."

"Fevers are nothing to mess around with," he said soberly.

"No, but they're also to be expected when children get sick. It means her body's fighting off the infection. Now stop worrying and go back to work. I'll take good care of her," Millie assured him.

"This wouldn't have happened if she hadn't been out in the cold," he grumbled.

"Nonsense! Tyler Brant, how a smart man can be so stupid at times is beyond me. She didn't get an ear infection skating on an outdoor pond. And you know it, so you can quit blaming Kristen Kellar."

"I still don't like the fact that these kids were allowed to be outside when there's a windchill factor," he contended.

"It never hurt you when you were her age."

"I wasn't as fragile as Brittany," he said, getting his overcoat from the closet.

"She's a normal, healthy six-year-old. Even the doctor says that," Millie pointed out.

"That doesn't mean I want her to take risks when it comes to her health."

"Attending a birthday party and going ice-skating is not a risk."

He paused before pulling his coat on. "You're on Kristen's side, aren't you?"

"There are no sides here, Tyler. Just a little girl who's trying hard to be like everyone else."

"I'm doing everything I can to make sure that Brittany has a good life." He couldn't keep the anger from his voice.

"I know you are, Tyler. I just wish..." She shook her head.

"Wish what, Mother?" he asked impatiently, tugging on the sleeves of his coat.

"That you didn't find it necessary to watch Brittany like a hawk. Ever since Susan died, you've been hovering over her a lot more than is necessary."

"You're wrong. It is necessary." He picked up his briefcase. "I'd expect you of all people to understand."

"I do understand. You forget. I've lived with you for the past five years."

He hated it when she used her mother-knows-best tone with him. It meant it was time for him to leave. "Keep me posted on how she's feeling, will you?"

"Yes, dear."

Tyler hated arguing with his mother. As hard as he tried to forget their conversation during the drive to work, he couldn't help but think about what she had said. Maybe he did keep a closer eye on Brittany than most parents did with their children. How could he not? Five years ago, he had walked away from an automobile accident without so much as a scratch, while Brittany had suffered burns on her legs and Susan had lost her life.

It was easy for Kristen to say he should loosen his hold over Brittany. She hadn't been the one to watch a car explode with the two people he loved the most inside.

Well, it didn't matter what Kristen Kellar said. She would no longer be a part of his life or his daughter's. There was no more need for her to stay with Brittany.

No need for him to see her at all.

KRISTEN DIDN'T SLEEP well the first night back in her apartment, troubled by what she had learned about

Tyler's past. Knowing that his wife had died in the same accident that had burned Brittany's legs explained why Tyler was so protective of his daughter. No wonder the man didn't sleep well at night.

It felt odd being back in her apartment. She had known her job was only temporary, yet she hadn't expected it would end on such a sour note.

As she wandered through her apartment, she tried not to feel melancholy at the prospect of being just plain old Kristen Kellar—ex-anchor, ex-fiancée, ex-nanny. The boxes of Keith's personal belongings were gone. Gayle had arranged to get them back to him. Kristen suspected she took great pleasure in doing the job. Gayle had never thought that Keith was the right man for her.

Kristen had avoided KC's column ever since reading the article about Keith and Janey's rendezvous in the Bahamas. She simply didn't care enough to pick up the paper and see how things were going with his current flame.

Gayle was right. Keith was not the man for Kristen. She needed someone she could rely on. Someone who didn't simply regard her as an asset to his career. Someone like Tyler.

She sighed at the thought. Was she foolish to even think of him in such a way? After all, she wasn't ready for another relationship with a man. It was too soon. She hadn't had time to heal emotionally. And it was obvious Tyler didn't want her in his life.

She tried not to think of him as she sifted through the accumulation of mail and phone messages, but it was hard not to remember all that had happened between them. By noon, she was restless, wishing there was something to occupy her time, to occupy her thoughts.

When the phone rang, she picked it up, hoping for something to distract her from her mood.

"May I speak to Kristen, please?"

She recognized Brittany's voice immediately. "Hi, Brittany. This is Kristen. How come you're not in school?"

"I've got an ear infection, so I had to stay home. Ms. Grayson doesn't want us in class if we have fevers. Mine was a hundred and two this morning."

Kristen felt a knot in her stomach. "You're sick?"

"Yup, but Gram says it's not from the ice-skating so you don't need to feel bad."

Yes, but what did Tyler think? Kristen wondered. "I'm sorry you're not feeling well enough to go to school. I know how much you like it."

"It's boring being sick. Do you think you could come and see me?"

"Today?"

"Uh-huh. I have to stay in bed and I thought you could come over and we could play Trouble on my bed tray...you know, like we did that one time."

Kristen could feel her heartstrings being tugged. When the tiny voice said, "Please?" she found she couldn't say no.

"All right. Tell your grandmother I'll be over later this afternoon, okay?"

"Okay."

As soon as Kristen had hung up the phone, she

questioned the wisdom of her decision. The last person she wanted to see was Tyler, yet she didn't want to disappoint Brittany. She'd have to make sure she left before he came home from work.

WHEN TYLER LEARNED that Kristen had stopped by to visit Brittany that afternoon, he frowned. It wasn't because he was annoyed that she had been to see his daughter. Rather, he was irritated that his first thought upon hearing the news was one of disappointment that she'd left before he could see her.

It didn't help that Brittany insisted on repeating every detail of the afternoon. When Tyler changed the subject, mentioning that it was time to get the Christmas decorations out and trim the tree, Brittany's whoop of delight was followed by a question.

"Can Kristen come over and help?"

Tyler tried to explain that Kristen was a busy lady. "She probably has a lot of things to do."

Brittany refused to take no for an answer. "Uh-uh, it's all right. She told me she wanted to help." She picked up her phone and pressed the number two.

"You've put her on speed dial?" Tyler asked.

"Yes. She's important."

As soon as Kristen answered, Brittany ignored her father. Her cheeks glowed and her eyes sparkled as she excitedly explained their holiday tradition. Then her animated face fell. Tyler knew Kristen was turning down the invitation and he felt a sense of helplessness watching his daughter go from exuberance to disappointment. By the time she hung up the phone, a tear was trickling down her cheek.

"She said she'd like to come over, but she can't," Brittany said, choking back a sob that tore at Tyler's heart.

"Did she say why she couldn't come?"

"Uh-uh." She turned big blue eyes moist with tears to Tyler. "I thought she liked me."

"She does like you, but you have to understand that this is a very busy time of year for everyone."

"But I wanted her to come," Brittany said, then began to cry. "She promised to show me how to make reindeer for the tree...the kind you stick a candy cane in and hang up like an ornament."

Seeing his daughter so unhappy motivated Tyler to do something he had longed to do all day long. As soon as he'd tucked her in bed for the night, he got in his car and headed to Kristen's apartment.

KRISTEN HAD JUST FINISHED her frozen meat loaf for one when Tyler arrived. "I suppose I should be used to having you pop up on my doorstep, but I'm not," she said as a greeting after she buzzed him in.

"If I had called, would you have let me come over?" he asked.

She didn't answer his question but stepped aside so he could enter. "Should I take your coat or is this just a quick visit to set a record straight?"

He removed his jacket and handed it to her. As she hung it in the closet, he said, "I came here because I thought we should talk about Brittany."

"Is she all right?" Kristen asked as she led him into the living room.

"Yes." He sat on the sofa and she automatically took one of the chairs, trying not to notice how handsome he was. Tonight he wore a dark green wool sweater over a white turtleneck. "Thank you for stopping by to see her today. She enjoyed your visit."

It was the last thing she expected him to say. For a moment, she could only stare at him, dumbfounded. "Is that it?"

"Is that what?"

"Is that why you drove all the way over here—to tell me Brittany enjoyed my visit?"

He leaned forward, his elbows on his knees. "Is there something wrong with my telling you that?"

"Usually when you blame someone for a person's illness you don't thank her for visiting her when she's sick," she said on a note of sarcasm.

"You're not responsible for her ear infection," he said, a hint of apology in his tone.

"That's not what you said last night," she reminded him.

"I'm sorry about last night," he said sincerely. "My mother says I overreacted."

"So you came over to apologize."

Her tone must have conveyed her disbelief for he asked, "Why do you find that hard to believe?"

"I don't," she denied. "I'm just surprised that you drove all the way over here to do it, that's all. You could have phoned."

"Well, that isn't the only reason I'm here." He tugged on his ear, looking sheepish.

Kristen's heartbeat accelerated. So he had wanted to see her. Excitement bubbled up inside her. His next words, however, burst the bubble.

"Brittany's grown rather fond of you. Tonight I discovered that she has you on her speed dial."

"Does that bother you?"

"Yes."

"Why?"

"Because I don't like to see her get hurt."

She gave him a puzzled look. "Why would I hurt your daughter? Tyler, I'm not a threat to Brittany."

"Maybe not intentionally."

"What's that supposed to mean?"

"She cried when you turned down her invitation to help trim the tree," he explained.

Kristen knew Brittany had been disappointed when she told her she wouldn't be able to decorate the tree, but learning that she was responsible for the little girl having tears in her eyes made her heart ache.

"You know why I had to turn her down," she said quietly.

"Because of what happened between us that last night I was home?" he asked.

She warmed at the memory. "No, because I know you didn't want me to accept the invitation. I know how uncomfortable I make you feel whenever we're in the same room together."

"You're wrong."

"Am I?" she challenged. "Why don't you just

admit it? As often as you try to convince me that you've gotten over the plane crash, the reality is that seeing me bothers you, doesn't it?''

"Yes, seeing you bothers me, but you're wrong about the reason why. It's not because you remind me of the crash. It's because every time I see you, I want to take you in my arms and hold you."

She half expected that with such a declaration he'd jump up, whisk her out of her chair and kiss her senseless. He didn't, but that didn't make it any easier for her to respond to his admission.

"We comforted one another," she said quietly. "We were talking about the crash and we—"

"What we did had nothing to do with the crash," he interrupted, pinning her with his gaze. "We both know there's been a tension between us ever since the first time I came over here. It doesn't matter why it's there. The point is it's there and I don't think it's likely to go away."

Judging from his tone, Kristen had a pretty good idea he'd been hoping it would just fizzle and he was unhappy that it hadn't.

She left her seat to stare out the living room window, not wanting him to see her face. She tried to keep her voice level as she said, "There's really no need to discuss this, Tyler. It was late at night and we got a little carried away, partly because—unlike you—I *do* get emotional about the crash."

"So you're saying you were seeking comfort?"

"Yes." It was a lie, yet she wasn't about to embarrass herself by admitting anything else. She turned to look at him. "Isn't that what you were doing?"

His face revealed nothing of what he was feeling, much to her dismay. More than anything, she wanted him to say that the reason he wanted to hold her wasn't because he wanted to comfort her, but because he wanted to make love to her.

He didn't.

He got up and came toward her. "When my wife died I decided that because of Brittany it wouldn't be fair for me to bring women in and out of her life. I haven't wanted to look for a replacement for Susan."

"You replace things, Tyler, not people," she reminded him.

"I know that. I also know that Brittany's extremely vulnerable when it comes to needing a mother figure in her life."

"Tyler, I'm not following you. Are you saying that you don't want me visiting Brittany because you're afraid she's going to become too attached to me?"

"No, what I'm trying to say is that I want you to come to dinner."

CHAPTER ELEVEN

"YOU WANT ME TO HAVE dinner with you?" she repeated, stunned by his invitation.

"With me and Brittany."

"You can't be serious!"

"Why wouldn't I be?" He looked perplexed by her attitude. "You know she wants you to help trim the tree."

"But you've just told me you don't want me around you or Brittany."

"No, I haven't," he denied.

"Yes, you have," she contradicted him. "Not that it matters."

He tugged on his ear again. "I guess I haven't done a very good job of explaining why I'm here."

"You said it was to apologize," she reminded him.

He sighed. "That's not the only reason. I didn't like the way your job as nanny ended."

"You mean with us arguing?"

He nodded. "When I saw how upset Brittany was that you couldn't help with the tree trimming, I knew that I needed to come over and see if I couldn't convince you to join us. But now that I'm with you, I realize that I'm not here only on Brittany's behalf."

"What are you trying to tell me, Tyler?" she asked, her heartbeat increasing.

"That my motives aren't entirely unselfish. That if you aren't a part of our trimming party, Brittany won't be the only one who'll miss you."

She couldn't deny the thrill of pleasure his words produced. Yet she couldn't forget what he'd said only minutes ago. "You just told me things are tense when I'm around."

"They are, but they're tense in a good way," he said, cracking a wry grin.

She chuckled sardonically. "Gee, you're really good for my ego, Tyler. I don't think I've ever had anyone tell me they like having me around so I can provide a little tension."

He reached for her hands. "You know what I'm talking about. You feel it, too. Admit it."

She knew exactly what he was talking about, but she did have some pride. After all, he had practically told her he didn't want to be attracted to her and now he expected her to be flattered by his admission that he liked being around her. She pulled her hands out of his grasp.

"So you'll tolerate this *tension* between us for Brittany's sake?"

"I already told you I'm not asking you to dinner for Brittany's sake. I'm asking you for mine."

The look in his eyes made her breath catch in her throat. It would be so easy to say yes, to let herself become a part of their family traditions, to let herself be a part of their lives.

"But if I'm there, you're bound to be constantly reminded of the plane crash," she told him.

"That's not a problem for me. Is it for you?"

She shook her head.

"So. Will you come to dinner and help us decorate the tree?" He moved closer to her, waiting for her answer.

"When?"

"Sunday afternoon."

She knew she couldn't say no. "All right."

He smiled then, a devilishly handsome smile that promised her she'd have a good time. "That's great. I'll pick you up at noon. Dress warmly. Part of putting up the tree is cutting it down first. We'll be going to a tree farm up near Zimmerman," he told her.

Long after he was gone, Kristen thought about how strange their conversation had been. He had made her heart race, both with anger and desire. It was obvious he was attracted to her, yet all the talk about not needing a replacement for Susan—was that his way of warning her not to think that anything serious could come of their relationship?

Maybe it was better if that was exactly what he meant. What she didn't need was to jump from one relationship into another. Even if Tyler Brant did make her heart beat faster, there was no way she was ready to become involved with him.

No, she'd have to make sure that there were no more opportunities to fall into bed with Tyler. She'd be a friend to the family.

For now.

ON SUNDAY, TYLER TOOK Brittany and Kristen to a tree farm thirty miles north of the city. There he cut down what Brittany described as the most beautiful tree in the world, tied it to the roof of the Jeep, then brought it home. If Tyler had expected there to be tension between him and Kristen, he'd been mistaken. It felt like the most natural thing in the world for the three of them to be together, and Brittany was delighted to have Kristen be part of the tree expedition.

The only awkward moment came when Kristen produced a small gift bag for Brittany. Inside was an ornament—a miniature pair of skates circled by a tiny wreath. They had just finished dinner and Tyler was busy trying to fit the tree trunk into the metal base when she gave it to Brittany.

"Daddy, look what Kristen bought me!" He paused to glance at the ornament Brittany held up for his inspection. "Isn't it beautiful?"

Tyler's eyes met Kristen's. "It's nice," he said guardedly.

"When I was a child, my mother bought me an ornament each year—something that was significant in my life. A miniature piano the year I started piano lessons, a tiny desk my first year in school," she explained.

"What a lovely tradition," Millie commented.

"So you bought me skates because I learned how to ice-skate, right?" Brittany said with exuberance.

"Yes."

Tyler didn't say a word but finished tightening the bolts holding the trunk in the metal stand. Then he set the blue spruce upright, angling it into the corner. "There's your tree, Brittany."

"It smells good," she said, taking a deep breath. "What should I do with this?" She once again held up Kristen's gift, looking to Tyler as if seeking his permission.

He knew the reason for her hesitancy, even if Kristen didn't. For the past five years they had trimmed the tree the same way Susan had—with exquisitely crafted glass ornaments that fitted the theme of her tree—gifts of the Magi. Every single ribbon, garland and bulb had been carefully chosen by her and not once since her death had they varied the selection.

Now Brittany stood waiting for her father to say something.

"We'll put it on the tree," he told her.

It was only when Millie opened the boxes of tree trimmings and the contents were revealed that Kristen said,

"I'm sorry. Maybe it wasn't such a great idea bringing Brittany an ornament. I can see that you've chosen your tree trimmings very carefully."

It was Millie who spoke up. "Nonsense. There's room for another ornament."

So Brittany hung the tiny pair of ice skates on the tree.

EVERY DAY TYLER looked at those tiny ice skates and thought of Kristen. One evening after Brittany had been tucked in for the night, Tyler sat in the family room reading a mystery, but the book couldn't hold his attention. He kept looking at Susan's tree, sparkling with silver and gold, its Magi so elegantly dangling from the green boughs.

"You look a million miles away," his mother commented as she entered the room. She glanced at the cover of the book. "Not as good as the reviews say it is?"

He shrugged. "Maybe the holidays aren't a time for murder and mayhem. I keep looking at the tree and remembering how Susan would fuss with the decorations. That first year we were married she drove to three different malls searching for just the right garland that would match her Magi," he said somberly.

"She was always a stickler when it came to fashion and color, wasn't she?" Millie reflected wistfully. "Always wanted everything to match." She walked over and fingered Brittany's ice-skating ornament. "Personally, I like an old-fashioned Christmas tree."

"You're saying you don't like this one?" He tried not to sound defensive.

"It's a beautiful tree, but maybe it's time for a change," she said pensively.

It was not a pleasant thought for Tyler. The Christmas tree had been a way to keep a part of Susan alive. The year she died he'd left the spruce up until the needles turned brown, as if not taking it down could preserve her presence in their lives.

"I can see by the look on your face that it's not something you want to do, is it?" his mother said when he didn't respond to her suggestion.

"I like the tree the way it is," he said. "And

you're the one who's always saying tradition is good. This tree is our tradition."

"No, it's Susan's tradition," his mother said quietly.

"And is there something wrong with that?"

She didn't answer right away, as if trying to choose her words carefully. "It made it a little awkward when Kristen gave Brittany the ice-skating ornament."

"Are you saying that because of an ice-skating ornament, we need to change the tree?" he asked with exaggerated disbelief.

"You know what I'm talking about, Tyler."

"No, Mother, I don't." Nor did he want to hear what it was. He could sense a criticism coming and wanted to nip it in the bud.

"We've been putting these decorations on our tree for five years and you've never mentioned that you're tired of the Magi."

"Because it's not my tree. But it is Brittany's and she might like to have a say in what goes on it."

"I let her hang the skates on the tree."

"Yes, for the first time in her life, she's actually got to hang something of her own choosing," Millie stated candidly.

"And what's that supposed to mean? She helps decorate the tree every year."

"Not with her ornaments."

He frowned. "What are you talking about?"

"The toothpick snowmen and Popsicle stick Santa she made last year. The little bell she got at nursery school," she answered.

He vaguely remembered Brittany coming home from school with a couple of handmade creations that he suggested she set on the fireplace mantel. Had she wanted to hang them on the tree?

"Why didn't you tell me she made them for the tree?"

"I suppose I should have, but I know how you didn't want anything to spoil Susan's tree."

And he still didn't. Just looking at the ice-skating ornament made him feel as if an intruder was trying to push aside treasured memories. Which was ridiculous.

"Brittany can put anything she wants on the tree," he told her.

"Good, because I think she's making another one in school this year. A clay star with her picture inside." Millie smiled. "It's too bad I didn't save the ornaments you made when you were a boy. We could have started a whole new tradition."

He groaned. "Thank goodness you didn't. They were awful."

"Beauty is in the eye of the beholder," his mother quoted. "You know, we don't have to completely redo the tree. We can add the new to the old."

His mother's suggestion was a good one; he did want Brittany to feel it was her tree, too.

"As long as we're on the subject of Christmas," his mother continued when he didn't say anything, "Marsh and Lynn won't be able to join us this year. And neither will your sister be coming, which means it'll just be the three of us…and Aunt Clara, of course."

"And you want to know what to make for dinner?"

"No, I want to know if you'd thought about asking Kristen to join us."

He *had* thought about it often in the past week. She had become a frequent visitor to the Brant home. Only yesterday she had ridden along as they drove down to Shakopee to see Beanie Baby Adventure Land and Santa's Village. Like Brittany, she had sat on Santa's lap and had her picture taken. She had gone Christmas shopping with Millie and Brittany and patiently listened as his mother demonstrated the art of making rosettes and crumbcake.

Not only had she found a way to Brittany's heart, but his mother's, as well. As he stared at the Christmas tree, he realized that she was not unlike the tiny ice-skating ornament hanging on the tree—suddenly a part of his life whether he wanted her to be or not.

"Well, Tyler? Are you going to ask Kristen to spend Christmas with us?" his mother wanted to know.

"I had to practically drag her over here on Thanksgiving. What makes you think she'll want to come for Christmas?"

His mother smiled rather sheepishly. "A lot has happened since Thanksgiving. You won't know unless you ask her."

"What if I told you I didn't want her here on Christmas?"

"I'd have to wonder if you were being honest with yourself. Brittany would love to have her. We both know that. She's become a friend to this family, Tyler, and I don't see why my mentioning the possibility of her joining us for our holiday dinner should make you frown,'' she scolded lightly.

''Maybe because I'm concerned Brittany may be getting too attached to her,'' he told her.

''*Brittany* getting too attached?'' she repeated with a lift of an eyebrow.

''Yes. She has her in the number two spot on the speed dial.''

Millie smiled and patted his hand. ''Don't worry, you'll always be number one.''

''I'm not jealous of her,'' he denied.

''No, you're falling in love with her,'' she stated in a mother's voice that said you can't fool me.

Tyler closed the book on his lap with a thud. ''I think you've been eating too much fruitcake. You're getting fruity on me.'' He set the book on the end table with a little more force than he'd intended.

''There's no point in slamming things, Tyler. Falling in love with someone is a perfectly normal thing to do.''

''I'm not falling in love with her and please don't suggest such a thing to Brittany. I don't want her to think there's a possibility that Kristen's going to be her mother,'' he warned.

''It's not such an outrageous possibility, is it?''

''She was engaged to another man only last month,'' he reminded her.

''Then it's a good thing she ended the engagement because he was the wrong man.''

''Mom, I really don't want to be having this conversation.''

"I know you don't. For the past five years you've shushed me whenever I've brought up the subject of your dating. I couldn't so much as hint that I thought it would be a good idea for you to fall in love again or you'd snap my head off."

"Because it's not a good idea. It hasn't been for the past five years and it still isn't. The only reason Kristen still visits is because of Brittany."

"Bunk. You can tell yourself whatever you want, Tyler, but the truth is you keep inviting her to spend time with us because you enjoy her company," she said in that authoritative tone he disliked.

"That doesn't mean I'm falling in love with her and I really would appreciate you dropping this subject." He tried not to sound irritable, but he knew he'd failed.

She didn't say another word but smiled smugly to herself, kissed him good-night, then went to bed.

Long after his mother had gone, Tyler sat staring at the tree, lost in his thoughts. He wasn't foolish enough to deny that he was physically attracted to Kristen. That was a given. What man wouldn't be?

But love? He would never fall in love again. Never. Whatever feelings he had for Kristen existed because of the plane crash. She evoked a protectiveness in him, sure, but love? No. He would only love one woman in his lifetime. Susan. Whatever was happening between him and Kristen, it wasn't love. He wouldn't let it be.

THE FOLLOWING MORNING, Brittany raced into the kitchen exclaiming, "Quick, Daddy, Gram! Turn on the TV. Kristen's gonna be on this morning. She told me.''

Millie switched on the small television on the kitchen counter. Just as Brittany predicted, Kristen was on the morning news. Only she wasn't the anchor, but a participant in a special story about a holiday party at the Children's Hospital.

''She's giving all the kids a cute little bear,'' Brittany announced. ''That's 'cause they're all sick.''

Tyler listened closely to the report. He noticed that Kristen wasn't the only celebrity at the Christmas party. Several members of the Vikings football team were signing autographs and passing out photos.

''What a lovely gesture on her part. I knew the minute I met her that she had a good heart,'' Millie said with admiration.

It was obvious from the way Kristen interacted with the young patients that she wasn't simply putting in an appearance for promotional reasons. He felt an odd little tug on his heart at the way she could make a sick child smile.

When the TV reporter shoved the microphone in her face, Kristen cheerfully answered the question about an upcoming charity event that was to be held to raise money for the hospital. The next question, however, caught her off guard.

''I'm sure you can relate to these children who are ill. It wasn't long ago that you were in a plane crash. Can you tell us how your recovery is coming along?''

Tyler could see that she wasn't prepared for such a question. Her face paled and he could feel his protective instincts surface. He wanted to reach into that TV screen and yank the microphone from the interviewer's hand.

He soon discovered, however, that Kristen didn't need his help. She managed to answer the question and skillfully direct the talk back to the subject of raising money.

When the brief segment was over, Millie said, "She's quite good, isn't she?"

"Yes, she is," Tyler admitted.

"Is it over?" Brittany asked.

"Yes, dear, it's over." Brittany ran out of the kitchen, only to return a few minutes later carrying a silver-and-red foil package that she announced proudly was a present for Kristen. Tyler cast an accusing glance at his mother, who only lifted her eyebrows and said, "She insisted on buying it with her own money."

After showing the package to Tyler, Brittany placed it under the tree. "What are you getting Kristen, Daddy?" she asked when she returned to the kitchen and sat down at the breakfast bar.

Until his conversation with his mother last night, he had thought about giving her something befitting a friend of the family. Now he had his doubts. Whatever the gift was, it would say something about how he regarded her and he wasn't sure what it was he wanted to say.

"I haven't decided, Brittany," he answered honestly. "Maybe some perfume."

"You don't need to buy her any perfume. She smells good all the time."

And didn't he know it. The minute she stepped into a room, he noticed her fragrance. Just the thought of it stirred his blood.

"I wish she could come over for Christmas. Then she can see all my presents. And maybe we could play games, too," Brittany added.

Tyler's mother shot him a knowing look that said, "See. Your daughter wants her to come."

"Well, maybe we can invite her to spend Christmas with us," Tyler said.

"She can't come." Brittany poured herself a bowl of cereal. "She has to work."

"Work?" That was the first Tyler had heard about her returning to her job. Why had she let Brittany know and not him?

"She told me someone's got to do the news, even on Christmas," Brittany said matter-of-factly. She changed the subject then, talking about her school break and all the fun things she hoped to do.

But Tyler wasn't paying much attention. His thoughts were on Kristen's return to work at Channel 12. Did that mean she'd be anchoring opposite Keith Jaxson?

He hated the idea of Kristen being anywhere near the guy. As he drove to work, he found he couldn't stop thinking about the two of them together. He finally picked up his car phone and called her.

"Brittany just told me you're going back to work."

"The doctor's given me a clean bill of health. There's no reason not to go back."

"Do you think you're emotionally ready to face all the pressures?"

"I think I am," she told him. "You should be happy, Tyler. I'm doing what you've been able to do. Putting the crash behind me and moving forward."

She was right. He should have been happy for her, but he wasn't. "When is your first day back?"

"Next Saturday."

"You're working weekends?"

"Management doesn't think it's a good idea to put me and Keith together. At least not yet."

That alleviated some of his anxiety. "Shouldn't he be the one who's on weekends?"

She sighed. "It doesn't work that way, Tyler. I'm the one who's been out of the viewers' sight for more than two months. And I don't mind working weekends."

But Tyler minded. "Does that mean you'll be working both Christmas Eve and Christmas Day?"

"Yes, but I don't have to do the six o'clock on Christmas Day, just the ten o'clock."

Which meant she'd be free all day. "I hope that means you'll be able to have dinner with us."

"Oh, thank you for the invitation, and I'd really like to come, but I've already accepted an invitation from my friend Gayle to have dinner at her place," she said apologetically.

Tyler felt like a high school kid who'd just been turned down for a date with the prom queen. "Brittany will be disappointed."

"She understands that work sometimes interferes with things we'd rather be doing."

He wanted to say, "Yes, but going to Gayle's isn't work, is it?" He didn't. He simply said, "Brittany bought you a present. She'll want to give it to you."

"And I have something for her, too. I could stop by on my way to Gayle's—if that's okay with you," she suggested.

"Sure. That would be fine." They arranged a time, then he said goodbye and hung up the phone.

But it wasn't fine. Tyler realized that he didn't just want a few minutes of her time on Christmas Day. He wanted her there with him for the entire celebration. For Brittany's sake, of course. Not for his.

Or so he told himself.

KRISTEN HOPED THAT Bob Yates's advice regarding her return to work would prove to be true. He assured her that it was like riding a bike. Once she got started, all her experience would come into play.

One thing she did know was that she couldn't change her mind again. This time, there was no turning back. Everyone at the station knew that she had been given a clean bill of health. A medical leave of absence was no longer an option, which made the pressure to perform all the greater.

Janey and Keith were comfortable with their relationship on screen and off. They were now the hot item in KC's column while Kristen was the rejected fiancée and demoted news anchor. Kristen needed to show everyone that she wasn't staying away because she was pining over Keith.

The first night she was on camera she couldn't hide her nervousness. After the broadcast, she refused to watch the videotape. She didn't want to see how badly she had stammered. She didn't want to see if she'd looked as uneasy as she'd felt.

The following night was an improvement, but she couldn't help wondering if she would ever regain her confidence in the job she had once done so well. By Sunday evening, she felt relieved that she had survived the first weekend.

Although most of the Channel 12 crew wanted to have the Christmas holiday off, Kristen didn't mind working. At least she didn't have to worry about how she would spend the holiday.

It wasn't that she didn't want to be with the Brant family. But Christmas was a time to share with the ones you love. She had grown very fond of Brittany and Millie Brant and could easily have spent the day with them. But then there was Tyler. He'd told her he liked having her around, yet when he called to invite her to Christmas dinner, he'd made sure she understood that it was Brittany who'd be disappointed that she couldn't attend. Not him.

And it seemed that way when she stopped at the Brant home on Christmas Day. She'd bought gifts for all three of them. Both Brittany and Millie hugged her after they exchanged presents. Tyler simply looked at her after opening his first-edition mystery novel and said, "Thank you."

From Brittany, Kristen received a tiny sand-cast schnauzer puppy figurine. Millie had made her one of her prize fruitcakes, but it was Tyler's gift that brought a lump to her throat. It was a small gold cross dangling from a gold neck chain.

She looked into his eyes and saw understanding. He knew exactly what it had meant for her to lose her cross in the plane crash. "It's lovely. Thank you."

Brittany reached inside the neckline of her dress and said, "See? Daddy gave me one, too."

Kristen smiled as Brittany held up the tiny cross, a smaller version of hers. When Kristen glanced up at Tyler, the compassion that had been there only moments ago was gone, replaced by a guarded look.

Kristen was puzzled. If he wasn't happy that Brittany was tickled to have a necklace like hers, why had he given it to his daughter?

"I wish you could stay for dinner with us," Brittany said when Kristen announced she had to leave, reminding her that the child's feelings were the reason Kristen was still a part of Tyler's life. She didn't doubt that he was partly motivated by his sense of responsibility, but the main reason he'd invited her to be a part of their family activities was because of his daughter's affection for her.

That's why when he called the day after Christmas and invited her to spend New Year's Eve with him, she naturally assumed he meant with him and Brittany.

"I have to work on New Year's Eve," she told him.

"What time are you finished?"

"Usually around eleven but—"

"Then I'll pick you up at eleven at the station."

"Isn't that a bit late for Brittany? Or do you usually let her stay up on New Year's Eve?"

He chuckled. "She'd never make it past ten. No, Brittany will be in bed long before the New Year starts."

Kristen's heart began to beat a little faster. "So you're asking me to spend New Year's Eve with you? Like on a date?"

"Yes." When she didn't say anything, he added, "If you've already made plans, just say so."

"No. It's not that."

There was another awkward silence and he said, "You'd rather not go out. I understand."

"No! I do want to go out. It's just that you usually invite me to do things with you and Brittany."

"Not this time."

She felt her body go all tingly as she remembered how close they'd come to making love. "Then this is definitely a date?"

"Yes."

Now her heart was really hammering in her chest. "What should I wear?"

"Whatever you normally wear when you're saying goodbye to the past."

"Is that what we're doing? Saying goodbye to the past?"

"It's a New Year and a new beginning. I think we should make the most of it, don't you?"

"Yes, I do."

"Good. I'll pick you up at eleven."

CHAPTER TWELVE

TYLER REGARDED HIS DATE with Kristen as an opportunity to prove that his mother was wrong. He was not falling in love with Kristen. He knew there was no point in denying the attraction between them. It had been there ever since the day he had carried her out of the river.

But it wasn't love. For two months he'd been telling himself any emotional connection between the two of them had developed because of the trauma they'd experienced together.

Of course, what complicated their situation was the fact that Brittany had become so fond of Kristen. It was hard not to feel some kind of emotion for a woman who was so good to his daughter.

The minute he saw her he felt the familiar rush of adrenaline. She wore black stretch pants and a red parka trimmed with black fur. A red-and-black-patterned ski band covered her ears; black gloves hid her hands.

"You said dress warm, right?" she asked when he didn't say anything.

"Yes. You look…warm," he said, his eyes roving over her in appreciation. He helped her into the Jeep before getting behind the wheel.

"I take it this New Year's celebration is out-doors," she said as he pulled out onto the highway.

"Appropriate for a guy from Minnesota and a girl from Wisconsin," he told her with a grin.

They made small talk, mostly about what it was like growing up in the Midwest.

When he pulled off the highway onto a narrow road leading into darkness, she asked, "A country New Year's celebration?"

"We're just about there," he said as they traveled down the snow-packed road, only pinpricks of light visible in the distance.

Finally, they came to a farm with a double strand of lights trimming the barn. Tyler parked next to half a dozen other vehicles.

"A friend of mine told me about this place," he said as he helped her out of the car. With an arm at her back, he steered her toward the light on the other side of the barn.

In a clearing beneath the light was a horse drawn hay wagon. Instead of wheels metal runners served to guide it across the snow. Already seated on the hay bales stacked on the wagon were at least a dozen people.

"You must be Mr. Brant," a man wearing a cow-boy hat and a shearling jacket called out to him. "You made it just in time. We're about ready to leave."

Tyler shook his hand and introduced Kristen by her first name only. Judging by some of the curious glances thrown their way, he figured that a few occupants of the wagon recognized Kristen, but to his relief, no one commented on her presence.

"If you two want to climb on board, we'll start our midnight ride," the driver told them.

Tyler boosted Kristen aboard the wagon where they shared a bale of hay near the front. The driver's wife, a woman named Sally, acted as hostess. She provided Tyler and Kristen each with a horn to blow and a noisemaker. As the hay wagon glided over the fields of snow, she offered champagne punch and hot apple cider. Kristen opted for the punch, Tyler the cider.

A portable CD player provided background music—a collection of country-and-western hits, most with a holiday theme. At one minute to twelve, Sally instructed her husband to stop the wagon, then she climbed on top of a bale where she stood with a noisemaker in hand. With an eye on her watch, she counted down the final ten seconds. Just as she shouted, "Happy New Year!" all the guests shook their noisemakers and blew their horns.

Tyler turned to Kristen. "Happy New Year."

"Happy New Year to you," she repeated, looking expectantly at him.

Even if the other couples around him had not been exchanging New Year's greetings in the traditional manner, Tyler would have kissed her. He covered her mouth with his, her lips warm and welcoming as they responded to his in a way that made him wish they weren't in public. But there were other people around them and he forced himself to control the desire that urged him to prolong the kiss.

Sally punched a button on the CD player and strains of "Auld Lang Syne" filled the air. Everybody began to sing along, including Tyler and Kristen. Before they had finished the first refrain, colorful bursts of fireworks lit the sky.

"Just as we promised, you're starting the New Year with a bang," Sally declared as the explosion of color created a spectacular display overhead.

"This is wonderful," Kristen enthused, clinging to Tyler's arm in a way that made him feel as if one of those Roman candles was exploding inside him. "It's too bad Brittany couldn't have seen this."

"She would've fallen asleep on the ride out here," Tyler remarked, glad that his daughter wasn't with them. He liked being alone with Kristen.

When the fireworks ended, the wagon made its way back to the barn. Tyler helped Kristen climb down, then brushed the hay off her clothes.

"Thank you for bringing me here. I haven't been on a hayride since I was a kid," she told him as they walked hand in hand back to the Jeep.

"You didn't get too cold?" he asked as the snow crunched beneath their boots.

"Uh-uh. It was fun. This was my kind of New Year's celebration."

"At least we didn't have to worry about the media shoving cameras in our faces," he said. "It's easier to be anonymous sitting on a hay wagon rather than dancing at a nightclub."

"I'm sure a couple of people recognized me, but they were polite enough not to say anything."

As they climbed into the Jeep, Tyler noticed the

rosy glow on her cheeks. Instead of starting the vehicle right away, he sat with his door ajar for a moment longer than necessary to stare at her in the dim light. She was so incredibly beautiful.

"Is something wrong?" she asked.

"No. I was just noticing that you look like someone who just came in from the cold, that's all," he answered, reluctant to tell her what effect she had on him. Despite the freezing temperature, he felt warm inside just from looking at her.

"It was rather invigorating, wasn't it?" she said, rubbing her hands together.

"Are you cold? I have a lap robe in the back."

"No, I'm fine."

He started up the vehicle and backed out of the parking area. They didn't talk much on the ride back, but it wasn't an uncomfortable silence. He stopped at the television station so she could pick up her car. Then he insisted on following her home. She protested, but he paid no attention. Staying close to her bumper, he navigated the city streets with the same caution she did. While she parked in the garage, he pulled up out front and waited for her.

"Would you like to come up for some coffee?" she asked when he met her outside the garage.

"Thank you. Coffee would be nice."

He took the keys from her to open the lobby door as well as her apartment door. Once inside, he helped her off with her jacket, hanging it up for her in the closet.

"Why don't you sit down in the living room and

I'll start the coffee,'' she suggested, but he stopped her by grabbing her hand.

''I don't need coffee. Do you?''

She shrugged. ''I just thought it might warm us up a bit.''

''Are you cold?''

She shook her head.

They stood staring at each other, their hands linked. ''It's a new year, Kristen. We can truly put everything that happened last year behind us.''

She nodded although he wasn't sure she believed him. ''Is that why you asked me out tonight? Because you wanted to make a new beginning?''

''I wanted a date with you. A real date.'' He lifted her fingers and brushed them with his lips. ''Tonight you weren't the person who survived a plane crash with me. And you weren't Brittany's nanny. You were just you.''

''And did you like just me?'' she asked.

''Very much.'' This time, his lips found her mouth and he kissed her slowly, deeply and with the passion he'd wanted to show her on the hayride. Only now there were no witnesses, just the two of them. There was no reason not to deepen the kiss.

She was warm and soft and willing. When he slid a hand beneath her sweater to cup her breast, she shivered with longing. Tyler could feel his control slipping away as they kissed and touched and stroked each other's body.

''I'm definitely not cold anymore,'' she whispered, her breath hot against his face, her lips swollen from his kisses.

He held her tightly to him, loving the feel of her in his arms. "I have a confession to make. When I asked you out, I had hoped that if we had a real date I'd discover that I'm not wildly attracted to you."

"And is that what happened?" Her lips brushed his once more in a tantalizing invitation.

For answer, he kissed her until they were both quivering with desire. "I can't stop thinking about you. At work. At home. When I'm in bed at night...especially when I'm in bed..."

Her hands caressed his chest, slipping inside his shirt, causing all sorts of havoc with his breathing as they crept toward his waist. He knew that if he intended to go home, now was the time to leave.

Reluctantly, he brought both her hands to his lips and kissed her fingertips. "It's late. I better go."

"You're leaving?" It was practically a plea.

Their eyes met. "I don't want to, but—"

She put her finger against his mouth to stop the voice of reason. "I don't want you to go."

Any willpower he might have had was chased away by the look in her eyes. It told him that she wanted him just as badly as he wanted her. Without another word between them, she led him down the hallway to her bedroom.

THE FIRST THING KRISTEN noticed the following morning was the note on the pillow next to hers. It read, "I'll call you. Tyler."

No "It was wonderful" or "Sorry I had to leave" or "Love, Tyler." Just four words.

Kristen wanted more. She wanted him to say that

last night had been wonderful. That he'd never had such a wonderful night in his entire life.

But she soon learned that Tyler was a man of few words when it came to feelings. He called her later that morning. All he said was that he'd enjoyed last night. Kristen didn't know if his cryptic tone was due to the fact that he was at the office and didn't want to risk anyone hearing their conversation or if that was all he had to say.

She saw him every day during the week that followed. Sometimes with Brittany, but often alone when they'd end up at her apartment making love. He never stayed the night, and Kristen assumed it was because of Brittany.

Kristen knew she was falling in love with him. So far, she had managed to keep their relationship out of KC's column, but several people at the station knew they were dating, including Gayle. She brought up the subject while they were having lunch one afternoon.

"Gee, I haven't seen much of you lately. I don't suppose it could be because you've been spending a lot of time with the Brant family?" she probed.

Kristen hoped her face didn't color at the question. "They're nice people."

"*They* are nice people?"

"Yes, *they*."

"So what did you do with those "nice people" on New Year's Eve?" Gayle asked in between bites of an orange.

"What makes you think I was with them New

Year's Eve?'' Kristen responded, snatching an orange segment and popping it in her mouth.

"Not them, *him*. And you can forget that innocent
act with me. Don Patchett saw Tyler pick you up
outside the studio.''

"Don's interested in my personal life, is he?'' she
asked when she'd swallowed the orange.

"You know he thinks of all the women here as if
they were his daughters,'' she said affectionately of
the night security officer. ''So come on. Give. Tell
me where you went. It must have been someplace
fancy. A man of his means, New Year's Eve…'' She
sighed dreamily.

Kristen sighed. ''Sorry to disappoint you.''

"Meaning?''

"No glitter, no glamour.'' She twisted the lid off
a carton of yogurt. ''We went on a hayride.''

"A hayride?''

"Mmm-hmm. It was fun.'' She told Gayle all
about the farm, the champagne punch and cider, the
country-and-western music and the fireworks.

"Sounds romantic to me.''

"It was.''

"So then there is something going on between you
two,'' she said in an ''I thought so'' voice. ''Are you
officially dating?''

Much to her dismay, Kristen felt her cheeks warm.
She scooped a spoonful of yogurt into her mouth to
avoid meeting Gayle's knowing gaze.

"You are.''

Kristen looked up to see a sly grin on her best

friend's face. "All right, so we are," she grudgingly conceded.

"For someone who's being courted by a good-looking, romantic guy, you don't look very happy."

"Because it's not as simple as it seems."

"You don't want him thinking of you in a romantic way?"

"Yes, I do, but..." She pushed a strand of hair away from her face.

"He's a single man, you're a single woman. You get along with his daughter and his mother. He saved your life, for Pete's sake."

She sighed. "That's part of the problem."

"You don't want a hero?"

"I'm not sure whether he's ready for a relationship and I certainly don't want him interested in me because he feels responsible for me. Gayle, look at how we met. We have all this...baggage between us."

"I thought you told me he had his neatly wrapped and put away," she said, dabbing at her mouth with a napkin.

"I thought he did."

"What makes you think he hasn't?"

"For one thing, he's been a widower for five years, yet he hasn't been in a relationship since Susan's death."

"You think that's because of his daughter? Or are you worried that he's never gotten over his wife?"

She shrugged. "I honestly don't know. He never talks about her." She took a sip of tea, then looked at Gayle over the rim of her cup.

Gayle eyed her thoughtfully. "Have you talked to him about any of this?"

"I've tried, but he doesn't want to talk about the past. Ever. He keeps saying we should start the New Year with a new beginning."

"It sounds like he's okay with things, but you're not," Gayle observed.

"You could be right."

She tossed her napkin onto the cafeteria tray and leaned her elbows on the table. "You want Mother Gayle's advice?"

Kristen chuckled. "I might as well say yes because you're going to give it to me anyway, aren't you?"

"Yes." Gayle grinned unabashedly. "Talk to the man. Make him talk about what's bothering you. It's the only way you'll be convinced that what the two of you have is real."

Gayle wasn't telling Kristen anything she didn't know. The trouble was getting Tyler to open up to her.

The following day when he phoned to invite her to dinner, she was relieved to hear they would be dining without Brittany. She'd use it as an opportunity to find out the answers to her questions.

The minute she opened the door, he pulled her into his arms and kissed her long and hard. Kristen decided that if she could just spend every minute in his arms, she would have no doubts. Unfortunately, when they weren't together, uncertainty invaded her thoughts.

"I'm glad you could see me at such short notice,"

Tyler said, keeping his arms around her in a way that made Kristen feel cherished. "I've made reservations at Eddie's."

"Would you mind if we stayed here and ordered in?" she asked.

His eyes gleamed approval and he tightened his hold on her. "You want to stay in?"

"It's probably better if we do. That way we can talk."

"Do you want to talk with actions or with words?" he murmured as he planted a trail of kisses along her jawline.

"Words."

"Why? We communicate through actions very well, don't you think?" he asked, a sexy glint in his eyes.

She eased herself away from him. "I'm serious, Tyler. We need to talk"

Seeing the look on her face, he released her, quickly masking his eyes in a way that was now quite familiar to Kristen. "Do you want to have this conversation before or after dinner...or maybe there won't be a dinner if we have it?"

She grabbed him by the arm and led him into the living room. "I don't make a habit of suggesting eating in and then telling my guest to get lost," she said, trying to add some levity to the conversation.

"Good, because I like the way things are going between us."

"I do, too..." She hesitated.

"But?" He pulled her down beside him on the sofa.

"Where are things going, Tyler?"

She could feel him stiffen beside her. "Are you looking for a commitment from me? Is that what this is about?"

"No. I'm not ready for that," she assured him. "It hasn't been that long since I ended my engagement to Keith, and then there's my job...."

She couldn't tell if her answer disappointed him or not.

"What about your job? I thought you said everyone at the station was happy to have you back."

"They are. I'm the one who's not happy."

"And why is that?" He lifted her chin with his finger, forcing her to look at him.

"I don't think I fit in that world anymore. And before you say anything about my face, I can tell you that it's got nothing to do with physical appearance."

"Then what is it?"

Before she could answer, the doorbell rang. To Kristen's surprise, it was Bob Yates downstairs telling her it was important that he talk to her.

"Maybe I should go?" Tyler asked.

"No, please. Stay," Kristen insisted. "I don't know why he's here, but it must be something about work. It shouldn't take long."

Had Kristen known the reason for her boss's appearance, she wouldn't have let him in the door. The minute he was introduced to Tyler he said, "This is perfect. You're just the man I wanted to see here."

Wary, Kristen asked, "What are you talking about, Bob?"

"You're never going to guess who called my office today.'' If Kristen didn't know better, she would've thought he'd won the lottery, his grin was so big. ''The executive producer of *Alive*.''

Kristen knew that *Alive* was a nationally syndicated program that reenacted disasters in which people had been successfully rescued. The very mention of the word and the fact that Bob had beamed when he'd seen Tyler in her apartment made her stiffen with anxiety.

''What does that have to do with me, Bob?'' she asked although she already knew the answer.

''This is the chance you've been asking for. You told me you've been wanting to produce. Well, here's your golden opportunity. *Alive* wants to do your story. Of course, it'll mean spending a few weeks in Chicago with their production team.''

''Wait a minute. What do you mean 'our' story?'' Tyler demanded suspiciously.

''The story of the plane crash,'' Bob answered. ''Of course it'll be a reenactment with actors and actresses, but the producers prefer to use the people involved. If not for the actual reenactment, then in an interview. And since Tyler's the hero—''

''No,'' Tyler stated firmly, then rose abruptly to his feet. ''If you'll excuse me, I can see this discussion doesn't include me.''

He started toward the door and Kristen hurried after him. ''Tyler, wait. Don't go.''

Behind her, Bob was saying, ''Maybe you ought to wait and hear what this is all about before you leave.''

Kristen could see how upset Tyler was by the way

he pulled on his jacket. "Tyler, please don't go. I'm not going to do this," she told him.

That brought forth an indignant protest from her boss. "Kristen! This is the chance of a lifetime. We're not talking locally produced stuff here. Do you know what kind of a limb I'm putting myself out on to get this assignment for you?"

Kristen did know. She was a local on-air talent with little experience as a producer, yet he had managed to get the producers of *Alive* to consider her for the show.

"Bob, I've already told you the crash is off-limits," she said, then made one last attempt to stop Tyler. It didn't work.

Saying, "I'll call you later," he left.

As soon as she was alone with her boss, she told him exactly what she thought of the idea. He didn't like what he heard and left shortly after Tyler.

"You better figure out what it is you want, Kristen," he said in parting. "Opportunities are not easy to come by in this industry."

She knew he was right. Turning down a chance to work on a program like *Alive* was probably a mistake. But like Tyler, she, too, had found the idea distasteful.

Long after both men had gone, she thought about calling Tyler, but every time she picked up the phone and started to dial, something stopped her. *He* was the one who had taken offense the minute the word *hero* had been uttered. *He* was the one bothered by the fact that he was her hero.

Which had to make her wonder if they would ever

get beyond the plane crash. Would she ever be the woman he loved or was she forever going to be the woman he saved from the crash?

TYLER WASN'T HAPPY with the way the evening had ended. After a restless night, he knew he needed to talk to Kristen. He was upset that he'd left her place in such a state, but the truth was that he didn't want to be called a hero. And certainly not in front of Kristen.

Helping her out of the plane crash hadn't been heroic. Anyone in his position would have done the same thing. Now saving his wife from a car that had exploded in flames—*that* would have been heroic.

But he hadn't done that.

So maybe he shouldn't call Kristen. After all, she, too, mistakenly regarded him as a hero. And he still wasn't convinced that that wasn't the only reason she had such strong feelings for him. He tormented himself with such thoughts until, unable to resist, he picked up the phone and called her from his office.

"I'm sorry about last night," he said as soon as she answered. "I shouldn't have left so abruptly."

"I'm not going to do the program, Tyler."

"I know. I just wish everyone would leave us alone."

"I feel the same way."

Those were the words he needed to hear. "We didn't get to have dinner last night."

"You owe me one. What about tonight?"

He groaned. "Can't tonight. I have a business

meeting, and tomorrow I have to leave town on business for a few days.''

She sighed. ''I'll miss you.''

''Not as much as I'll miss you.'' He paused, then took a deep breath before saying, ''I love you, Kristen.''

''Oh, Tyler, I love you, too. And if you were here, I'd show you just how much.''

Her words caused him to ache with longing.

''We'll have to plan a very special evening when I get back,'' he said huskily.

''We will,'' she promised.

As Tyler hung up the phone he felt like a young kid in love. He didn't know how long he sat with a lovesick grin on his face, just staring at Kristen's name, which he'd scribbled on a piece of scrap paper.

When one of his employees poked his head into his office and said, ''Whatever you had for lunch, I want it tomorrow if it makes you feel that good.''

Kristen did make him feel good. Now all he had to do was persuade himself that he deserved to feel that good.

''WHEW! THAT WAS a good workout. You must be a hundred percent recovered if you can keep up with me,'' Gayle said as she and Kristen came to a halt at the end of the cross-country ski trail.

''It feels great to be able to do this again,'' Kristen told her as she released the bindings on her boots and stepped off the skis. ''I was worried my leg might give me problems.''

They loaded their equipment into the back of Gayle's pickup, then sat on the open tailgate. Gayle unscrewed the cap of her thermos and asked, "Want a sip of hot chocolate? I brought an extra cup."

"Sounds perfect," Kristen replied, flashing her a grateful grin.

Gayle poured each of them a cup of the steaming liquid. "Doesn't this remind you of our college days?" When Kristen murmured her agreement, she added, "We spent more time on our skis than in our shoes. As long as there was snow, we were out there practicing."

"Only because there were so many cute guys on the ski team," Kristin reminded her with a wistful grin.

Gayle smiled. "Those days seem so long ago now. Who would've thought that ten years later we'd be working for the same television station?" She took a sip of her chocolate, then said, "Life is funny, isn't it?"

"Mmm-hmm." Kristen was glad Gayle had introduced the topic of work. "I need to tell you something. I'm thinking about quitting."

Her friend seemed unfazed by Kristen's announcement. "I wondered how long you'd last on weekends," she said.

"It isn't because I'm on weekends."

"Then what is it? You're not still self-conscious because of your face, are you?" Gayle asked with concern.

"No, but I won't miss having to apply all that makeup every day."

"And what kind of work are you thinking of doing?"

"Producing. Actually, producing a different kind of news program."

"Are you talking about one of those magazine-type shows?"

"No. Keep in mind this is something that's still in the thinking stage, but while I was taking care of Brittany, I realized that on Saturday mornings the main television entertainment is cartoons."

"You want to do a children's program?"

Excitement bubbled up inside her and she nodded. "News reported *by* kids *for* kids. It could pretty much follow the format of the sunrise program we do each morning, only with a child's perspective."

"Are you talking about using kids for the talent?" Gayle asked, her skepticism showing in her face.

"Yes. We could get students from local schools to audition. We both know that most of the area schools have cable access and are already producing their own programs for their students. Just think how neat it would be for them to have something on network TV." When Gayle didn't comment right away, Kristen said, "You don't think it will fly, do you?"

"I think it might, but I'm not sure how you'll get management to listen. You know what a big risk new programming is," she warned.

"I do," Kristen admitted. "That's why I have to put together a great proposal. Gather statistics from markets where they have this type of programming and show them numbers. You know it always comes down to numbers."

Gayle nodded. "What you need to do is talk to someone who's already producing this type of program."

Kristen smiled. "I have. Remember Jessica Tarver? She was a year ahead of us in college." Gayle nodded, and she continued, "She does a similar program in the Chicago area."

"Is that where you went this week? To Chicago?"

"Tyler was out of town on business, and since I'm only working the weekend spot, I thought I'd drive out to see her."

"And was she able to give you the information you needed?"

"Hmm-hmm. She told me they had a segment on weekends where they have local students do a five-minute spot. They call it *Kids' Corner*."

"You do know Keith did something similar at the cable station he and I used to work at," Gayle told her.

"He never told me that." Kristen couldn't hide her surprise.

"Yes, well, I guess there are a lot of things he didn't tell you, aren't here?" Seeing Kristen frown, she quickly added, "Sorry."

Kristen waved away her apology. "No, you're right. I was so naive. I think I must have been in love with the idea of being in love."

"So now you're older and wiser. And the wiser part of you should make the most of your professional connection to the man. Go pick his brain. Find out what worked and what didn't work with the kids segment," she advised her.

The whole idea sounded distasteful to Kristen. "No, I'll figure this out without his help. Besides, there's not much point in picking a brain the size of his."

Gayle smiled. "Good point. Now, tell me all about your love life."

Kristen couldn't help but smile as she said, "Things are going pretty good."

Gayle refilled her cup with hot chocolate. "Then it's definitely moving forward."

Kristen stared out at the snow-covered landscape, thinking how peaceful it looked. "Oh, yes, we're moving forward."

"From that silly look you get on your face every time the subject comes up, I'd say you're in love, girl."

"I am," she confessed. "I know it shouldn't be possible. I mean, only a couple of months ago I thought I was going to marry another man, but I've never felt this way before."

Gayle finished her hot chocolate, then jumped off the tailgate. "Do you think he's the one you might want at your side the rest of your life?"

"I guess I haven't wanted to think that far ahead," Kristen answered honestly. "He's such a rock. It kind of scares me."

"Why?"

"Because it'd be so easy to lean on him. Let him take care of me, and believe me, he *would* take care of me. You should see the way he protects the women in his life."

Gayle pushed the tailgate shut and reached in her

pocket for her keys. "We all need someone to lean on every now and then," Gayle noted.

Kristen agreed. "I know, but first I need to prove to myself that I can stand alone."

"Better make it quick. If Tyler is the prince you claim he is, it won't take long for other women to discover he's not a frog."

CHAPTER THIRTEEN

"I WON'T BE HOME for dinner this evening," Tyler told his mother at breakfast.

"Not another business meeting? You've been gone for three days. Don't you think you should spend some time with Brittany?" As usual, she didn't hesitate to speak her mind.

"Are you going to eat supper with Kristen, Daddy?" Brittany wanted to know.

"I'd like to, but maybe you'd rather have me eat with you?"

"Can't Kristen come over here and eat with us?"

As much as he wanted to see Kristen, he knew that his mother had a point. He needed to spend time with his daughter.

"How about if we invite Kristen to come over another time and tonight it'll just be you, me and Gram?" he suggested, not missing the approval that flashed in his mother's eyes.

Tyler knew it really wasn't much of a sacrifice to make. Since it was a school night, Brittany would be in bed early and there would still be plenty of time to visit Kristen.

"While you were gone, I heard from Bernice. Unfortunately, she needs to have more surgery," Millie told Tyler.

"And you want to be there?"

"I should be. She is my only sister," Millie reminded him.

"Then go, Mom. Don't worry about us. We'll get along just fine," Tyler assured her.

"Does that mean Kristen gets to be my nanny again?" Brittany asked, her eyes lighting up at the thought.

"That won't be necessary," his mother answered before he could say a word. "It's the week you two go to Florida for spring break."

"Then you won't be coming with us?"

"You don't mind, do you?"

"No. It won't be as much fun, but we'll manage to have a good time," Tyler assured her, then tugged on a strand of Brittany's hair saying, "Won't we, Brit?"

She giggled, then asked, "Can Kristen come with us to Florida, Daddy?"

"It's funny you should ask because that's exactly what I was thinking," he answered.

He was puzzled by the look on his mother's face. Obviously, she didn't think it was a good idea. "Have you talked to her about it already?" Millie asked.

"Not yet, but I'll give her a call today."

"It's awfully short notice. She might have a problem getting the time off."

Brittany crossed her arms over her chest. "Why do grown-ups always have to work so much?"

"Everyone has a job to do, Brittany," he said patiently.

"But I want her to go with us. She's been to the Magic Kingdom and knows all the good stuff to see. It would be funner if she went with us."

"More fun," her grandmother automatically corrected her. "And you'll have fun with your father. Now, finish your cereal. The bus will be here before you know it."

"All right. But I still want her to come with us. And I know Walter will want her to come, too."

Tyler didn't have an answer for that. Fortunately, his mother changed the subject to the homework assignment Brittany had completed. Then the usual morning flurry as she gathered her backpack and her lunch, pulled on her snowsuit and boots and gave her father and grandmother hugs and kisses precluded any talk of vacations or Kristen.

"All right, Mom. What is it?" Tyler asked as soon as they were alone. "Ever since Brittany asked about inviting Kristen to Florida, you've been looking at me in a strange way. Why don't you want Kristen to come with us on vacation?"

"It's not that."

"Then what is it?"

She put down the dishes she'd been clearing and said, "If you must know, I'm afraid Brittany might get hurt. And you, too."

"You didn't think that a few weeks ago when you urged me to give her a chance as Brittany's nanny," he reminded her.

She pursed her lips. "Well, things are different now."

"Why? Because I'm in love with her?"

She grimaced. "I wish you hadn't said that."

"Why not? You're the one who pointed out to me that I was falling in love with her and you never voiced any disapproval then."

"Well, maybe I should have."

He shook his head. "You're not making any sense. What do you have against Kristen all of a sudden?"

"Well, she's a celebrity for one thing."

He chuckled. "She always was a celebrity. What has that got to do with anything?"

"You know what people are like in show business. They're fickle." She sat down beside him. "I just don't want to see either you or Brittany get hurt. Especially not Brittany. She's vulnerable, you know. Not having a mother. It's easy for her to get attached to a mother figure."

Tyler placed his hand over hers. "I worry about that, too, Mom. I don't think Kristen would ever hurt Brittany. Or me."

"I hope you're right," she said, then got up to finish clearing the table.

The last thing Tyler needed was to second-guess Kristen's motives. He wished his mother hadn't mentioned her reservations about people in the media. "I'd better get to the office. Do you mind if I take the rest of the paper?"

"No, go ahead."

He scooped up the sections scattered across the

countertop. "By the way, where's the entertainment section? I want to check the theater listings."

"Isn't it there?"

"No. It was missing one day last week, too. Must be a new carrier. I'd better give the circulation department a call." He tucked the newspaper under his arm and reached for his briefcase.

"Have a good day," his mother called out to his departing figure.

Tyler was determined to make it a better day than the way it had started. As soon as he reached Brant Electronics, he asked one of the mail clerks in the office to hunt down a copy of the entertainment section. He couldn't have dinner with Kristen tonight, but he'd get theater tickets for tomorrow night and take her to a quiet but elegant restaurant in downtown Minneapolis. Being with her would put all those nagging doubts his mother's comments had aroused to rest.

When he reached his office, he found a copy of the newspaper lying in the employees' lunchroom. He pulled out the section he wanted and took it to his office. He had just made a quick check of local theater listings when the headline of KC's column caught his eye. Is It Bye-bye Kristen? it asked.

Curious, Tyler read the small print. According to KC, Kristen had gone to Chicago in search of a job. Rumor had it that she would be resigning from her anchor position to pursue other aspects of the television industry. Producing.

Chicago. Tyler had a sick feeling in the pit of his stomach. *Alive* was produced in Chicago. Bob Yates had told her he'd pulled strings to get her a job as a producer for the show....

Tyler didn't want to believe that Kristen had accepted that job...not after telling him she wasn't going to do it. It had to be a rumor. She wouldn't have gone to Chicago without telling him. She'd said she liked the way things were going between them. She loved him.

No, she would never accept a job in Chicago without telling him, and certainly not *that* job.

He reached for the phone and dialed her number. He got her voice mail. He was about to leave a message when he noticed the pink slip on his desk. It was a phone message taken by his secretary. It said, "Sorry. Had to go to Chicago to see an old college friend. I'll be back on Friday. Call me. Kristen."

Tyler dropped the phone back on the hook without leaving a message.

KRISTEN HADN'T WANTED to go back to Chicago— and especially not when Tyler would be coming home just as she was leaving, but Jessica Tarver had arranged for her to visit the set of a children's news program. It was an opportunity Kristen couldn't turn down even if it did mean having to spend sixteen hours in the car.

Although the trip would have taken an hour by air, she opted for the eight-hour drive, which also added two extra days of travel to her schedule.

By the time she returned at the end of the week, she was full of enthusiasm and feeling more positive about her chance for success. The first thing she did when she stepped into her apartment was to check her voice mail to see if Tyler had phoned. He hadn't.

Disappointment washed over her. She had hoped he'd call while she was gone and leave a message so that when she got home she'd hear his voice. She'd missed him terribly and wanted to hear his familiar voice, see his sexy smile and feel his strong arms around her.

Yet there were no messages from him. The only Brant who'd called was Brittany. She had phoned three times and each time the message was the same. "Walter wants to talk to you." Kristen couldn't help smiling. But she needed to talk to Tyler before she spoke with his daughter.

Kristen called Tyler's office only to be told he was in a meeting. When the day passed and he hadn't returned her call, she tried again. This time, he wasn't available. No excuses. No explanations.

Later that evening, she tried calling his home. According to his mother, he was working late at the office. However, when she phoned his office number, there was no answer there, either.

When she couldn't reach him the following day, she began to suspect he wasn't getting her calls or else he didn't want to return them. She didn't think it was the former.

Again she called his home, this time connecting with Brittany, who enthusiastically regaled Kristen with details of the plans for their upcoming trip to Florida. When Kristen asked about her father, Brittany told her the same thing Millie had said. He was at work. Kristen made sure she reminded Brittany to tell her father they had talked.

After several days of driving herself crazy wondering why Tyler no longer seemed interested in her, Kristen got in her car and drove over to Brant Electronics.

When she arrived, she was surprised to find that his office was not some plushly carpeted, oak-paneled room tucked away on the top floor of the building, but a cubicle on the same floor as the assembly line. Noticing her reaction, Tyler's secretary informed her that he was the kind of CEO who wanted his employees to feel comfortable about coming in to talk to him.

He was also in a meeting in the conference room—which was in another part of the building. When Kristen asked if it would be okay if she waited, the secretary pointed to a row of chairs outside Tyler's office and offered to get her some coffee.

Kristen felt as if she were on display. She had little doubt that most of the people who had seen her come in knew who she was. And since she'd been a guest at the company Christmas party, she figured that most of them also knew she was dating Tyler. No one who passed by looked surprised to see her sitting outside his office.

Tyler, however, was taken aback to find her there. He returned from his meeting accompanied by another man. "Kristen. This is a surprise," he said, his eyes darkening briefly before becoming guarded.

She stood, suddenly feeling awkward and out of place. She didn't miss the curiosity on the other man's face. "I took a chance I could have a couple of minutes of your time, but if you're busy, I can come back."

Before he could answer, the man at his side said, "You don't have to leave on my account. I'm only here to pick up a couple of reports and then I'll be gone."

He smiled as he and Tyler walked past her into his office. Within a couple of minutes, they came out, folders in hand, the other man smiling again as he walked by her.

"You'd better come inside," Tyler told her in a voice that was anything but warm. He closed the door behind her, but because the upper part of the cubicle walls was made of Plexiglas, Kristen felt as if she were in a fishbowl. Although no one appeared to be looking in their direction, she felt as if dozens of eyes had fastened on the two of them.

"You're certainly right in the middle of things, aren't you?" she said a bit uneasily as she glanced out at the assembly line.

"I like to be where the action is." He sat down behind his desk and addressed her as if she were one of the employees instead of his lover.

Kristen longed to wrap her arms around him, but it was obvious he didn't want her affection. She understood that this was neither the time nor the place. She just wished he would at least smile at her.

"Why did you come here, Kristen?"

"I want to know why you're not returning my phone calls."

This time, he was the one who looked uneasy. He

began to play with the papers on his desk. "I haven't been home much." He lifted a pile of papers in emphasis as he added, "We've got this big project under way and it's taking much more of my time than I expected."

"And you couldn't take even five minutes to return my calls?" She didn't want to sound angry, but she was. Was this his way of giving her the brushoff? "Look, if it's over between us, at least have the decency not to lie to me."

His eyes darkened. "Lies? You're accusing *me* of lying?"

"What's that supposed to mean?" She could feel her heart beating rapidly in her chest.

"You told me you weren't going to take that job with *Alive*...that you didn't want anything to do with producing a story about the plane crash."

She moistened her lips. "It's true, I don't."

"And the trip to Chicago?" The words were as cold as ice, like his eyes.

"Was so I could visit a college friend of mine."

"So you said in your phone message." His words were laced with derision.

"You don't believe me?" She could only stare at him in disbelief. "Why else would I go to Chicago?"

"Maybe to talk to the executive producer of *Alive*." He fixed her with an accusing glare.

"You think I went to take that job?"

"Didn't you?"

"No! Where would you get such an idea?"

"In KC's column, it said—"

She laughed in astonishment. "KC's a gossip columnist."

"And, as the saying goes, where there's smoke, there's fire," he challenged her.

"Well, not in this case. Tyler, I don't want to produce a story about that awful day in our lives. When I told you I was doing some serious thinking regarding my career, I meant it. I've been working on a project involving children and the news. An old friend of mine from college has experience doing just that. She lives in Chicago, so I went to see her."

He got up from his chair and came around to her side of the desk. "Why didn't you tell me this?"

"Because I wanted it to be a surprise. I wanted to show you that I'm working hard at putting my life back together."

He raked a hand through his hair. "But if I'd known you were going, I could've arranged for someone to look out for you. I know people in Chicago."

His thoughtfulness touched her heart. "That's very sweet, but I don't need anyone to look out for me. I can take care of myself."

He reached for her hands. "But I want to take care of you, Kristen. I'm in love with you."

She glanced around nervously. "Aren't you worried that someone might see—"

"See what? Me kissing you? Let them," he said before pulling her into his arms.

When the kiss finally ended, she said, "I'm in love with you, too."

He smiled then, and for the first time in several

days, Kristen truly felt as if everything was going to work out between them.

"Since it's been a while since we've seen each other, how would you like to come over for dinner this evening?" he asked, returning to his seat. "Brittany has something going on at school. A music program, I think."

"Sounds wonderful," she said, knowing that Gayle would understand when Kristen called to beg off their plan to attend a seminar.

Later, listening to Brittany's class reciting two poems and singing a song about friends, Kristen was glad she'd come. She loved the look of fatherly pride on Tyler's face.

After the concert, they stopped at an ice-cream parlor. Then, when Brittany had been tucked into bed, Tyler drove Kristen home. Seated beside him on her sofa in front of the fire, she told him about her ideas for a children's news program. He seemed to share her enthusiasm. He smiled and offered suggestions. Gone was the guarded look that had been in his eyes all evening.

She couldn't resist wrapping her arms around him and hugging him. "Thank you."

"For what?" he said when she'd released him.

"For believing in me," she said quietly, looking down at her hands.

He placed a finger beneath her chin and made her look at him. "I told you a long time ago that you're a strong woman, Kristen. You can meet any challenge there is out there."

"When I'm with you, it feels that way."

He placed a kiss of reassurance on her lips. "Good, because I plan to be with you a lot. You know how Brittany talked nonstop about her trip to Walt Disney World and invited you to come along? I want you to come with us."

Kristen couldn't think of a single thing she'd rather do more than spend a week with the two of them. But there was something she had to find out before she could accept the invitation.

Tyler pulled her into his arms and held her close to him. "I'm not rushing you, am I? In our relationship, I mean?"

He was giving her the opportunity to be honest about the doubts troubling her. "Sometimes I worry that maybe you feel a sort of responsibility because you saved my life."

"You think what's happening between us is a result of my feeling responsible toward you?" He shook his head as if reproving her. "You're wrong, Kristen. Maybe the crash did bring us together, but it's not keeping us together now."

"Good. I needed to hear that."

He looked into her eyes and said, "You're the first woman I've made love with in five years. It isn't just sex between us. At least it isn't for me."

"Nor for me, either."

"We've lived through something not many people will ever share, but to say we fell in love because we were the only two people to survive that plane crash is wrong."

"You're right." She got up and went to stare out the window. Her gaze followed the swiftly moving light of an aircraft flying overhead. "So much time has passed and the crash is still getting in the way. It's like a demon stalking me all the time."

"Maybe it's time you put the demon to rest."

"And how do you suggest I do that?"

He got up from the sofa and came to stand beside her. "You haven't been on an airplane since that day, have you?"

"You don't even need to ask that question," she said sarcastically.

"Maybe it's time we both did. Together. Come with us to Florida."

"I don't think I'm ready," she said, her voice wobbly.

He reached for her hands. "Not even if I'm with you?"

She didn't answer right away but stared into his steady eyes. She wanted to say yes. Whenever he held her in his arms, she felt as if she could do anything.

"What if I make arrangements for a short flight? Just you and me on a clear day. Will you do it?"

"I want to…" she began uncertainly.

"Then say yes. If we want our relationship to move to the next level, we'll have to meet the challenges out there, Kristen."

She knew he was right. She couldn't spend the rest of her life being afraid of flying. "Okay. I'll do it."

He kissed her then, and she knew she'd given him the right answer. Now all she needed to do was figure out how she was going to get on that plane.

THREE DAYS LATER on a cold, sunny afternoon, Tyler parked his car at the Crystal airport. Despite a wind-chill making the temperature feel well below zero, Kristen was sweating. Her palms. Her face. Even her feet.

Tyler was as solicitous as a man taking care of a sick child, treating her with the utmost patience and care. As he helped her out of the car, he squeezed her gloved hands.

"You're not nervous at all, are you?" she asked him as they walked toward the charter company's small office.

"Yes, I am. Why do you suppose I've been driving to Hibbing?"

She took little comfort in his confession. She was too tense to get beyond anything but her own fear. As they rounded the corner and caught sight of the small plane on the tarmac, she halted in her steps.

"I can't do this."

"Yes, you can." He gently pulled her by the arm into the office. Once inside, they were greeted by the pilot who did his best to put the two of them at ease. It didn't help. Kristen's fear continued to mount.

As they started out toward the plane, Kristen again stopped suddenly. "I can't do this."

Tyler tried to urge her forward, but she yanked her arm out of his grasp.

"I can't," she repeated stubbornly.

"Kristen, I've already paid for this man's time and for the use of the plane," Tyler said, trying to reason with her.

"I'm sorry. I can't do it."

"Listen, why don't you two talk for a few minutes? Just come over when you're ready," the pilot said, and headed for the plane.

Tyler placed his arm around her shoulders. "I'm going to be right here beside you. If you want, I'll keep my arm around you the whole time."

She shook her head. "I can't. Please understand that. Don't make me do it, Tyler. Please."

For several minutes he tried to convince her to get on the plane. When he realized that it was useless, he said, "All right. I won't make you come with me."

"You're still going?" Fear had her clutching his arm.

"Yes. I'm not doing this just for you, Kristen. I'm doing it for me, too."

"But I don't want you to go without me."

He held out his hand to her. "Then come with me."

She wanted to take his hand. She tried to make her hand go into his, but it simply wouldn't move. "Please don't go, Tyler."

"It's just a quick trip, up and down. I need to do this, and you do, too." He stood with his hand outstretched, waiting. When she didn't take it, he finally let it drop. Without another word, he started for the plane.

She watched him walk toward the small aircraft, her heart racing. When he climbed aboard, her mouth became dry and she felt as if all the air in her lungs was being sucked out. When the clerk in the office stuck his head out the door and suggested she wait inside, she didn't move.

She couldn't. She was rooted to the spot, watching the small airplane head for the runway. Fear such as she'd never known paralyzed her as the plane began to gather speed, then lift into the air.

Although Tyler had told her the flight would be short, it felt like an eternity to Kristen. Just when she thought she would explode with anxiety, the plane taxied to a landing. As Tyler walked toward her, she ran out to meet him.

Tears streamed down her face as he wrapped his arms around her. Unable to speak, she sobbed into his coat.

He cradled her trembling figure in his arms, swiping at her tears with his gloved finger. "Have you been outside the entire time?"

She nodded.

He gave her an extra hug, then led her to the car and bundled her inside. By the time they arrived back at her apartment, she had regained her composure. He invited her to come home and have dinner with him and his family, but she declined.

"I think I'll try to get caught up on some stuff around here."

"Are you sure you're all right?"

"Sure. I'm fine."

"We're going to make it, Kristen," he said before leaving.

As those final words echoed in her ears, she only wished she could believe them.

KRISTEN SAW TYLER often during the following weeks. He didn't mention the Florida trip again, but whenever she was with Brittany, the little girl talked about her visit to the Magic Kingdom.

Kristen thought that if it weren't for the Florida trip, everything would be perfect between them. She could hardly stand to think of spending a whole week without seeing Tyler.

Life was finally beginning to feel normal again for Kristen. With the prospect of starting the children's news program, she felt as if she'd managed to put the crash behind her and get on with her career.

Everything should have been perfect. But it wasn't. She knew it and Tyler knew it, too. Something kept them from talking about commitment to each other. She suspected his feelings for Susan were the reason…that he'd never truly gotten over losing her. Kristen hoped that in time he'd be able to love her as deeply as she loved him. For she did love him, which she made sure he knew every time they were together.

"I know you and Brittany will have fun but I wish you weren't going," she murmured one night after they'd made love.

"You know I don't want to, especially not now, when everything is so good between us."

"It *is* good," she agreed dreamily. "For the first time in ages, I feel whole again, Tyler. Alive, and not afraid to live."

He nuzzled her breasts with his lips, then covered her mouth in another long kiss. "That's why I fell in love with you. You're a strong, sexy woman."

"Thanks to you, my hero," she said lovingly. "You've been so patient with me."

One minute he was caressing her, the next he was out of bed, pulling on his clothes. "It's getting late." The words were said abruptly, almost harshly.

She scrambled off the bed and came up behind him, wrapping her arms around his waist. "Why does it bother you so much when I call you my hero?"

"Because I'm nobody's hero," he answered, keeping his back to her.

"You're wrong. You're mine. And not just because you pulled me from the wreckage of that plane. When I needed understanding and support, you were there. Keith ran away. You stayed."

"And that's why you're with me?"

"No, I'm here because I fell in love with a man who was willing to let me have a few imperfections. You allowed me to find out for myself who I am, and not once did you ask me to be something I wasn't. Keith was in love with the way I looked, not the woman I am."

Tyler turned around to trace the fading lines of her scars with his fingertip. "These aren't imperfections. You're beautiful, Kristen, inside and out. It doesn't take love to see that."

"Spoken like a true hero," she told him, her voice full of love and admiration.

He groaned and backed away from her. "I wish you'd quit using that word."

"Why do you hate it so much?"

"Because it doesn't apply to me," he said. "Not now and not when…"

"When what? When Susan was killed? Is that what you were going to say?"

"What do you know about what happened to Susan?" he snapped.

"Your mother told me about the accident," she said gently, reaching out to stroke his arm.

"And did she tell you I'm the reason my wife died?"

There was so much pain in his voice she found herself on the verge of weeping. "I know it's hard not to blame yourself when stuff like that happens, but it wasn't your fault."

He didn't answer but continued pulling on his clothes.

"Tyler, you say you love me. Talk to me, please," she pleaded. "I love you."

He dropped onto the bed, his shoulders slumped. "You wouldn't love me if you knew…" He shook his head.

"Knew what?" she persisted, falling to her knees in front of him. She gathered his hands in hers. "Please tell me what's tormenting you. You pretend to have everything from the past neatly packaged and put away, but you don't."

He raked a hand through his hair. "I don't deserve your love."

"Yes, you do. Is it because you were in the car with your wife when she was killed? Is that why you feel this way?"

"I was driving. We had stopped at a railroad crossing. A car slid on some ice, rear-ending us."

"That happens in poor driving conditions," she consoled him. "Sometimes it's unavoidable."

He shook his head. "You don't understand. I got out of the car. I wanted to check the damage. That's when a second car slid into us. It must have punctured the gas tank. Our car burst into flames."

This time, she couldn't stifle the gasp. "I'm so sorry, Tyler."

"Brittany was in the back seat, Susan the front. Brittany was just a baby and I thought Susan would be able to get out, but her seat belt jammed. So I..." He couldn't finish.

"You got Brittany out first. That's what anybody would have done," Kristen said, tears trickling down her face.

"But I had insisted Susan stay inside after the first car hit us...it was below zero and I didn't want her to get cold." His face was full of agony as he spoke.

Kristen straightened and sat down beside him, wrapping her arms around him. "Oh, Tyler, I'm so sorry. But you can't blame yourself. You were the one who told me we can't make sense out of something so horrible."

"I thought I had managed to put the past behind, but then the airplane crashed...." His voice was tormented. "I didn't want to fall in love with you. I shouldn't have...I don't deserve you."

"That's not true," she said firmly. "You're a good man! Just look at the good things you've done."

"I've done nothing."

"I wouldn't call saving my life nothing. I'm proof of your good deed. And so are the people of Hibbing. They've benefited by your commitment to put a plant in their small town and create jobs for their people. Tyler, you can't spend the rest of your life beating yourself up for something that wasn't your fault."

"How do you know? You weren't there."

"No, but I was in a plane crash with you and I know how you reacted. And I know the kind of man you are. If there was any way for you to save Susan, you would've done it."

He gently pulled his hands away from hers and finished putting on his shoes.

"Tyler, do you love me?"

He turned around and kissed her. "Does that answer your question?"

"Am I worth fighting for?"

He smiled then. "Why is it when I'm with you, I think anything's possible?"

"Because it is," she told him and only hoped that she could convince him, too. "You need to forgive yourself, Tyler. As you said to me, it's time to put those demons to rest." She kissed him tenderly.

"You're the first person I've talked to about this," he confessed.

"Oh, Tyler." She couldn't prevent the tears that streamed down her face. "That must mean something, don't you think?"

He kissed away her tears. "It means I'm willing to share my soul with you, Kristen. Are you willing to share yours with me?"

She looked at him, knowing what he was going to say next.

"Come to Florida with me and Brittany. I won't press you now. Just think about it. For us."

CHAPTER FOURTEEN

TRUE TO HIS WORD, Tyler didn't press her. She should have been happy, but she wasn't. The thought of Tyler and Brittany getting on the jumbo jet terrified her as much as the thought of getting on the plane herself. Yet she couldn't let her own fear stop them from traveling the quickest and safest way available. At Gayle's suggestion, she enrolled in a class to help her overcome her fear of flying.

On the Friday evening before Tyler and Brittany were scheduled to leave, Millie invited Kristen over for a farewell dinner. Listening to Brittany chat on about what she expected to find in the Magic Kingdom reminded Kristen about her own visits to Florida as a child. But neither the fond memories nor the prospect of a week with Tyler proved enough to get her past that hurdle of fear.

She hadn't told Tyler about the class she'd completed. Even though her instructor had said she'd been a model pupil, willing to overcome her fears and wanting to succeed, on the last day of class she had failed the final test. She hadn't been able to get on the plane.

Kristen had been hoping that after dinner Tyler would accompany her back to her apartment on his last night in town. He didn't. She went home alone, with nothing but her anxiety to keep her company.

After the warmth of the Brant home, her apartment felt cold and lonely. She stared at the school pictures Brittany had given her, thinking what a lovely child she was, so full of life. So much like Tyler.

When the doorbell rang, she rushed to the intercom, thinking it might be Tyler. It was Keith. Disappointment made her reluctant to let him come up.

"I brought over some tapes I thought you could use," he told her when she opened her apartment door. "Bob told me about your idea for a children's news program. I did some phoning and came up with a few more sources for you."

She was taken aback by his generosity. Maybe he was trying to make amends for the way he'd treated her.

"Thanks. I'm sure they'll be useful," she said, accepting the stack from him. "But you could've left me a note at the studio, and I would've picked them up."

"Then I wouldn't have had the opportunity to see you."

"Why would you want to see me?"

He shifted uneasily and looked sheepish. "I guess I deserve that."

"I wasn't being sarcastic. Why *would* you want to see me?"

"Because I've missed you. We were good together."

At one time, those words would have sent tingles

of pleasure through her. Not anymore. "We were good on the air," she agreed.

"And in real life, too," he added.

"No, we weren't."

"How can you say that? We had planned our wedding and we'd still be engaged if it hadn't been for that plane crash," he insisted.

She faced him, her hands on her hips. "Keith, the plane crash isn't the reason we broke up."

"Yes, it is. Everything was perfect between us until you took that flight. Then everything changed."

"Not everything. Me. I changed."

"Of course you did."

There was a glimmer of understanding in his eyes, but Kristen knew it had come much too late.

"As I look back, I realize now that you needed time to come to terms with the fact that you had nearly died. And—I'm not proud to admit this—I didn't know how to handle the situation."

"So you distanced yourself from me emotionally?"

"You didn't seem to want me around."

She made a sound of disbelief. "You were the one who didn't want to be around me. Hospitals made you uneasy. *I* made you uneasy. You were so worried about the effect of my absence on your career. Worse, you were worried about how I *looked*. Well, you know what? I was feeling pretty crummy myself and what I needed from you was support."

"I know, and I'm sorry I wasn't there for you," he apologized, "but I was scared and didn't know how to help either of us."

She didn't doubt the truth of his words, but they didn't change what had happened between them. "I didn't need your help, just your understanding. Didn't you think that maybe I was scared, too? I wanted to run away, Keith. But I couldn't. I had to learn to face my fears."

"Look, we probably both made some mistakes. All I can say is I'm sorry." He tried to take her in his arms, but she shrugged away from him.

"Okay, I accept your apology. But we can't go back and pick up where we left off. I don't love you, Keith. Actually, I'm not sure I ever did."

He winced as if she'd dealt him a physical blow. "After everything we meant to each other, you can say that?"

"We meant so much to each other that you went off to the Bahamas with another woman while I was home recovering from a plane crash that nearly ended my life."

He stared at her silently for several seconds, then said, "You really have changed, Kristen. You never used to be so cold...and full of anger."

She chuckled in disbelief. "That's great, Keith. Because I tell you the truth and it's something you don't want to hear, you think I'm cold."

Again there was a silence. "Well, I guess there really is nothing more to say, is there?"

"Not when it comes to our personal lives. Go back to Janey, Keith. She's a nice person." She walked over to the door and opened it, waiting for him to walk through it.

He started to leave but stopped. "You really don't want to give us a second chance, do you?"

"Good night, Keith," she said, then closed the door.

Long after he was gone, she thought about their conversation. Maybe Keith didn't know how to deal with the changes that had occurred in their lives because of the crash, but she did.

Tyler had been right. Although it had taken her a while to realize it, she was a strong woman. Strong enough to face whatever lay ahead.

She knew now what she needed to do. She called the airline and booked a seat on the same flight as Tyler and Brittany. Then she pulled out her suitcase and packed. She couldn't wait to see Tyler's face when he discovered she was on the plane. It was going to be such a wonderful surprise.

ON SATURDAY MORNING, Tyler led Brittany by the hand through the airport in search of the departure gate. As he passed through the concourse crowded with people, he saw several families—moms, dads and kids eagerly anticipating traveling together. He didn't want to be a single father taking his daughter to Florida. He wanted a wife at his side, a mother for Brittany. He wanted Kristen to be that woman.

"Daddy, our plane won't crash, will it?" Brittany asked as they walked down the long corridor.

"No, sweetie. The plane I was on was a smaller one. These big jets are safe," he reassured her.

"Mandy Mosely at school says her daddy doesn't like to fly, so they always drive when they go to Walt

Disney World,'' Brittany commented as they rode the moving walkway through the terminal.

"It's a long way to go by car and I only have a week's vacation. You wouldn't want to spend half of that time driving, would you? Not when you could spend those extra days with Mickey and Minnie.''

"No, but maybe Kristen would've come if we went by car. I heard her tell Gram she doesn't fly anymore. She only takes a car, like Mandy's daddy.''

And if it's all right for Mandy's daddy, why isn't it all right for Kristen? Tyler knew the answer to that question. It *was* all right. For weeks he'd been pressuring her into flying because he felt it was what she needed to do. He'd been trying to control her feelings about flying the same way he tried to control everything else in his life. Maybe he'd been wrong. Just because he'd forced himself to get back on a plane didn't mean she needed to fly again.

Just as they reached their departure gate, he made a decision. Instead of taking a seat in the waiting area, he yanked Brittany's hand and stepped back onto the moving walkway.

"Daddy, where are we going?'' Brittany wanted to know as he dragged her behind him.

"To the parking lot.''

"Why?''

He looked down at her and said, "To see if Kristen will come with us if we travel by car.''

"We're not going on the airplane?''

"Nope. We're going to get Kristen and go in the car,'' he stated with a grin, feeling as if the weight of the world had been lifted from his shoulders.

He thought he could feel Brittany's laughter in his heart.

KRISTEN TOOK A CAB to the airport, tipping the driver for getting her through what had to be one of the worst traffic jams she'd ever seen on the freeway. With only a few minutes to spare, she went straight to the departure gate where the airline attendant had just announced the last call for boarding.

Out of breath, Kristen rested her elbows on the ticket counter while the clerk checked her identification and issued her a boarding pass. She was grateful she had only packed a carry-on suitcase, which she dragged behind her as she hurried through the jetway to the plane.

She'd been assigned a seat in the front of the plane. With the flight attendant urging her to be seated for takeoff, she barely had a chance to scan the sea of unfamiliar faces in the seats behind her. There was no way she could see to the rear of the plane and reluctantly did as the attendant requested. She stowed her suitcase in the overhead compartment and took her seat, knowing she'd have to wait until the plane was airborne to find Tyler and Brittany.

It wasn't what she wanted to do, especially since her entire body was shaking. More than anything, she needed Tyler's strength to support her. She needed to hold his hand and hear his calm voice. She shut her eyes, fighting the urge to rush for the exit.

"Are you all right?" the flight attendant asked.

"I'm f-f-fine," she stammered, wishing she didn't feel as if she were about to pass out.

"You're awfully pale," the woman said gently.

"That's because I'm on a mission. My boyfriend's on this plane and he doesn't know that I bought a ticket at the last minute. I'm going to surprise him," she said in a rush, her voice close to hysteria.

The attendant smiled. "No wonder you're shaking. How romantic."

"Yes, and the sooner I let him know I'm on board, the sooner I'll be able to relax," Kristen told her.

Just then, the plane began to taxi toward the runway. "You can't get up now, but once we're in the air, I'll do what I can to help you make it a very special surprise," the woman said with a smile, then gave Kristen's shoulder a pat of encouragement.

In the air. Kristen swallowed with difficulty. How would she manage to survive going up in the air? Her body was shaking so badly the man beside her reached across to cover her hand with his.

"Everything will be fine," the elderly gentleman said.

"I know," she squeaked. Tyler was somewhere in the mass of seats behind her. She could do this. She could, she kept repeating to herself.

She closed her eyes and leaned back, fingering the gold cross he had given her for Christmas. Then she visualized the look on his face when he discovered she was on the plane. And she thought about Brittany and the joy that would light the little girl's face when she saw the Magic Kingdom.

So lost was she in her thoughts that she didn't realize the plane had taken off. When she felt a gentle hand on her shoulder, she opened her eyes to see the same flight attendant at her side.

"The captain's turned off the seat-belt sign. You can get up and look for your fellow," she said with a smile. As Kristen fumbled with the seat belt, the woman asked, "Is this a special occasion? I mean, this isn't your way of accepting a marriage proposal, is it?" Excitement danced in her eyes.

"Nothing quite that romantic, just special."

"If you tell me his name, I can give you his seat assignment," the attendant offered.

"It's Tyler Brant. And his daughter's Brittany. They're both on the plane," she told her.

"Going to Walt Disney World, I bet," the woman said with a knowing smile. She excused herself only to return a few minutes later with a list. "It says here Mr. Brant and his daughter were supposed to be in 32A and B, but they never checked in."

Kristen could feel the blood drain from her face. "What?"

"I'm awfully sorry, but they're not on this flight."

TYLER AND BRITTANY'S luggage went on ahead to Orlando. By the time he had retrieved the Jeep and driven to Kristen's apartment, he was so excited he could hardly breathe.

Some of that excitement disappeared when he buzzed Kristen's apartment and received no answer. He tried several times, each time waiting. And waiting. And waiting. Finally, Brittany said, "She's not home, Daddy."

"No, she isn't." He thought for a moment, then

said, "I'll tell you what. We'll leave her a message and then we'll go home and wait for her to call. Okay?"

Once they were back in the Jeep, he dialed Kristen's number on his car phone, took a deep breath and said, "Hi, Kristen. It's me. Brittany and I are at home. We didn't leave for Florida. We couldn't leave without you. We're driving down in the Jeep and want you to come with us. So please call as soon as you get home."

Brittany was tugging on his arm the whole time he was speaking. "I want to leave a message, too, Daddy." Tyler passed her the phone. "Hi, Kristen. It's Brittany. I just wanted to tell you not to forget your swimsuit. And your sunscreen. It's sunny down there."

When she would have talked beyond the allotted tape time, Tyler took the phone from her. "She'll get the idea. Don't worry."

Then they were back at the house where Tyler had to use a key to get in since his mother's flight to Kentucky had left that morning. The first thing he did was to check his answering machine—on the chance that Kristen had returned immediately after they'd been to her apartment.

To his joy, the message light was blinking. He listened to several clicks, one a call from a friend of his mother's, and then he heard Kristen's voice.

"Tyler, it's me. Where are you? I'm on flight 1145 and you're not here."

Her voice sounded weak and a bit frightened. Tyler couldn't believe what he was hearing and re-

played the tape several times before accepting that
what it said was true. She was in the plane flying to
Florida and he was in Minnesota!

Brittany walked into the room while he was listening and exclaimed, "Kristen's on the airplane!"

A feeling of helplessness soon had him pacing as
he tried to figure out how to reach her. He glanced
at his watch. The plane was about to land. There was
only one thing to do. He called the airline and asked
that Kristen be given a message upon landing.

Then he waited. It was the longest wait of his life.

Finally, the phone rang. "Kristen?" he asked
without saying hello.

"Tyler, how come you weren't on the plane?"

"Because I didn't want to go without you. Brittany and I drove over to your place to tell you we
would drive down to Florida if that's what it took to
get you to come along."

"You were willing to do that for me?" He could
hear the astonishment in her voice. Then she started
to cry. "Oh, Tyler, that is so sweet."

"No, what's sweet is you getting on that plane
because you thought Brittany and I were on it. Are
you okay?"

"I'm fine. Tyler, I did it! I flew in a plane!" The
sobs became exclamations of joy.

More than anything, he wanted to be with her. "I
knew you could do it," he said, his voice full of
admiration and love.

"The question is, now what do I do? I'm standing
in the middle of an airport with nowhere to go."

"You just stay right there. Brittany and I will catch the next plane down."

He could see his daughter jumping up and down beside him. "Let me talk, Daddy!"

"Just a second. Brittany wants to speak to you." He gave her the phone.

"Is the sun shining, Kristen?" There was a pause and she said, "Oh, good. Will you teach me to swim?" She passed the phone back to Tyler and said, "Kristen says she'll show me how to swim but only if you say it's okay."

Tyler held the receiver to his ear. "I think there are a lot of things we can learn while we're in Florida, don't you?"

"Oh, Tyler, I can't wait for you to get here. I know you said that New Year's was a new beginning for us, but this truly will be a chance for us to start with a slate that's finally clean."

Tyler slid his arm around Brittany's shoulders and hugged her close. "The three of us are going to have a great life together. This journey will have a happy ending. I promise."

"Don't miss this, it's a keeper!"
—**Muriel Jensen**

"Entertaining, exciting and
utterly enticing!"
—**Susan Mallery**

"Engaging, sexy...a fun-filled romp."
—**Vicki Lewis Thompson**

See what all your favorite authors
are talking about.

Coming October 1999 to a retail store near you.

 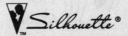

 **HARLEQUIN®**
Makes any time special ™

WIN A DREAM

In celebration of Harlequin®'s golden anniversary

Enter to win a *dream!* You could win:

- A luxurious trip for two to
  The Renaissance Cottonwoods Resort
  in Scottsdale, Arizona, or
- A bouquet of flowers once a week for a year
  from **FTD**, or
- A $500 shopping spree, or
- A fabulous bath & body gift basket, including
  K-tel's *Candlelight and Romance* 5-CD set.

Look for **WIN A DREAM** flash on
specially marked Harlequin® titles by
Penny Jordan, Dallas Schulze,
Anne Stuart and Kristine Rolofson
in October 1999*.

FTD
RENAISSANCE.
COTTONWOODS RESORT
SCOTTSDALE, ARIZONA

K·TEL

HARLEQUIN®

SUPERROMANCE

COMING NEXT MONTH

#864 MY BABIES AND ME • Tara Taylor Quinn
By the Year 2000: Baby
She's a goal-setting, plan-making kind of person, and one of Susan Kennedy's goals is to have a baby by the age of forty. That's coming up fast. A couple of problems, though. There's only one man she can imagine as the father of her child. And that's her ex-husband, Michael. She gets pregnant on schedule, but then there's another problem—well, not really a problem. She's expecting twins!

#865 FAMILY REUNION • Peg Sutherland
The Lyon Legacy
Family means everything. Scott Lyon's heard his great-aunt's words forever. But now Margaret's disappeared, and the closer Scott comes to finding her, the more family secrets, betrayals and deceptions he uncovers. And then he meets Nicki Bechet, whose grandmother knows more about the Lyons than she's telling.

Join Scott and Nicki in this thrilling conclusion to the Lyon Legacy as they search for the truth and learn that family—and love—really do mean everything.

#866 A MESSAGE FOR ABBY • Janice Kay Johnson
Patton's Daughters
Abby's the third Patton sister. The baby. The one everyone said was privileged, spoiled. But childhood with a harsh, unapproachable father and only a vague memory of her mother wasn't easy, even if she did make it look that way. So now Abby's determined to live up to her image and have fun. Then she meets Detective Ben Shea—and he has news for her. *Sometimes it pays to get serious.*

#867 A RANGER'S WIFE • Lyn Ellis
Count on a Cop
Lawmen know that everything can change in an instant. The smart ones don't take their lives or their promises for granted. At least, that's what Texas Ranger Ty Richardson believes. Before his best friend, Jimmy Taylor, died in the line of duty, Ty promised to take care of Jimmy's wife and young son. And Ty intends to honor that promise—to help them, protect them, be there for them. But he'll never forget that they're Jimmy's family, not his—no matter how much he loves them both.

#868 EXPECTING THE BEST • Lynnette Kent
9 Months Later
Denver cop Zach Harmon's finished with raising kids. As the oldest of eleven, he spent too much time helping out with his siblings. But then, he never expected to fall so hard for Shelley Hightower—who understands his feelings all too well. *Now* he has to convince her that raising their child together is exactly what he wants to do.

#869 THE RESCUER • Ellen James
Dr. Alexandra Robbins may be a successful psychologist in Chicago, but her own marriage wasn't a success. She's in the middle of a messy divorce. So it's a relief for her to escape to Sobriety, Idaho, and complete her research on type R men—rescuers, compelled to risk their lives to save others. Colin McIntyre, the object of her study, fascinates her big-time, but the more he attracts her, the more frightened of him she becomes. And she doesn't understand why....

HARLEQUIN • CELEBRATES

FIVE DECADES OF ROMANCE

In October 1999,
Harlequin Intrigue®
delivers a month of our
best authors, best miniseries
and best romantic suspense
as we celebrate Harlequin's
50th Anniversary!

Look for these terrific
Harlequin Intrigue® books
at your favorite retail stores:

STOLEN MOMENTS (#533)
by B.J. Daniels

MIDNIGHT CALLER (#534)
by Rebecca York

HIS ONLY SON (#535)
by Kelsey Roberts

UNDERCOVER DAD (#536)
by Charlotte Douglas